Wylde Strangers

Wylde Strangers

Wylde Hearts Book One

Josie Juniper

Copyright © 2021 by Josie Juniper

All rights reserved. This book or any portion thereof
may not be reproduced or used in any manner whatsoever without the express
written permission of the publisher except for the use of brief quotations in a book
review.
This is a work of fiction. Any resemblance to folks living or dead is
coincidental.

Cover art by Sean Fleckenstein

www.josiejuniperauthor.com

ISBN: 978-0-578-32537-8

acknowledgments:

Massive thanks for generous support and encouragement goes out to Linda and Beau James, and Barry Cooney. To my incomparable critique partners/editors—Donna Derington, Carman Webb, and Lisa Larkins—eternal gratitude. I could not have done this without you all! And to Sean Fleckenstein, the hero of my own timeless romance (and collage artist extraordinaire), so much love and thanks. We are Infinite Like Pi.

chapter one

Griffin winced and grabbed his brother Byron's wrist as he was about to toss a box into the back of the crowded van.

"Whoa there... nothing on top of the ones with the vinyl. That one especially." He took the box from Byron's arms and nudged aside a big carton that said *towels/sheets*. "It's got my Japanese import EPs."

Byron rolled his eyes—a gunmetal gray, matching Griffin's— and pulled the hood of his sweatshirt tighter against the late-September rain. "Sorry, your Hipster Highness." He sat on the protruding bumper of the van and took a cigarette from the pack in his shirt pocket, leaning back to keep it dry. "And you're welcome, by the way. You know asking people to help you move is pretty much evil." He lit up. "I didn't even get pizza."

"You owed me, for your clever little joke with the van." Griffin swung one of the two rear doors shut, eyeing the bright purple paint job. In his mind, he'd started referring to the old produce company van as "The Grape of Wrath."

Josie Juniper

Byron laughed, smoke puffing from his nose. "You distinctly said, '*any* color.' And now you'll never lose it in a parking lot."

Griffin sat on the bumper too, leaning his head back against the wet door, eyes closed. He ran a hand through his damp auburn locks. "When I pull up to the rental in Wylde, people are going to expect me to jump out and start making balloon animals. It looks like a clown drives this."

"A clown *does* drive it."

"Remind me why I'm letting you stay in my apartment? Stop being an asshole or you can go back to couch-surfing." Griffin wiped the side of his face on one raised shoulder. He watched Byron smoke for a minute, and struggled to choose his next words. "Not trying to sound like the killjoy big brother here, but please use this opportunity, y'know... *wisely*. Okay? Show up to the new job. Save your money—I'll still be covering rent and bills, so you can rack up a few grand while I'm gone. Whipping that crappy little small-town bar into shape won't take more than four months—I'll be back in January, for sure—but that's plenty of time for you to get on top of your finances."

"I know, I know. Gotcha." Byron's gaze followed a tight-skirted brunette clicking down the sidewalk in high heels, a small orange umbrella held high over her head.

Griffin waved a hand in front of his face to get his attention. "And stay away from Nix and Marco, got it? I'm not kidding. Just... go to a meeting instead, if you feel tempted to hang out with them. You've got three months clean and sober. Don't screw it up while I have my back turned."

"Quit hassling me." Byron squinted against the smoke blowing back into his eyes. "Are you coming up for Christmas?"

"Probably not." He avoided Byron's eyes. "Doesn't feel the same since Mom died. And I don't think Dale would miss me, as long as you're there."

"If I don't get any decent presents because you're hiding in that hick town," Byron said, clearly trying to lighten the mood, "I absolutely blame you. I asked Santa for a pony."

Wylde Strangers

Griffin grabbed Byron in a headlock. "Yeah? I'll send you a bag of horse shit. Close enough?"

"Knock it off!" Byron laughed, wrestling free. "Man, you bent my smoke."

"Good. Those things should be next to go. I quit, and you can too."

"Sure." Byron smoothed his hair, then his shirt, in mock affront. "Did you kick heroin too? Because unless the answer is yes, I'm not impressed." He took one last unsuccessful drag off the broken cigarette and tossed it into the rainy gutter. "Leave me *something* to enjoy—a man deserves one vice."

"You've got the phone numbers of half the women in Portland," Griffin said. "That's plenty to keep you busy."

A white pickup crept to a stop beside them, and the driver's side window rolled down. "How much longer are you gonna be in that space?" a dough-faced middle-aged man called out.

"We're done," Griffin told him.

"Then move it! Don't sit there scratching your ass all day," he barked.

Griffin rolled his head in the direction of his brother. "You know what I'm going to miss about the city? The friendly people."

***

The loading zone in front of Gold Lizard Lounge was open, and Griffin swooped into it at an angle. Dougie, one of the cooks, was standing out front with his hands in his girlfriend's hair, delivering a prolonged goodbye kiss. He looked up when Griffin got out of the van, then spun the girl around and gave her a pat to set her in motion.

"Howdy, boss-man," he said to Griffin.

"Hey." Pocketing the keys, Griffin threw a glance through the big front windows of the stylish bar. He could see Cleo talking to Anton the bartender, standing close and relaxed.

"You heading south now?" Dougie asked.

"Yeah. Just stopped by to give Cleo the extra keys."

Josie Juniper

Dougie leaned against the brickwork between the windows and door. He gave Griffin a look of cautious sympathy, shoulders drawn up, hands in the pockets of his stained white apron. "For what it's worth, man, we're all sorry to see you go. Even if it's just for a few months." He gave a backwards nod to indicate Cleo. "She runs the place great, don't get me wrong. But she ain't a laugh like you."

Griffin shot another glance through the window. "She's good with the numbers." *But not with people.*

As co-owners, they'd always had a "stern mom, fun dad" vibe, and the arguments it had caused over the past five years had gotten closer together, until there was nothing *but* arguing. She'd accuse him of being too easy on the employees, handing out pay advances like candy. But Cleo had been raised a rich girl, and couldn't understand, the way Griffin did, how it felt to be broke and panicked days before the next check.

After their breakup, she'd bought out his half of their second bar, Velour, and they'd kept Gold Lizard fifty-fifty. With the money from the buy-out, Griffin had invested in an acquaintance-of-a-friend's bar in a little Southern Oregon town called Wylde.

He took his phone from a pocket and checked the time. "I should get going. It's a six hour drive."

Dougie clapped him on the shoulder. "Good luck, man. Give 'em hell."

"Thanks." Griffin put one hand on the long brass door handle and paused. "And don't let Byron get away with anything just because he's my brother. If he doesn't give a hundred percent, or…" Griffin stared across the street, weighing how to phrase it. "If you see any sketchy types with him, text me. I don't want to sound like I'm asking you to spy, but…"

Dougie delivered a knowing nod. "Will do, boss."

Inside, classical music was playing. Griffin went to the stereo to switch it to an indie streaming channel, jabbing the button hard in annoyance.

"I was listening to that," Cleo said behind him.

He didn't turn, just picked up a stack of mail beside the stereo and sorted through it. "It's fifteen minutes 'til opening, and it sounds like tea-time-for-the-elderly in here."

"Wow, nice. Thanks."

Griffin took the set of keys from his pocket and held them out sideways. In his peripheral vision, he saw Cleo put a hand under the key bundle, and he dropped them into her palm.

"I'm taking cash from the safe," he told her. "The bank closed an hour ago."

She leaned on the counter. "Sounds like poor planning on your end."

"Packing up took a long time. I'll sign the money out. Do you need it all? It's a Wednesday—it's not going to be busy."

"Just... do what you want, Griff. You always do."

He snorted. "Looks like that's *your* game."

She folded her arms, and he finally looked straight at her. She was wearing the drapey pearl-gray sweater he loved—the one that showed off her pale shoulders, and the graceful line of her neck. Her pink-tipped chestnut hair was swept around to one side, fanned across her collarbone.

"Passive-aggressive much?" she asked.

He tossed the mail down. "It just surprises me that someone with your pathological regard for rules is... so openly cozy with an employee. At best, it looks sloppy, and at worst, we've got a sexual harassment lawsuit on our hands."

She closed her eyes on a sigh. "Anton's not going to *sue me* for dating him."

"Easy to say when you're still in the honeymoon phase."

She flapped an impatient hand at him. "Okay, *bye*. Delightful talking to you. Don't bother letting me know when you get down to Redneck-ville. And thanks again for saddling us with your junkie brother."

Griffin turned on her. "That's a cheap shot. Byron's working hard at recovery—"

"*Again*," Cleo inserted under her breath.

Josie Juniper

"—and he's always been nice to you, even when you don't particularly deserve it. Could you maybe try to be as good a human being as you are a manager?"

He walked away, ignoring her indignant growl as he headed for the office. He took two banded stacks of twenties from the safe and signed out the withdrawal before pausing in the office doorway. He gazed across the bar. The new Sputnik-sphere drop-lights looked great—Griffin hated to admit it. Cleo had a stylish eye, he had to give her that much.

A great eye, but a crappy heart, he thought to himself.

***

He'd first heard about the struggling Wylde Saloon five months before, when he'd attended the wedding of his friends Sadie and Weston in a little rural town just north of the California border. Land was cheap there, and his friends had bought a few acres and built a big log cabin.

The bar was owned by a fiery woman named Delilah Kelley, who was... less than thrilled about the merger. She'd grudgingly agreed to it, and had even been the one to contact him, as a result of a conversation about bar ownership they'd had at the wedding reception—during which she'd told him that everything he thought was idiotic. His opinions on food, cocktails, décor, music... all asinine, according to Delilah. And she hadn't approved of his casual wedding attire of black jeans and a Radiohead t-shirt either.

Griffin had no idea what to expect in Wylde. But he felt confident that if Delilah Kelley would let him take the lead, he could turn her old-timey tavern into a trendy hotspot worthy of Wylde's ever-increasing influx of tourists and transplants.

He rubbed a hand over his face, careful to keep his attention on the road, and took another drink of soda. A few more hours of freeway driving to go. His eyes were heavy, but his brain was a buzzing stew of apprehension over the uncertainty of his new investment, and irritation over Cleo's out-of-character romance.

Wylde Strangers

Anton was only twenty-six—seven years Cleo's junior. It was… possibly tacky?

Anton. His stupid vintage suits, his perfect hair and straight white teeth, his Bad Boy neck tattoos. *Ugh.* It had only been six months since Cleo and Griffin's breakup. That wasn't long, was it? After seven years together, it seemed too soon.

Yeah, no. *Fine.* Not too soon.

Griffin switched on the stereo to stay awake. The first song was The Thermals' "Here's Your Future." He chuckled and raised his soda.

"A toast—to my next disaster." He took a sip. "Let's do this."

chapter two

Delilah knew it was Abe coming through the door without even glancing up from the pint glasses she was drying. Because despite the fact that he'd been coming into the Wylde Saloon since he'd been old enough to drink, and also despite having dated Delilah for two of those nine years, he never failed to pull on the door—clearly marked "push"—with a clatter.

"We're not open yet, Abe," she called out.

"I know it, girl. But you should pour me a drink to celebrate."

She looked up as he brought a cellophane-wrapped bundle of pink-and-blue-dyed daisies from behind his back. On the edge of the wrapping, Delilah saw a discount sticker. The color of the flowers said "baby shower," and the color of the sticker said it was from the grocery store where Abe worked, and he'd likely gotten them for free. *So clueless.*

He swaggered across the well-worn hardwood floor, his boots thumping out a backbeat to the Dixie Chicks song on the old jukebox. Resting against the bar, he gave the daisies a sniff, then tipped the bundle toward her.

"I'll take a shot of tequila." He set the flowers down and pushed aside some of the overly-long dark hair sketching a diagonal across his forehead.

"You aim to pay for it?"

He grinned and rubbed his cleft chin. "Is that anything to ask a man who got promoted from frozen foods manager to... *assistant store manager*?"

He waited for a reaction, his smile as sweet and frozen as a cheap pie. Delilah held his gaze, one eyebrow raised, then reached for the most bottom-shelf tequila and poured out a shot.

"Congratulations—drink up and hit the trail. I've got a lot to do before this city boy shows up to ruin my bar with a bunch of arugula and microbrews."

Abe laughed. "Man, he's got his work cut out with you."

"With *me?* The other way around, maybe." She gave a sniff like someone spoiling for a fight and ready to swing. "I'll take his money—it all spends the same—but he seemed like a damned fool when I met him."

Abe leaned across the bar, showing off his muscular forearms with the sleeves rolled up. "We're all fools for you, Miss Kelley."

She rolled her eyes and flipped aside her strawberry-blonde waves. She saw Abe's gaze follow the action, sliding over her shoulders in the tight green top that matched her eyes.

"All men are fools anyway," she grumbled. "Did you have a reason to come in here bragging up your promotion with stinky second-hand flowers?"

He put a hand on his chest in a parody of woundedness. "And here I thought daisies were your favorite."

She conceded a smile and picked up the flowers. "I do like daisies." Turning away, she stripped the wrapping off and ran water in a jar that had once held cocktail onions, using it as a makeshift vase. "But you've got a twinkle in those blue eyes. Get to the point, or toss that tequila back and shove off."

Josie Juniper

She set the jar of flowers at the end of the bar and fluffed the blooms out. Abe raised his shot glass in a toast and polished off the contents, then set it down very quietly, rather than with the showy smack Delilah had expected.

"Hear me out…" he began.

"Oh, *this* should be good."

He held up a hand. His smile faltered, and he met her eyes with a painful earnestness that made Delilah's heart sink.

"I know a big part of why you quit seeing me was… well, you might have been… expecting a ring. And I dragged my heels. I heard through the grapevine that you said you ain't got time to wait around, since turning thirty. Your clock's ticking and whatnot."

"My clock is no one's concern, Abel Ferguson. And if you're headed where I think you are with this, you can stuff that egg right back up the chicken."

The jukebox started skipping as it changed to Garth Brooks' "The Dance," and Delilah hopped onto the bar, pivoted, and dropped down on the other side, her heart-pattern cowboy boots smacking the floor. She stalked over and gave the machine a kick, on the scuffed dent that had been imprinted in it from a thousand previous kicks. She took her time walking back.

Abe got off the barstool and met her halfway, taking her hands and moving them into position for slow dancing. His smell was so familiar—Aramis cologne and the grocery store scent that was a combination of spices, baked goods, and Freon. She looked at him, moving purely by habit in a swaying circle to the music. She could see a tiny razor-nick on his chin and realized he'd shaved before coming over. Suddenly she was very worried that there was a ring in his pocket.

"Abe, wait…" she began.

His hands drifted up to cradle the sides of her head. "At least let me say my piece."

Delilah took a step back, holding both his hands in hers. "No, please. I mean it, Abe." The way his face fell made her chest cramp. She rushed on. "There's too much blood under the bridge."

Wylde Strangers

"You know how sorry I was about the thing with Michaela."

"I do believe you were sorry. But it wasn't just that—it was a hundred other little things." She squeezed his hands. "We've known each other all our lives, Abe. You shared your animal cookies with me on the first day of kindergarten," she said with a light laugh. "We're near to brother and sister."

"I don't want to be your brother. Hell, girl, are you telling me that's how you feel now? Because I thought we were, y'know... pretty hot together." He winked and kissed the back of her hand.

Delilah pressed her lips into a line, unsure how to respond without hurting his feelings. The sex had been... perfectly nice. It wasn't exactly *bad*. But the truth was, Abel Ferguson was part of the landscape of the tiny town where they'd both grown up. Three years before, at twenty-seven, she'd decided *Good enough—he's a nice guy.* And the wedding dresses in the magazines had started to look appealing. But the spark was never there. Abe was too familiar, too predictable. All Wylde and no *wild*.

"You're so handsome," she said with an encouraging smile. "I know you're going to make the right girl happy."

His shoulders slouched like a raft losing air. "But you're saying that girl ain't you."

She gave him a quick hug, her pelvis far away, the way one would hug a stranger. "I'm sorry, Abe. I'm glad you got that promotion. I'll bet this time next year you'll be manager of the whole store. A real catch."

He shook his head. "Don't you want to get married, have babies? Katie told me—"

Delilah stepped back with a scornful flip of her hand. "How the hell would I have time for a husband? I have a bar to run, and the sewing work on the side—I need the extra money for Pop's care... plus I'm tired to death from taking care of him when Maria can't be there. Where would I find the energy for one more person?"

"My job's got real good benefits," Abe tried, his eyebrows raised in hope. "If we was married, that'd pay for the Colonel's nurse."

Josie Juniper

Delilah's father, Moses Kelley, was known in town as The Colonel. An elderly Vietnam vet, he and Delilah's mother, Wanda, had started a family late in life. Wanda had died before she got to see her daughter graduate high school.

Delilah shot Abe a cynical look. "Not unless you plan to marry my dad, it won't. I may be a hard-ass, but I'm not so cold that I'd marry someone just for the medical insurance."

Abe's gaze dropped. "*Just* for the insurance? You couldn't marry me for love?"

She gave him a light sock on the shoulder. "You know I'll always love you like a friend. And when—"

The door rattled as someone pulled on it, and Delilah jumped back as if she'd been caught standing too close. The door opened. Framed in the rectangle was a tall lanky man with disheveled auburn hair and an unshaven two-day stubble. He wore a t-shirt with a picture of Godzilla framed by Japanese writing, faded black jeans, and black Converse sneakers.

"Your door's hung backwards," he announced.

"It says 'push' right on it," Delilah replied coolly. "Don't they teach you to read up there in Portland?"

Griffin stuffed his hands in his pockets and ambled over. "That kind of handle is for a pull-door. So I'm guessing whoever installed it is the one who can't read."

She glared at him, poking at a molar with her tongue. "Aren't you clever," she said, mercilessly flat. Her attention shifted back to Abe, and she nodded toward Griffin. "Abe, this is the city boy who's gonna be working for me."

Griffin extended a hand and shook with the shorter, stockier man. "Working *with*, not for. I'm half owner," he corrected. "Nice to meet you. Abraham...?" He waited for a surname.

"Abel. Ferguson," Abe said. His eyes were narrowed in something that stayed just on the polite side of suspicious.

Delilah was almost surprised Abe didn't challenge Griffin to an arm-wrestling match right there, he seemed so wary of the good-

12

Wylde Strangers

looking newcomer. She had to admit, Griffin Isaacs was easy on the eyes. In a scruffy loser kind of way.

"Okay, cool—Abel. Nice to meet you."

Griffin surveyed the room, the dusty décor that had been unchanged since Colonel Kelley had bought the place in the early seventies. It was every inch a cowboy bar—a dark, rustic space where people came to soak their aches in beer at the end of a hard day, share a dance or two, and play a game of pool on the old table balanced by matchbooks slipped under two of the legs.

"Wow," Griffin breathed. "This is a time-warp." His hands returned to his pockets and he began a leisurely circuit of the room. "But it's got potential."

Delilah saw the unmistakable flash of competitive hostility in Abe's slate-blue eyes, though he was doing his best to keep an amiable good ol' boy smile on his face.

As Griffin stopped in front of the stuffed moose head that Abe's grandfather, Otis Ferguson, had donated to the Wylde Saloon decades before, he laughed, then turned and pointed back at it with a thumb, as if to say, *Hilarious*.

Delilah stood on her toes, and near Abe's ear, she joked, "The minute he mentions arugula, I'll let you kick his ass."

chapter three

Peering through the curved glass, Griffin inspected the CD jukebox. He heard Delilah exchanging murmured goodbyes with Abe. He could tell by the tone that the words were critical, and most likely about him, but he didn't take it personally. As the new kid in town, he knew he'd be gossip-fodder for a few weeks until the sleepy little map-dot found something else to talk about. Maybe someone would get a new pickup or... shoot an especially large deer? What the hell did people do out here in the sticks?

Griffin threw a look over his shoulder. "This thing is awesome," he called out to Delilah. "How many CDs does it hold?"

"Three hundred." She grabbed a rag out of a bleach-bucket and wrung it out, then made her way across the room, wiping down tabletops and straightening chairs—four per table—to sit at precise right angles to each other. Cleo had done the same thing, and Griffin hadn't been above pivoting them crookedly sometimes behind her back, just to annoy her.

Wylde Strangers

"Nice. Three hundred's pretty good."

Delilah gave an indifferent grunt. "I've been listening to the *same* three hundred songs here since I was about twelve. It gets old."

Griffin folded his arms and leaned back against the jukebox. "Why don't you change them?"

"It hasn't opened in almost twenty years. And if you crack that glass with your behind, I will put the rest of you through it too."

He stood upright. "What's this dent on the front?"

"Skips sometimes, and I have to kick it."

Walking slowly to the table Delilah was cleaning, Griffin pulled out a chair, spun it around, and sat on it backwards. "Just a guess, but that might have something to do with why it won't open." He gestured to the chair opposite. "Let's talk. I had a lot of ideas while I was driving down last night."

"I'll just bet."

Before sitting, she dropped the rag on the table and wiped her hands off, smoothing them down her hips and thighs, which had a curve that had drawn Griffin's attention more than once already. He noticed the fabric was lighter in that area of her jeans, as if from constant dampening with bleach water. Despite Delilah's similar fondness for precision, she was different from Cleo, who never would have allowed her clothes to get damaged. Delilah's nail polish was chipped and her boots faded. As she sat, she pulled her peachy-golden hair up and snapped it into a quick messy bun with the black elastic that had been around her wrist.

"So, this morning I spent a few hours going over the numbers," Griffin said. "I feel confident that we could be in the black after… maybe six months? But there'll have to be remodeling. Probably need to close for about three weeks. Oh, and a name change. I started a list…" He dug in his pocket for a folded piece of paper, also removing a green lid-stopper stick from Starbucks and putting it in his mouth, toothpick-style.

"We're not changing the name."

Josie Juniper

Griffin paused while unfolding the page. He shifted the plastic stick to the other side of his mouth. "It's not expensive," he said. "Fifty bucks."

"It has nothing to do with the money." Her arresting green eyes narrowed. They were surrounded by a heavy black ring around the irises, which reminded Griffin of that famous old National Geographic photo of the Afghan girl.

The possible reason for her resistance caught up with him, and he gave her what he hoped was a winning smile. *These country types are... traditional,* he reminded himself. *She's being sentimental. I'll have to sound understanding.*

He held up both hands. "I know how you feel. This is a lot to throw at you. But in a decade, Wylde is going to be a real tourist town—maybe even a 'destination.' Beautiful high desert, an hour from the Shakespeare festival, good rock climbing over at Rattlesnake, it's—"

"You... *know how I feel?*"

The dishwasher in the kitchen shut off, leaving only the warble of some country music siren. Something about it was more unnerving than silence. He cleared his throat. "Yeah, that's probably bullshit," he admitted. "So maybe you could tell me."

She scoffed. "Why?"

He took the stick from his mouth. "Because I'm not a mind-reader." He knew if he let her intimidate him during this first summit, the stain of it would seep in, and it'd be all she'd ever see. He set his jaw the way he did when he had to be tough with Byron, and clamped the stick between his teeth again, hoping for a dash of noir film tough-guy.

He finished unfolding the page, slowly, watching her. "Here's the thing. 'Wylde Saloon' is just... descriptive. It's like having a dog named Dog. A good title, just like on a movie, makes people *curious*. It teases a story. The narrative—" He paused, seeing her blasé expression. "Do you know much film theory?"

"Do I look like I know film theory?" she bit out slowly. "My favorite movie is *Bullitt*."

Wylde Strangers

Griffin's eyebrows tugged up in surprise. "Steve McQueen? No shit?" He nodded, impressed. "I would've guessed more like... I don't know, *Love Actually* or something."

Delilah snorted. "You don't know anything about me."

"True." He took a slow breath. "Okay, let's try something different. I'll list off things that should be done. Then we sort them into categories: things you're cool with, things to discuss further, and total deal-breakers."

She shrugged—an insolent roll of her shoulders. He pulled his focus away from the smooth wings of her collar bones, outlined beneath the tight shirt, and glanced at the paper in his hand.

"New décor inside," he began. "Floors refinished. Put in a few big windows. An outdoor seating area, with landscaping and a fire pit. Upscale menu. Signature craft cocktails. Advertising. New music in the jukebox—not all that 90s country crap. And... yeah, *new name.* Something edgy. Not a generic place-holder that makes it sound like a cowboy watering-hole."

"It *is* a cowboy watering-hole."

"All right, you're making me say it, but... *one that's going under*."

"You ready for your, uh... what did you call it? Categories?"

He swept an arm. "Be my guest."

"The floors do need a shine. The rest of it can go hang."

He took the plastic stick from his mouth—the tip now bent and mangled—and set it in an ashtray. "Right, right. Okay, cool. I almost forgot, there's the option you obviously want: everything stays the same while I throw money at you and cover the bills, property taxes, insurance, employee pay... until you go out of business anyway."

Delilah stood up as Reba McEntire's "Fancy" started to skip. "I agree something needs to change. I just hate your ideas." She went to the jukebox and gave it a backwards kick, with an almost graceful twirl.

"Excellent. Good talk." Griffin stood up. Pointing at the ashtray on the table, he said, "Great place to start with some changes. You're letting people smoke in here? Illegal since 2007, in case you missed

17

the memo. You know what the fine is? Five hundred bucks a day." He snatched up the paper on the table and shoved it in his pocket, crumpled. "I won't pay it. That's on you."

Delilah's jaw went hard, mirroring his. The thought drifted through Griffin's head that the expression accentuated her full lips, with their hint of pink gloss, in a way that made him unsure who he was more annoyed at—her, or himself.

"You think I'm going to tell a hard-working man, when he comes in half-dead after a long day at the plant, that he can't have a smoke with his beer?"

"Uh, *yes*. Obviously," Griffin said. "There are rules." He sketched an exaggerated rectangle in the air. "You're still located in the larger world—not fantasy-land."

Delilah snatched up the bleach rag and stalked back to the bar, dropping it into the bucket. Locking his hands on top of his head in frustration, Griffin followed.

"Be reasonable," he tried. "This is actually a great argument for outdoor seating."

"Most people *do* smoke outside—we're not a pack of savages, like you seem to think. It's just a few of the older guys. They're tired, they're sore, and as long as no one around them minds, I'm not going to bust their balls about it."

Griffin gave a bitter laugh. "I don't think you have *any* problem busting balls, lady. You're doing a first-class job on mine." He grabbed a pen out of a plastic cup beside the cash register, and snatched an old order-slip off the ticket-holder carousel in the service window. "Here's the address of the rental where I'm staying," he said evenly, writing on the back of the slip. "Text me when you want to come over and have a sane conversation about *our* bar." He handed it to her and strode toward the exit.

"Or you text *me*, when you want to come back in to *my family's* bar with a list of better ideas! The ones you've got now are a bunch of flashy nonsense, and none of it would fly here. I'd get laughed out of town. I still have my dignity."

He turned back to her. "Awesome. Hope it serves you well in bankruptcy court. But you'd better come to *me first,* if you want me to sign checks for your staff on Friday. Otherwise, maybe you can try paying them in 'dignity.'" He pushed on the door, only to have it jar in the frame. He closed his eyes, fuming over having his dramatic exit thwarted by the stupid backwards door. He swung it open and walked out, squinting into the glare, ignoring Delilah's taunting laugh behind him.

chapter four

Delilah turned her father's hand over, gently but efficiently, and started to wipe it down with the damp washcloth.

He pulled away. "Cold," he complained, the word thick and whispery.

"It is not." She opened his fingers to swipe between them. "I ran the tap 'til it was warm."

"Too hot," he mumbled.

"Oh, it was too cold a second ago, and now it's too hot? Nice try, Pop." She attempted to get under his fingernails a little, and he jerked his hand free and gave hers a smack. "Nice reflexes," she told him. "Fine—we're done."

She went and dropped the washcloth into a laundry basket. The front door opened, the bells hanging from the knob—placed on every door to let Delilah know if her father tried to open one—jangling like perpetual Christmas.

"Good morning!" Maria sang out, heading for the kitchen. Delilah could hear her put something in the refrigerator. She came into the living room, where Delilah was turning on the TV for her father. "I brought some of that banana pudding with vanilla wafers," Maria told Delilah. "You hear that, Colonel?" she said to Delilah's father, dropping a plump hand onto his shoulder. "A treat, for after lunch!"

He ignored the news, tired eyes fixed on the flickering TV images.

"Thanks, Maria. I can pay you back for the ingredients."

"You don't pay for the pudding," Maria said with a wave. "I was making it for my grandson already. I like to share." She took her big tapestry-style craft bag off her shoulder and dropped it onto a recliner, knitting needles protruding.

Delilah drew Maria aside and lowered her voice. "Can you try to cut his fingernails today? He fights me too much."

"Of course." Maria put an arm around Delilah's shoulders and walked with her toward the front door. "Have you seen that investor again? Graham?"

"Griffin." Delilah took her purse off a coat peg and dug for her keys. "No, we haven't talked since day-before-yesterday when he came in. It's sort of a standoff." She pulled out the keychain, a pink Swiss army knife. "I'm stopping by his place on my way in. He's renting the apartment above the old tool-and-die works." With a frown, she added, "Looks like I have to blink first. The guy's an idiot, but he's the idiot holding the purse strings."

Maria gave Delilah a squeeze. "You'll find a way to meet in the middle."

Delilah took a wrinkled white envelope from her purse and handed it to Maria. "Half of your pay for the week. I promise I'll have the other half tomorrow night—Fridays are usually good. Howard's doing a taco special."

"Don't you worry. Take your time, *mija*."

Maria's smile under her elaborate crown of salt-and-pepper braids was relaxed and grandmotherly, but Delilah knew Maria's family struggled financially as much as many people in Wylde. Her husband Luis had a small pension from his Forest Service job, but their house had been damaged in a fire a year before and they were still doing repairs, as well as raising their 10-year-old grandson.

Shortly after leaving, Delilah drove along what locals called the High Road—though the street name was actually Towhee, a fact asserted by a few faded signs. This ran parallel to the so-called Low Road. The two streets were yards apart, separated by a culvert. Most of Wylde's businesses were on either the High Road or Low Road. A fork at the west end branched either to the K-12 school or the industrial area. Delilah hung a right toward the factories, stopping at a tall brick building that read *Cudahy Tool & Die* in faded letters above arched windows.

She climbed out of her dirt-tanned white hatchback, walked up to the door, and pulled on the ring-shaped handle. Locked. To the right of the door was a buzzer dangling from a wire. Next to it, swaying on a nail protruding from the bricks' mortar was a rain-wrinkled 3x5 card with an arrow pointing toward the ground. Delilah's gaze followed the arrow and saw a pile of acorns.

Above, she heard a window clatter open, and Griffin looked out.

"You're supposed to throw them at the window," he explained.

"What?"

"The acorns. The landlord put them there, like it was just… totally normal."

She laughed. "He's old. He doesn't understand texting."

He ducked back in, disappearing for a few seconds, then popped his head out again. "I'll be right down."

A minute later the huge door creaked open and Griffin beckoned. Delilah followed him in, and he locked the door after her.

"Sorry about that," he said, pointing toward the lock. "Probably seems creepy. I wish I could just keep it open, but Mr. Cudahy is convinced that 'kids'll get in here and drink and get up to no good' if the downstairs is unlocked."

Delilah followed Griffin across the wide room to the stairs against the far wall. "That's not a bad Al Cudahy impression," she admitted.

"The guy makes it easy," Griffin said. "He sounds like… if a gravel truck ran on chewing tobacco." He opened the door at the top of the stairs. "After you."

His feet were bare, and he wore gray hiking shorts with frayed pockets, a t-shirt with some sort of complicated-looking math equation on the front, and a black hoodie. Delilah pointed at the shirt as she passed him in the doorway. "What's that all about?"

"A math geek friend gave it to me," he said, padding toward the open kitchen. "He says it makes a graph that's something obscene. I told him not to tell me, because frankly I kinda dig the mystery." He picked up a mug and took a sip of the contents. "Coffee?"

"No thanks." Delilah realized her shoulders were high and tight, and she consciously relaxed them and began an investigative circuit of the room, as Griffin had done in the bar. The ceilings were high, the walls exposed brick. There were sections partitioned off by black-painted plywood, presumably a bedroom and bathroom. Two space heaters stood at either end of the room. Along the wall in the center were kitchen fixtures, and a long island with mismatched stools, running parallel. Across from that was an entertainment center faced by a gold sofa. Half-unpacked boxes were open in front of it.

"The big furniture was already here," Griffin said, following Delilah toward the entertainment center. "I just brought smaller stuff, since I won't be here long."

She nodded and took a few books out of a box—*The Complete Stories of Flannery O'Connor* and Faulkner's *As I Lay Dying*.

"Went through kind of a southern author kick recently," Griffin said, sitting on the arm of the sofa.

Delilah grunted and set the books back in the box. "That why you decided to move to a rural town?"

His eyebrows went up. "Huh. Maybe?" He shrugged. "There is something romantic about places like this." He took a sip of coffee, then amended the statement. "I mean romantic in the sense of literary. Not, uh… sexual."

Josie Juniper

Delilah cut a look at him. "I went to school—I know that 'romance' originally just meant stories." She leaned on the sofa's other arm. "So. Let's talk about your stupid ideas for my bar."

"*Our* bar," he said quietly into his coffee mug.

"I know I can be a little… prickly. I'm used to doing things my own way. My father's the same—all the Kelleys are." She picked at the peeling nail polish on one thumb. "But I understand there have to be changes."

"You *are* prickly. At Sadie and Weston's reception I heard someone say you're an asshole." He smiled. "Can't claim I wasn't warned."

"Who said it?" she growled.

"Uh, *no*. I'm not setting off world war three. Suffice it to say it was a woman, and she's probably just envious of you, because…" He trailed off. "You know." He made a circular wave, encompassing Delilah.

She was surprised to feel her face go hot at what might have been an arrested compliment. As she labored to push her train of thought back onto the tracks, Griffin's phone chimed from his pocket. He took it out and looked at the screen.

"Sorry, hold that thought. I have to take this." He walked toward the bedroom. "Dougie," Delilah heard him say. "What's going on?"

There was a long silence, in which Griffin listened, and Delilah sat down on the floor and started taking books out of the boxes and perusing them.

Griffin let out a long, defeated sigh. "Okay, and he left with them?" More silence. "All right. No, it's cool. I'm glad you told me. I'll give him a call. Thanks, man." He stuck his head out of the curtain-draped bedroom doorway. "Hey, Dee?"

Delilah looked over. "What, me?"

"Yeah. I need to make a quick call. Two minutes, tops."

"Not a problem." She held up a book as proof that she was sufficiently entertained. He ducked behind the curtain.

"Byron!" Griffin said a few seconds later, in a tone of false heartiness. "Anything you wanna tell me about?" He waited. "Oh, y'know. Just wondered if you left work halfway through your shift, with Nix and Marco." There was a span in which the person on the other end seemed to be monologuing, punctuated by Griffin's *uh huh, sure, mmhm, right*. Finally he broke in. "Look, cut the bullshit. I can't help you if you lie to me. I need—" There was another pause, and Griffin's voice dropped. "Okay, stop. Byron, *stop*. Jesus Christ, you're going to make me feel bad, and I'm pissed at you right now." He sighed again. "Look, I'll call you back in five minutes, and you'd better pick up, got it? No, I *don't* hate you. Pull it together. Five minutes."

He came out, walking slowly and staring at the wood floors. Delilah stood up.

"I'll let you, uh, deal with your thing," she said. "We can talk bar stuff later. Come by tomorrow night and see what a Friday looks like. I can introduce you to people."

"Sure, cool." He stuffed his phone in the hiking shorts' knee pocket, and it started to fall out of the ragged seam at the bottom. He switched it to the opposite side.

Delilah gave a reluctant half-smile. "My other job is sewing," she said, pointing at the pocket. "I'm guessing you're being a total guy and won't get rid of those because they're your 'lucky shorts' or something. But I could fix the rips."

He pulled his head back. "You'd do that for me?"

"I'll tell you what: if you can figure out how to get the jukebox open, I'll fix your seams and pockets. Deal?"

He put his hand out to shake. She took it, surprised at how hard and muscular it was, edged with calluses. She turned it over in both of her own. "How did you get laborer's hands?"

"Rock climbing."

She chuckled, turning and heading for the door. "Sounds like the kind of fool hobby you'd have. Imagine, hanging off a cliff on purpose." She shook her head.

He opened the door and leaned against its edge, and their eyes locked as she paused before leaving. "I like the uncertainty," he told her. "Figuring out where to put my hands and feet next… it's a puzzle. A riddle."

"Maybe so," Delilah said. She started down the metal steps. "But if you guess wrong, you fall."

chapter five

Because the apartment covered the entire upper floor of the defunct tool-and-die works, there were windows on every side. They were huge paned casement windows, and Griffin loved opening them as soon as he woke up. The cross-breeze drifted through the apartment from all four directions, bringing in the scent of dry grass, sun-warmed rocks, faint syrupy hints of the nearby diner, and a not-unpleasant motor oil astringency from the factory down the road.

He made coffee and a quick fruit salad, listening to Built to Spill on the big stereo he'd finally set up, and picked up his phone.

Griffin: *Hey are there thrift stores around? I want to get CDs for the jukebox*

A few minutes later, as he was chasing a stubborn red grape around his bowl with one fork-tine, she replied.

Josie Juniper

Delilah: *Why are you asking me? Google it*

Griffin: *Well good morning to you too*

He set his phone down, annoyed, and went to wash his bowl and pour another cup of coffee. When he sat back down, there was a message.

Delilah: *The three I go to are in Klamath Falls. 40 min drive from Wylde, but worth it.*

Griffin: *You don't strike me as the thrift store type*

Delilah: *Then why did you ask me??? I don't go to be cool. Only an idiot buys everything new. I get fabric for sewing.*

Griffin: *Ah. Cinderella*

Delilah: *?*

Griffin: *she uses that stuff the stepsisters threw away, and makes a ball gown*

Delilah: *Was never into princesses. Didn't get the reference.*

He took a sip of his coffee, imagining Delilah as a kid. Something told him she'd been all tangled hair, scabby knees, and fistfights. She struck him as a loner—the kind who'd build a treehouse and not let anyone else in. Just sit in there with a bag full of peanut butter sandwiches and a stack of comic books.

Griffin: *Were you a tomboy?*

She didn't reply for long enough that he wondered if he'd offended her somehow by asking. He went and took a shower and got dressed. When he passed by the kitchen island again, there was a message.

Delilah: *Guess you could say that. But mostly don't like the princess thing because happily ever after is a bunch of BS. Also don't spend money on CDs until you know whether the jukebox will open. You're going about this ass-backwards.*

Griffin: *There's a method in my madness. If I shell out the money first, I won't give up. Easier to blow off a challenge if there's no investment. I like a little risk*

Delilah: *That explains your weird thing for dangling off mountains. Can't really back out when you're holding on to some crack a mile off the ground. You have to figure it out.*

He laughed, sitting back and staring at the phone for a minute.

Griffin: *you might be the first person who ever noticed that. YES. That is it EXACTLY*

A few minutes passed. His phone buzzed as he was locking the door to leave and drive into Klamath Falls.

Delilah: *You're welcome.*

***

Griffin felt the young woman behind the counter at the thrift store watching him surreptitiously as he made his way around the room. The fluorescent lights emitted a subdued buzz, and the store had that familiar smell unique to second-hand shops—fabric softener and the doggy tang of old sofa, mingling with the beige mustiness of books. It wasn't until she smiled that he realized she was watching him *not* to see if he was shoplifting, but in what Cleo called "a boys-and-girls way."

He approached the counter with a stack of tolerable 90s alt-rock CDs, a garlic press, and a vintage 80s San Diego Zoo shirt that said "You Belong in the Zoo." He set them down and took out his wallet as the girl—short and curvy with two long brown braids—picked up the shirt and gave it a flap before folding it.

"Good find," she said.

"I feel bad for only paying three bucks. You could get thirty or more on eBay."

"Your lucky day." She started ringing up the purchase. Holding up the garlic press, she asked, "Are you a good cook?"

"I do all right. I work in kitchens sometimes, so..." He shrugged.

"You're a chef?"

He leaned against the counter and took another green plastic stopper-stick out of his wallet along with his credit card. "No, I... just do a bunch of things." He handed over his credit card and put the plastic stick in his mouth.

She swiped the card and looked at it. "Interesting name—*Griffin*. I'm Hazel."

"Nice to meet you." He offered a hand. Hers was small, warm, and slightly rough, like picking up a freshly baked cookie.

She pointed at the stick he was chewing. "I'll bet you just quit smoking."

"Yep."

"Miss it?"

"Oh hell yeah. But I wanted to climb better."

She laughed and nodded. "I thought I recognized your calluses." She held up her own hands. "I do a little bouldering, but I'm not, like, impressive."

"No shit?"

"Yes shit. Been to Lost Rocks? I went last month."

"Heard of it, but haven't been there. I mostly free climb these days."

Wylde Strangers

A customer holding an armload of baby clothes made her way up, and Griffin stepped back. He scanned the counter for a piece of paper, and not seeing one, took a bent business card from his wallet. He picked up a pen and crossed out the number for Gold Lizard, then circled his personal number.

"Just put this in the round file if I'm being a creep, but that's my number if you want to talk more. I'm staying over in Wylde for a couple months."

Hazel picked up the card and tucked it her pocket. "Not going in the round file," she said, ducking her head with a smile.

***

Delilah had the guy backed up against the door of the bar kitchen's walk-in refrigerator.

"On a *Friday?*" she shrilled at the tall beefy man in the stained apron. Though she barely came up to his shoulder, he cringed back as if cornered by a wolf spider. "I just dropped two hundred bucks on taco fixings, and you're bailing on me?" She swept an arm at the long metal table where the provisions sat. "I'm tending bar, and Jack can't handle the kitchen alone. Even if Petra ignores the dishes and helps, the whole thing'll go tits up."

"I can't help it! Amber's being a flake about her night with the kids."

"Spare me the sob story," Delilah snapped.

Howard scowled. "I'll keep prepping for another hour. But then I have to go."

"You walk out that door, you'd better keep walking!"

Griffin conspicuously shook the crinkly white plastic bag in his hand as he entered the kitchen. There was no way to pretend he hadn't overheard—distant satellites had probably picked it up. Delilah's head whipped around to glare at him.

Setting the thrift store bag on the metal table, Griffin gave Delilah a nod and extended a hand to shake with the cook. "Howard, right?" he asked. "I've heard you make a hell of a BLT. I'm Griffin Isaacs."

Josie Juniper

Howard grinned, showing a steel crown on one of his canine teeth. "The new owner! You're younger than I expected."

Griffin chuckled. "And probably younger than I feel, most days."

Delilah started unpacking the taco fixings, an air of menace around her like smoke from a wet campfire. She smacked down jars of salsa and cans of black olives as if crushing roaches with them.

"Wanna know my secret on the BLTs?" Howard asked, leaning toward Griffin conspiratorially. "I toss the lettuce in a touch of oil-and-vinegar, and add garlic powder to the mayo."

"Damn, that's smart." Griffin opened the plastic bag and withdrew a manila folder, out of which he took a stack of legal-sized envelopes and handed one to Howard. "Paychecks," he said. Delilah's focus snapped up in his peripheral vision. "And, uh… if you want to walk me through how you like the tacos, I'll cover your shift tonight. I was going to be here anyway, getting to know everyone."

Howard's eyes slid toward Delilah. "Are you… sure?"

"Totally. You'd be doing me a favor, giving me something to do." He went to the shelf with the linens and grabbed an apron.

"Thanks, man!" Howard started feeding slabs of cheddar through the rotary grater. Griffin picked up a #10 can of olives and clamped it into the jaws of the opener. Delilah peered into the white thrift store bag.

"Aren't you supposed to be fixing the jukebox?" she asked.

"This is a little more pressing," he replied with a raised eyebrow. "Besides, that was a trade, right?"

"I could hardly sew them while they were still on your ass."

He looked up from where he was draining the can into the sink. "I would have taken them off for you," he replied with a teasing spark.

Delilah leaned against the counter and shot a look toward Howard, who was whistling as he whipped the handle around on the grater. "You're just encouraging him to blow off work next time some minor snag pops up. He made the same excuse last week."

Wylde Strangers

"Doesn't mean it's not true. I'd rather believe in people and be wrong than *not* believe in them and be wrong."

"That's the philosophy of a born sucker."

He set the can on the table and studied Delilah. "Said the born cynic."

"I'm a realist."

Griffin snorted. "Whatever. At any rate, you wanted me here, I'm here. And making tacos is fun."

"I suspect you're gonna be that guy—*the fun boss.*"

"And I suspect you're not *the fun anything.*"

She gathered her hair and piled it into a bun, stabbing a ballpoint pen through it to keep it in place. Her profile, as she turned to look through the service window with a proud lift to her head, reminded Griffin of a pre-Raphaelite painting—the strong round chin, long nose, and bee-stung lips wearing a sullen pout.

"I don't have time for fun," she muttered. Snatching up a short black bar apron, she wrapped it around her trim waist and stalked out of the kitchen.

Howard came up beside Griffin and set down a tub of shredded cheese, covering it with plastic wrap as he eyed Delilah. "You know that saying about 'Hate to see her go, but I love to watch her walk away'? With that one, I *love* to see her go, *and* watch her walk away." He shook his head with a chagrined smile.

Griffin started unwrapping heads of lettuce. "She dating some poor beleaguered bastard?"

"Used to see a guy named Abe." Howard looked sidelong at Griffin and jabbed a playful elbow. "But don't go getting any ideas there."

"What, *her?*" Griffin sucked his teeth skeptically. "Yeah, *no*. Not my type."

As he sharpened a knife to chop lettuce, Griffin smiled, thinking of the text message from Hazel he'd found on his phone when he'd pulled up to the Wylde Saloon.

33

Josie Juniper

Hi! I forgot to put your garlic press in the bag. I suppose I could bring it to you. Show me how well you can use it. Dinner?

chapter six

On opening night at Gold Lizard, five years before, Griffin had felt a rush of joy looking out at the crowd—the murmur of voices, trills of laughter, perfect music on the stereo, the chime of glasses and plates—steeped in the heady feeling that *he had made this*. He and Cleo had stood behind the bar wrapped in each other's arms, surveying their newly launched venture, and she'd pressed her lips near Griffin's ear and said, "This is you! It's your vision." She'd clasped hard against him and added, "I want you so much right now…"

Two years later, the opening of Velour had been a similar thrill. Business was good, and they'd bought a condo in a new building just blocks from Gold Lizard. Walking between home and work, or down the fashionable boulevard, he'd felt woven into the fabric of the neighborhood. There had been a definite sense of knowing where his life was headed, a crisp and certain alignment.

Tonight, face flushed with heat from the grill as he slid another order of tacos through the service window, Griffin felt…

disconnected. The music was a sugary country drawl that made him tired, Petra dropped as many plates as she successfully washed, and Jack wandered over to flirt with her so often that he was more of a hindrance than a help in the kitchen.

But it was also the first time Griffin heard Delilah laugh. The sound caught him off guard—it might as well have been a cat opening its mouth and singing like a nightingale. It was a rich, unapologetic laugh. A spill of sound, trailing off into something like a moan, which had the unfortunate effect of immediately making Griffin wonder what Delilah was like in bed.

"Hey, Portland," she called at him through the service window. "Get out here and meet the mayor. This is Missy Owen."

Griffin rinsed off his hands and dried them on his apron before coming out to shake hands with a tall, thin, eccentric-looking older woman—maybe sixty-five—in a floppy black felt hat with a twisted pink bandana serving as a hat band.

"Nice to meet you," he said, surprised by the woman's iron grip. "I didn't even know Wylde *had* a mayor. I thought it was an unincorporated town."

Missy's eyes, settled deep into a road map of friendly fine wrinkles, seemed to twinkle like sunlight on moving water. "Informal mayor. Really I'm a professional busybody. People just got to calling me 'mayor' at some point, and it stuck."

She wore a baggy pinstriped suit with a pink dress shirt. Out of her breast pocket, in the place where a handkerchief would traditionally protrude, was the top of a roll of Necco candy wafers.

"Busybody, my ass," Delilah scoffed. "This town would barely run without you." Her focus shifted to Griffin. "Fundraisers, volunteer groups, nagging the county until they get off their tails and fix things... none of it would get done without Missy. Plus everyone comes to her for advice. And she owns the fix-it shop."

Missy drew the Necco roll from her pocket and flipped through a few of the powdery little discs until she found a black one. She eyed Griffin amiably and placed the candy on her tongue with the delicacy of one accepting Communion. "I hear you're fixing to shake things up around this place."

"Yeah?" Griffin cut a tense smile toward Delilah, just as someone down the bar called out for a drink, and she hurried off.

His eyes followed her smooth swagger, the way her movements flowed into each other, making the simple act of pouring drinks look like some sort of water ballet. She was a study in contrasts—the low voice that growled more than it purred, set against that bright laugh. He dragged his gaze away. "I don't know how much 'shaking up' I plan to do," he told Missy. "I'm just trying to save the bar, not set the world on fire. But I get the feeling she's going to fight me at every turn, purely for the sake of it. You have any pointers?"

Missy cocked her head toward Delilah, who was laying out shots with the brisk efficiency of a pin-setter, and navigating three simultaneous conversations without missing a beat.

"If you want to earn her respect, don't duck when she shoots from the hip. Half the time it's blanks. And don't believe that she can't be hurt. She talks tough, but I've known that gal since she was born, and she has a tender heart."

Griffin thought of Delilah, just hours before, screeching at Howard. It was hard to believe a warm-and-fuzzy side hid within that noisy armor. "Maybe," he replied noncommittally. "But it might not be a bad idea for her to earn *my* respect too."

***

A decorative plaque hung on the wall behind the bar. It was beveled and painted with the words *"Pick up your car tomorrow (and if you argue about it, don't come back),"* and had six latching cup hooks screwed into the wood. Customers knew that if Delilah held out her hand and said, "You're hooked," you'd best hand over your car keys without complaining, and find another ride home.

There were only two hooks occupied that Friday night—Shep Nash and Ira Bailey. Delilah was just managing to usher them out the door under Missy's care as Griffin took off his apron. He executed a perfect jump shot across the kitchen and into the linen hamper, and was only mildly disappointed that Delilah had been too busy to notice. Jack and Petra had already left, hands lodged in each other's back pockets.

Picking up a battered red toolbox, Griffin wandered over to the jukebox to start in on the repairs.

"Ah, you're a sweetheart, Lilah," Shep crooned, his arm dropping from Missy's shoulders to circle back and offer Delilah a hug. "And pretty as a picture."

She gave him a bracing smack on one shoulder, then spun him toward the door. "Don't you try and sweet-talk those keys out of me, you old sinner. You know I'll make good on kicking you out of here for keeps. I won't miss your skinny hide one bit." The words were gruff, but her smile gave her away.

Shep careened into Ira and they locked arms as Ira launched into the chorus of the old Tom Jones hit "Delilah." Missy gave them both a shove through the door.

Griffin scrolled through the YouTube videos saved on his phone, which showed how to change CDs on that jukebox model. He sat on the floor and watched a video while Delilah wiped down tables and turned chairs up. Empty of customers, the room had an odd echo— there was only the sound of the rasp and clunk of chairs, the hum of the ice machine, and the drone of the video.

At the end of the tutorial, Griffin switched on a small flashlight and inspected the edges of the loading hatch on the jukebox. He grabbed a flathead screwdriver and ran it beneath the lip of metal, twisting and poking. Within a minute he had the front of the machine open. Delilah's boots clopped across the room with a leisurely tread, as if she could hardly be bothered.

"Huh." A chair squeaked as she sat down. "I could've done that myself."

"Yep. But you didn't." Griffin leaned inside and inspected, then pulled a bar towel from his back pocket and started wiping away the grime. "I can see why this thing skips. It's filthy inside. You won't have to kick it anymore."

Wylde Strangers

She gave a small sigh of laughter. "You can be my replacement target."

"So funny." He ducked out from under the hatch and reached for the CDs he'd bought. "Any preferences for which songs I get rid of?" he asked.

"Not particularly." She sprawled her feet out and rotated her ankles as if her feet were tired.

"I'll keep it simple and start with the A's." He brought up another video on his phone and started watching the instructions on initializing new CDs.

"Just—" Delilah cut herself off after the first word.

Griffin glanced up, and seeing the look on her face, hit *pause*. He leaned on one of his hands, studying her face. She stood up, the chair barking back so hard it started to tip before righting itself.

"What is it?" he prompted.

"Nothing. I was just going to say… keep A5. You can swap out the rest." She headed for the kitchen.

Griffin stood and searched the faded and curled tags for A5— Kenny Chesney, "She's Got It All." Feeling for a quarter in his pocket, he nearly dropped it in the jukebox to play it before thinking better. He threw a look over his shoulder at the kitchen. Delilah stood in front of the utility sink filling the mop bucket, motionless, her expression anguished. One hand clutched the edge of the sink. Thick billows of steam rose around her, as if Hell itself had opened beneath her feet.

chapter seven

The hardest thing about closing down the bar was falling asleep at four o'clock and getting up at eight, when the Colonel generally woke. Maria snoozed in the guest bedroom after putting him to bed on nights when Delilah closed, waking at six to drive home and start breakfast for her grandson and husband.

The routine had become more exhausting since the Colonel's second stroke the previous year, but Delilah was used to it. Moses Kelley hadn't been a tall man even at the peak of health, and was now thin enough—despite Maria's calorie-laden cooking—that he wasn't too difficult to move. At five-nine, Delilah was exactly her father's height. And she'd towered over her mother, who'd been five-foot-one.

"Come on, eat those eggs," she nagged her father as she wiped out the cast iron skillet and set it aside.

"Spoiled," he griped in a papery rasp.

She leaned against the counter, planting one wet hand on her hip. "What's spoiled? The eggs, or you? Because those eggs are from

Bailey Farms—they couldn't be fresher if the chicken was standing on your placemat." She picked up a piece of toast with peanut butter and took a bite. "*You*, on the other hand…"

Delilah's phone chimed with a message from her best friend Katie.

"Door!" Moses barked, responding as he always did when Katie's doorbell text tone sounded. He pushed his plate away, knocking over a cup of milk.

Delilah swept up the spill with a dishrag and grabbed her phone. Her father had been a handful since he'd awakened. Though his sense of time was all but nonexistent now, Delilah felt that he still knew when it was a doctor visit day, and woke up agitated.

Katie: *Your 4:30 is the last appt of the day. Want me to come over after? I could help you get the Colonel into the car and follow you back, pick up wine at Sunny's and we could watch that mystery show on HBO*

Delilah: *Aaauuuggghhh I wish but I've gotta close the bar again whyyyyyyyyy*

Katie: *Can't the new guy do it? What use is he if you still can't take a night off?*

Delilah: *He's Daddy Warbucks. Signs the checks haha*

Katie: *Ah. That's something I guess. Is he cute?*

Delilah: *No*
Delilah: *I mean sort of, if you like that kind of thing, the douchey hipster type who's like "Do you know much about film theory?"*

Katie: *Omg please tell me you're making that up. He didn't say that.*

41

Josie Juniper

Delilah: *He did*

Katie: *LOL NO, GROSS*
Katie: *g2g, Mrs Vicks just got here and you know she's such a hypochondriac. Last week her eye twitched and she swore she had Mad Cow! I should get a raise every time I have to deal with her*

Delilah: *Ok see you this afternoon. And Pop's in a mood too, so I'll bring a present in lieu of a raise haha*

***

Sweet Dreams Coffee had that cozy small-town atmosphere, with its puff-topped pink curtains, padded chairs, cheery tile floors, and the lush scent of vanilla that spread for a two-block radius. The pink sign affixed to the roof had been made by Shep Nash, who was the cousin of the café's owner, Tammy. Delilah herself had sewn the curtains, Abe Ferguson's brother Noah had done the floors, and Katie's uncle had installed the kitchen equipment.

These little threads of connection were some of what Delilah loved about living in Wylde. Every person felt like a brushstroke in the mural, and there was no place that wasn't thick with personal history. For the two years Delilah had gone to college in Eugene—as much as she'd enjoyed "the big city" of 150,000 people—she'd missed Wylde, with its stories and characters, its gentle pace. When her father had the first stroke, she'd had to drop out of school to take care of him and run the bar. Though mixed with a longing for the wider world, coming home had been a relief in many ways.

She got out of the car, and spotting Tammy's youngest son leaning against a porch post staring at his phone, called to him.

"Ethan, will you keep an eye on the Colonel for a minute while I grab coffee?" she asked him.

He gave her a salute in reply and moved one porch post closer, adjusting his baseball cap. Delilah opened the door—with its stained-glass muffin-and-coffee-cup design—just as the customer at the counter apparently delivered the punchline to a joke. Tammy erupted into her trademark screeching laugh, capped by a series of snorts, and slapped one hand against the counter. Looking up, she waved at Delilah and immediately tipped a twelve-ounce paper cup off the stack to start her drink.

"Howdy, Miss Lilah," she sang out. "I've got the peppermint syrup in. You want a mint mocha, extra whip?"

"Please. And a raspberry latte for Katie—I'm heading over to Doc Anand's."

Tammy made the drinks, humming along with the Shania Twain song coming from the speakers. Delilah threw a glance over her shoulder to check on her father in the car.

"That kid who bought into your saloon has been in here every morning," Tammy said, spiraling a veritable mountain of whipped cream onto Delilah's drink. "Real generous tipper! If I was twenty years younger, I'd fall right into those dreamy dimples of his. What a smile on that boy…" She fanned herself with a hand. "If he's still single by December when Molly comes home from UCLA, I'll throw that girl right into his axle and see if she knocks him over."

"How do you know he's single? Maybe he has a girlfriend back in the city."

"He doesn't. I asked."

Delilah laughed. "Of course you did." She dropped a few dollars into the tip jar. "But she's too young for him. Griffin's thirty-three."

"What's twelve years? Besides, how often do we get fresh blood in this town?" Tammy pushed the first drink across the counter and set the lid beside it so Delilah could enjoy the extra whip before covering it.

"I'm sure Molly has enough 'fresh blood' in Los Angeles." Delilah took a sip of her mocha and swiped a bit of whipped cream off her upper lip. "Besides, he isn't staying. Just a few months, then back to Portland. He's not a small-town type."

"Why on earth would you say that?" Tammy asked, raising the steam pitcher high to pour Katie's latte. "He's real friendly. Just a peach."

Josie Juniper

Delilah made a face. "Comes off arrogant."

Tammy looked up through her fake lashes with a knowing smile. "Not with everybody. You bring out the fight in a man, Delilah Kelley."

Delilah lowered her drink. "What are you saying?"

"Oh, don't get your back up." Tammy capped Katie's drink and put a flower-shaped sticker over the hole. She grabbed a pastry bag and snapped it open, then dropped in two pale orange cookies. "Here—one for you and one for Katie. Pumpkin spice macarons. You gals let me know if they're any good." She held out the bag, an obvious peace offering to smooth away the indignant frown Delilah realized she was still wearing.

She slotted the bag between the cups wedged in the cardboard carrier, then put the top on her own drink. "Thanks. Don't mind me this morning—I'm tired because the Colonel woke up on the wrong side of the bed."

"I know, hon. What you need is a vacation. You should take some time off, now that you've got a partner. I'm sure he'll be real useful. The other morning he helped me when the bowl got stuck on the Hobart mixer. Un-stuck that thing and lifted it like it was a feather." She winked. "Nice muscles too—you can't help but notice."

Rolling her eyes, Delilah brushed her long braid aside. "I *can* help but notice. Still… he did fix the jukebox, I guess. For all the good it'll do. Filled it half up with crappy songs no one around here knows."

Tammy cradled her chin in one hand on the counter. "Something new might be nice though, right? You always complain about those same old songs. And some of 'em you don't even let people play because of Caleb—" The older woman stopped halfway through the thought, nervously picking up a rag to wipe the steam wand on the espresso machine.

Hearing the name paralyzed Delilah for a moment, then she pushed herself into motion and picked up the drink carrier. "You have a good morning, Tam," she forced out, trying to keep her tone light.

"You too, Lilah. And, um… sorry for bringing him up."

Delilah paused with her back against the door. "It's better than when *no one* brings him up. Maybe that's why it still shocks me to hear his name." She leaned against the glass and nudged it open. "Because it feels like everyone forgot him after he died."

***

Despite being almost eighty years old, Moses Kelley still grinned like a teenager when he saw a pretty face. And Delilah's best friend Katie MacNair had one of the prettiest in town. Delilah rolled his wheelchair up to the receptionist station at Doctor Anand's, and Katie greeted them with a radiant white smile. Her hair was inky black, smooth and heavy like something from a shampoo commercial—the type that looks like it should be swaying in dramatic slow motion.

"Sorry I'm late," Delilah said. She took Katie's drink from the removable cup holder hanging from the back of the wheelchair and set it on the counter. "There's an offering—almond milk, raspberry, no whip." She took a step back and waved at her jeans and formerly sage-green sweater, newly splashed with beige. "I'm wearing mine. Because *someone* threw a tantrum when it was time to get into the chair."

"You're the best!" Katie said, picking up the drink and peeling the sticker off the opening. "And you, Colonel Kelley, are the absolute naughtiest." She shook a finger at him, and he winked in reply. She took a sip of the latte, and her darkly fringed golden-brown eyes dropped closed in delight. "Perfect. Thank you!"

"There were cookies too, but they got knocked into a puddle when Pop was freaking out." Delilah scrunched her mouth in disappointment. "Pumpkin spice ones. Next time you see Tammy, just tell her they were amazing."

Rhonda, Doctor Anand's nurse, opened the door to the exam room and came out to collect Delilah's father. "I'll have him back in two shakes," she promised.

After the door closed behind the backwards-moving wheelchair, Delilah sank into a seat in the empty waiting area. "Take your time. *Please*," she sighed.

Katie went and turned off the sign above the glass door and flipped the lock, then came and sat beside Delilah, both of them slithering down in their chairs the way they had when they'd ridden the school bus together as kids. Delilah could feel Katie inspecting her profile. Her best friend reached and gave her a pat on one coffee-stained knee.

"You know what? I'll go home and change and come to the saloon tonight, drink a few rum-and-Cokes, hang out and keep you company while you work."

"Oh god, Kate—no. You look as tired as I do."

"No one in town is as tired as you are. And I want to get a look at this Griffin character and weigh in on the debate."

"Oh, man. You'd better be prepared with three witnesses to say you had both hands visible at all times and never so much as smiled at the new man in town. Otherwise Eli will throw fits when he gets back from his long-haul. You sure you want to risk it," she joked, "showing up at the saloon unsupervised like a tramp?"

Katie flapped a dismissive wave. "I'm sick to death of his jealous BS. He can take a flying leap." She bit her lip, hands tangled in her lap.

Following the movement, Delilah noticed that Katie's little engagement ring wasn't on her finger. She gasped and grabbed Katie's hand.

"Don't make a big deal about it," Katie said, her voice catching.

"What happened?" Delilah breathed.

"I'll pay you back for sewing the dress..." Her voice tightened.

"Katie-bear, no!" Delilah pulled her friend into her arms. "I don't care about that—I'd sew a hundred wedding dresses for you." She smoothed a hand down Katie's back. "Why didn't you tell me?"

"I just decided this morning," Katie sniffled over Delilah's shoulder. "I haven't even told Eli yet—not really. I texted him and said we have to talk when he gets back, and he said 'That's never good,' and I said 'No it isn't' and left it at that." She reached for a tissue from a box on the magazine table.

Knowing the situation could change over the course of a day, Delilah chose her words carefully. "I'm here for you no matter what." She brushed a strand of Katie's long hair away from her face with the tenderness of a mother. "But... I think you're making the right decision," she couldn't help adding. "Eli doesn't deserve you. And you know what? Screw it—I *am* taking the night off." She dragged Katie into another embrace. "We may be a couple of dateless bitches, but tonight we've got a date with a crappy bottle of chardonnay and a TV murder mystery."

chapter eight

Sadie and Weston had been the first of Griffin's Portland friends to join the Millennial homesteading movement. Land "out in the boonies" was affordable and appealing to fed-up city-dwellers, and for many, it was time to put those lumberjack beards to the test and start roughing it—so long as "roughing it" included internet service to stay connected to remote jobs and online shopping.

"I can see why you had the wedding down here and not in Portland," Griffin said, crossing his ankles on the deck railing and leaning back in his chair. He tipped his beer bottle up and took a drink, admiring the red-and-orange sunset. "It really is pretty."

Overhearing Griffin as she brought Weston another bottle and sat on his lap, Sadie said, "We got married in Wylde because Wes is a cheap bastard. Let's not romanticize it."

"I'm plenty romantic," Weston said easily, brushing her red hair aside and kissing her neck. "But also practical."

She took his dark-bearded chin in one hand and kissed him. "Also the six-hour drive separated the real friends from the dabblers. It's not far enough to have been a 'destination wedding,' but enough of a hassle to discourage people we don't give a damn about anyway."

"Aha, a test." Griffin raised his bottle in a sort of toast. "I passed. Winner!"

"And you got a new bar out of it," Weston said, pointing.

"Such as it is," Griffin replied with a sigh.

"How's that going?" Sadie asked.

"Eh. It's only been two weeks, so we'll see. I know you guys don't even know Delilah that well, but I wish someone had warned me that she's so cranky."

"You just have a chip on your shoulder about stubborn women because of Cleo," Sadie said. "Delilah's always been sweet to us. She did an amazing job with my dress—she's a wizard with upcycling. Gets all her fabrics from thrift stores. I like her. I wouldn't have invited her to the wedding if I didn't."

"But I can't help but notice you're not *friends*-friends," Griffin pointed out.

"We see her when we go into town, in passing and stuff. And we've gone to the bar a few times, just to enjoy the local color—y'know."

Griffin chuckled. "Slumming for kicks."

"Griff!" Sadie gave him a playful smack on the arm. "You're terrible."

"Sure, but I've got your number."

"You know what? I'll invite her to dinner, next time you're coming too."

Griffin held up a hand. "God, no. Please. Don't make me spend time with that woman outside of the bar." He polished off the last of his beer. "I don't mean to sound like an asshole—I know her life isn't a bed of roses. Her best friend was at the bar last night and we got to talking, and I heard a few things that put it in context."

"Do tell! Spill the local tea—I'm starved for gossip," Sadie begged. "I've started binging reality TV just to hear people dish."

Josie Juniper

Weston's work phone rang and he scooted out from under Sadie and went into the house to take the call.

"Here—gimme his beer before it goes to waste," Griffin said. Sadie handed it over, and Griffin settled into the Adirondack chair. "Two things: she's got an elderly invalid father she's been taking care of for almost a decade, and..." He took a long drink and frowned, feeling like the second detail might be too personal to share. "And apparently she had this boyfriend who died, like when she was eighteen."

Sadie covered her mouth. "Oh, no..."

"Yeah. The same year her mother croaked."

"What happened? You know, I thought there was something melancholy about her—like, sort of haunted."

"Well, her friend Katie—gorgeous girl, by the way—didn't say anything specific about the mother, so I'm sure that was something totally normal. But the boyfriend, they were like high school sweethearts—though he was older, and a drop-out. Typical small-town bad-boy: rode a motorcycle, bounced in and out of jail, but always small-time, never did more than cool his heels. And he was a drinker. 'Acres of charm,' Katie said. Snuffed it on his bike. There's a song on the jukebox that was 'their song,' and Delilah won't let anybody play it, but wouldn't let me change it either."

Sadie peeled a hand away from her mouth. "So tragic!"

Weston walked back out onto the deck.

"You're in demand—work calls at seven o'clock?" Griffin said.

Shoving his phone in a pocket, Weston sat on the arm of Sadie's chair. "That was, uh, Cleo."

Griffin's bottle stalled halfway to his mouth. "Why's she calling you?"

"I'm doing a new website for Velour. Because of the changes."

Trying to sound casual, Griffin asked, "What changes?"

"She hasn't talked to you about it?" Weston exchanged a look with Sadie.

"Why would she?" Griffin took a drink. "Not my bar. We don't talk, unless it's something specific about Gold Lizard."

Wylde Strangers

"She wants to go locally-sourced *only*. A hundred percent."

"With... everything? Seriously?" At Weston's nod, Griffin laughed. "That's crazy. It'll be too limiting. She won't be able to get a bunch of basic things."

Weston shrugged. "Dude, I hear ya. She's going to change the menu a lot, focus on local seasonal items like mushrooms, nuts, apples—"

"Okay, but what about the booze? There's only a handful of decent distilleries in the Northwest. And she's—?" Griffin cut himself off and waved a hand. "Whatever. Not my problem, not my money." He took a long drink. "And not my girlfriend. Her jailhouse-tattooed poser boyfriend can console her when the place tanks."

"Anton?" Sadie chimed in.

Griffin raised his eyebrows. "Alrighty then. Looks like she's talked to you about him."

"I mean, not a ton..." Sadie fiddled with the hem of her cardigan.

"But enough." Running a hand through his hair, Griffin watched the last of the sunset melt against the serrated horizon. "It's fine. I don't want to make you feel weird."

"This shouldn't be a 'his side/her side' thing," Sadie said, her voice faintly pleading, putting a hand on Griffin's knee. "Cleo and I have known each other since college."

"I know. Ignore my bullshit." Griffin gave her a tired smirk. His gaze roamed the rough painted shadows of the desert, and he felt a million miles from home, marooned as if he was on Mars. "But if it comes up, you're free to mention to her that I'm happy here, and I've gone on two dates with a girl who looks like a brunette Jennifer Lawrence. Hazel and I hiked up Mt. McLoughlin a couple days back."

"Oohh, you know what *that* means," Sadie teased. "The next one is date three. Third-date rule!"

Leaning back and examining the smear of stars brightening in the dark sky, Griffin smiled. "It's up to her. But I sure as hell hope so."

Josie Juniper

***

Griffin and Delilah sat across from each other at one of the tables which had been stashed under the overhang on the bar's back porch. The rest of the tables were crowded like pinball bumpers in the dirt, covered with tarps. From inside the bar came the steady grinding drone of the floors being sanded down for refinishing.

"As long as we have to be closed for two days, we might as well take the opportunity to buy new tables and chairs," Griffin said, tucking the pen he'd been using behind one ear. "Ones that match."

"Too expensive. And people like these. They have favorites. It's more homey if they don't match."

Griffin pulled a skeptical grimace. "*Favorites?* Are you for real?" He laughed. "Okay, cool idea—maybe none of the glasses could match either. We'll get a bunch of crazy shit from a thrift store, and customers can arm wrestle for who gets to use the best beer mug. They can fight like siblings! It'll be fun."

Delilah sipped her coffee. "You have no sense of loyalty—that's your problem."

"I have plenty of problems, but an absence of loyalty isn't one of them, thanks. And what the hell does that have to do with these broke-down chairs and wobbly-ass tables?"

Delilah rotated her cup, avoiding Griffin's eyes. "When you love something—even inanimate objects—they're like family. You have… a relationship with those things. A history. You don't throw them away when they get ugly. You fix them. Did you know Wylde is one of the last towns in Oregon with a fix-it shop? Missy can repair anything with moving parts."

Griffin rubbed a hand slowly down his face. "That's very quaint. But normal bars—*successful* bars—have matching furniture."

"A good-looking four-top runs about three-hundred-fifty. And we'd need twenty. More, if you want to do that outside-seating idea."

Griffin's eyebrows shot upwards. "Behold, a miracle! Through your pessimism I spied the fact that you're receptive to making a nice back patio."

She shot a sour look his way. "I didn't say I was receptive to the idea."

He broke off a bite of zucchini muffin inside the pastry bag on the table and ate it. "You didn't have to," he noted with a *gotcha* grin.

She flipped him off with a half-hearted smile, and Griffin couldn't resist a *Breakfast Club* quote. "Obscene finger-gestures from such a pristine girl!"

She tossed the next line back at him. "I'm not *that* pristine."

Griffin cracked up and raised a hand for a high-five, surprised when Delilah reciprocated. Her palm was warm when it touched his, and softer than he'd assumed it would be. He felt a faint flush of heat touch his face, and took the pen from behind his ear, tapping the legal pad on the table. "Right. So. Wanna drive to the restaurant supply place in Medford today?"

She shook her head adamantly. "I have to get home, and we don't need seven-grand-worth of new furniture."

Griffin leaned on his folded arms. "Gotta spend money to make it. If we don't start implementing changes, what I'm doing here isn't an investment—it's charity." Seeing Delilah's jaw go hard, he sat back. "Look, you may know this place, but I know bars in... like, a larger businessy sense. So I need your input. I don't want to go to Medford and come back with something you hate. We're not keeping the mismatched shit—that's all there is to it. Are you going to help, or just throw handfuls of marbles under my feet while I tap dance?"

"Customers won't like it. People around here like comfort and familiarity."

"I get that. But there aren't enough locals to support this place anymore. Wylde residents are moving away. I'm buying tables for the customers of the future, as tourism expands and the town starts to grow again. People like Weston and Sadie, who are snapping up all this cheap acreage, and want cool places to hang out once they're here, so they don't have to drink at home."

Delilah stood up with a look of disgust. "Weston and Sadie Bloom are nice folks—don't get me wrong. But I'd be lying if I said I don't resent the wave of outsiders poised to take over my town." She slapped a hand against her chest. "It's the town where I grew up. Not a quirky project for pampered city folk, coming out here staring at the real residents like it's some redneck petting-zoo."

"The 'wave of outsiders' is coming, like it or not. Ride it or drown. Your choice." He stood and grabbed the legal pad and pastry bag. "You coming with me?"

"To Medford? No. Just text me pictures. I told you, I have to get home."

On an impulse, Griffin asked, "Taking care of your dad?"

Delilah gripped the top of her chair. "What do you know about it?"

"Just something I heard, from your friend Katie." He took another bite of muffin, chewing contemplatively. "Is it supposed to be a secret? I mean, everyone in town knows. But I'm just an 'outsider,' right?"

She pushed the chair in, hard. "Damned straight, you are. You don't even plan to stay." She strode toward the back door and yanked it open. "Everyone leaves."

As the rusty screen door screeched shut behind her, Griffin wondered whether Delilah's boyfriend Caleb would have been one who'd left or stayed, had he lived.

chapter nine

"This place is fantastic," Hazel said, turning around in a circle to take in all of Griffin's apartment. Her gauzy retro black skirt belled out and fluttered back to her calves, which were clad in striped tights. "I didn't think spaces like this existed anymore. It looks like something from an eighties movie. You know, like how everyone lived in an industrial loft?"

"I have a chair in the shower where I practice my *Flashdance* routine," Griffin said. He opened the refrigerator and started setting out snacks on the kitchen island—olives, hummus and carrots, crackers and homemade cilantro dip. Hazel meandered over and inspected the offerings.

"Fancy. Almost as fancy as your dress-up outfit."

Looking down at the repaired hiking shorts and San Diego Zoo shirt he was wearing, Griffin protested around the olive in his mouth, "This is the shirt I bought at your store! I figured that'd get me points."

"Not quite as many points as if you'd put on pants and a decent shirt, like a human. But you're kinda ridiculously good-looking, so I'm gonna let it slide."

He held up a finger. "Just wait until you taste the pomodoro. Major points. I even got fresh pasta. *'Cause I'm classy.'*" He pronounced the last sentence in an exaggerated New Jersey accent.

"Are you Italian? You sorta look like you could be."

"I'm a bunch of stuff. Maybe there's some Italian in there—who knows. My last name, Isaacs, is Jewish. But also sometimes Welsh, I guess?" He picked up a bottle of red wine and opened it with second-nature efficiency. "Here's the funny part: it might even be misspelled. My mom knew my dad for basically a minute, and he was long gone by the time I was born. She still put his name on the birth certificate, but wasn't sure if Isaacs was spelled with a C or a K, or even if it actually had the S on the end." He poured wine into two glasses and handed one to Hazel. "I'm practically made up."

"That's quite the origin story." They toasted, leaning toward each other on either side of the island, and Hazel took a sip. "All right, this makes up for you looking like you got dressed out of a free-box. You can definitely pick a nice wine."

"Owning a bar has to be good for something other than debt, insomnia, and flat feet."

A languid smile spread across Hazel's face, and her gaze moved from his eyes to his lips. His own smile bloomed, and he straightened and took a few lazy steps backwards, resting against the refrigerator with one foot back flat against it. They watched each other, and Griffin had a suspicion that he might end up cooking dinner later than he'd assumed if he didn't start immediately.

He looked away first, turning on the burner under the pasta water and taking his phone from his back pocket. He opened the music app and pushed his phone toward Hazel with a fingertip. "You want to pick something?"

Her eyes narrowed as if to say she recognized his game—pretending not to notice the invitation in her expression. She picked up a cracker and nibbled on it, scrolling through the music on the phone for a few minutes. She put on Bon Iver and set the phone aside, taking another sip of wine.

"I know I'm such a girl, but I never get sick of this album."

"We're both such-a-girl, because same." Griffin looked up briefly, then dropped a handful of garlic cloves into olive oil heating in a pan.

"That's a ton of garlic," Hazel said.

"Oh, shit... do you not like it? I should've asked."

"No, no, I love it. I'm just thinking, what if I want to kiss you?"

He raised his eyebrows. "Then it's a good thing we're both eating it."

She hid behind her glass with a pleased smirk, then hopped off the wicker-topped stool to go inspect the book shelves.

"So," Griffin began. "You told me on the mountain last week that you've lived in San Francisco, Seattle, Chicago, and a while in... was it Atlanta?"

"Yup." She slid a book out and opened it. "And three months in New York. But that doesn't count. I didn't have my own place—I was staying with people."

He nodded. The knife *thwocked* against the cutting board as he quartered the tomatoes. "I've lived all my life in Portland, which is a half-assed big city. Now I'm in Wylde, a place with roughly four thousand people, and... I can't imagine actually staying here for real. It's so tiny, so culturally different. How can something just a few hours away be this whole other world? What I'm curious about, from you, is... you grew up in Klamath Falls, which is, what, twenty thousand?"

"Give or take, uh huh."

"But then you went out adventuring and lived in real cities. So... why'd you move back to Klamath Falls? A place with two Starbucks?"

"One and a half. One of them is a kiosk in the Albertsons."

"Fair point." He tossed the tomatoes into the pan. "I guess what I'm really asking is—and please don't think this is meant to sound condescending, because I've had that thrown at me about a hundred times in the past three weeks—but what's the draw of a small town? I feel like I need to understand it, or I'm going to screw up the bar. Delilah has me insecure about it. Everything I suggest to her is seen as some attempt to defile not just the bar's identity, but *hers*, and possibly the entire town's."

Hazel circled back to the island and took another drink of her wine. "That's an interesting question."

"Thank you."

"And only a tiny bit condescending."

He laughed. "I'm willing to own it," he said, popping a chunk of tomato into his mouth.

"Give me one," Hazel said, opening her mouth.

Griffin held up a bite of tomato in question, then put it between her teeth, touching her lower lip as he drew away. She licked the spot he'd touched, then smiled.

"We're gonna hit all the eighties films," she joked. "*Nine-and-a-Half Weeks* is next."

"Will that scene be less sexy with oat milk?"

"Definitely." She jerked a thumb toward the door. "I'll be leaving now. It's been swell."

Their eyes locked, both of them laughing, and this time Hazel looked away first.

"So, okay. Small towns," she said, picking up a carrot stick and pushing it around in the hummus. She chewed for a while, lost in thought as Griffin worked on the sauce. "I'm thinking a million different things. First are the obvious ones—lower cost of living, less crime and pollution, yadda yadda. Then the hokey shit, like community. But as dumb as that sounds, accountability is *huge*. Knowing everyone'll hear about it if you're a jerk makes people nicer. It just does."

"I buy that."

She ate an olive, thinking again. "But then I kind of want to say, 'Oh, but you also can't generalize, because small towns are individuals, like people.' It rang true when you said Delilah thought you were messing with the town's identity. I know you think she's being some conservative whacko, but it's hard to relate if you didn't grow up in a place like this. You come to depend on certain types of... consistency? The same way little kids look at their parents."

"Isn't that kind of infantile?"

She raised an eyebrow. "I see why she keeps dinging you for being condescending."

He winced. "Sorry."

"And also, *no*, it's not. I'm just explaining it wrong."

He dropped the cooked pasta into the sauce and tossed it, flipping it neatly in the pan, showing off a little. "I think you're explaining it beautifully."

"And I think you're kissing up because you don't want to look like an asshole."

"Well, yeah."

"And also because you might want to get in my pants."

He bit his lip. "Is it working?"

Hazel drained her glass and came around the island. She took the pan from his hand and set it on an unlit burner. "Did somebody tell you I'm a goddamned sucker for lip-biting? Because that is so cute I can't stand it."

Griffin wove his fingers into her hair and leaned to kiss her. Their mouths leisurely found every angle as the music moaned and the running dryer behind the bathroom partition tapped and churned metallically in the quiet background. After another minute, Griffin's hands grazed down to Hazel's waist. They tightened as he lifted her onto the counter, and she gave a surprised squeak.

"You're tiny," he said against her mouth.

She dragged his t-shirt off and dropped it. "We'd be the same height lying down."

***

The bedroom cubicle was surprisingly cozy for being a partition in a large space. The heater poured out a steady radiance, and the bed was a sprawling king which Griffin had bought the previous week, after determining that his back wouldn't survive months on a futon.

Hazel reclined into Griffin's chest, his arms around her loosely and his cheek resting on top of her head. She matched the calluses on their palms and third finger-joints, then sighed with a luxurious stretch. Griffin glided his fingertips up one of her raised arms, enjoying the shifting of her smooth back against him. She was small and compact with an hourglass waist, and rounded leg muscles. Her shoulders had a beautiful angularity, with a scar over one collarbone where she'd had a bad break.

"I love the look of a wrecked bed," Griffin said drowsily against her hair.

She gave a hum of libidinous laughter and reached over her shoulder to touch his face. "We pretty much destroyed it."

"Are you hungry?"

"Starving. Weren't you supposed to feed me?"

"I mean... I tried." He tilted her head and dipped to kiss her temple from over her shoulder. "You distracted me. The pasta's going to be mushy and it's completely your fault."

"Worth it."

Griffin eased out from behind her and stood up. "I'll bring the food in here. Don't move—you look amazing exactly like that." He paused at the doorway. "More wine with dinner, or do you want water?"

She laughed. "You're low-key bragging, implying that I need water."

Griffin made a half-bow. "At your service."

"Water's good. Don't get dressed."

He grinned and headed for the kitchen. The music had stopped, and when he got to the counter he twisted his phone around to put on another album. There were two texts from Delilah. He switched the burner on under the skillet to reheat the neglected food, and opened the messages while he waited.

Delilah: *Doc Anand said it's not a match bc it turns out I'm blood type B, not A+ like I thought. Also the heart problem complicates it. We'll take it as it comes, but it's a 40 min drive both ways 3x a week. I wish I didn't have to ask you this. I know it's a lot.*

Delilah: *Hey Portland, sorry about that. Wrong recipient obviously. Meant to tell you the new chairs and tables actually look great. Had 3 ppl last night tell me how comfortable they are.*

He stared at the messages for a minute, brow furrowed. Dragging his focus away, he pulled the pan off the burner and swirled pasta into two shallow bowls with tongs and threw a bit more torn basil on top.

"You want parm?" he called out to Hazel.

"Tons. Yes."

He topped the pasta with cheese and picked up the plates, then set them down again. Swiping his phone open, he typed a message back.

Griffin: *I know I bullied you into it, but the furniture's success is all you. I would have gone with the brushed steel and you were 100% right about the heartwood.*

Griffin: *Also, my blood type is A pos. Who's sick?*

chapter ten

As the cacophony of cheering and bells rose in a crescendo, Delilah marched into the living room. Her hand shot out to grab the remote from her father. He flinched, and she stepped back and took a deep breath. More slowly, she reached for the remote, which he clutched against his chest in thin knobby fingers. The roar of *The Price Is Right* assaulted Delilah in a wave.

"Pop, I can't hear myself think," she tried, her voice barely audible over the jingles and screams. She looked over her shoulder at Maria in the kitchen. "Maria's baking you a pie," she went on. "Let's not distract her with this racket, okay?"

She made another grab for the remote, and her father slapped her arm hard. She sucked in a gasp, tears springing to her eyes as she resisted the automatic impulse to slap back. She went to the knick knack shelf and lifted the lid on a cut-crystal dish, then took out a yellow buttermint and returned to her father. She held it up between her thumb and forefinger. The Colonel's eyes—red-rimmed, but still dark and cutting as obsidian—fixed on the sweet prize.

"Two," he demanded, the word visible but not audible over the clamor.

"Two at once isn't good for your blood sugar."

"Two!"

A contestant on the show won a new car, and the shrieking and applause pushed Delilah over the edge. She whirled back to the candy dish, snatching a second buttermint. Dropping them into the Colonel's hand, she took the remote none too gently, turned the volume down and switched on the subtitles. She carried the remote with her toward the kitchen.

Before she'd made it through the archway, she heard thumping as the Colonel kicked the coffee table.

"Can't read it!" he protested.

Delilah went into the kitchen and put the remote in the fruit bowl, then covered her face with both hands. A moment later, she felt Maria's warm touch on her shoulder.

"*Mija*, don't cry."

"I'm not," Delilah said from behind her hands. "I'm just frustrated." Her palms slid down and she looked out the window. Across the quiet street, she saw the neighbors' Halloween decorations—a floppy scarecrow, jack-o-lanterns, three gauzy ghosts swaying from the oak tree.

Maria smoothed a hand down Delilah's spine. "I'm making your favorite pie—pecan."

Delilah gave Maria a hug. "Thank you. My fat ass doesn't need it, but my stingy Grinch heart could use some sugar."

Maria patted Delilah's cheek. "You're not a Grinch. You're just tired." She paused, a careful expression on her face. "Maybe you should consider the care center Doctor Anand recommended…"

"I'm not sticking him in an old folks' home."

"You're already stretched too thin, and this is only going to get harder."

"I'll be fine. No rest home."

The thumping from the other room got louder. Delilah spun back toward the doorway, and Maria gently took her wrist.

Josie Juniper

"Why don't you go for a walk, *mija*? You used to love walking in the autumn." She turned Delilah and propelled her toward the front hallway.

Delilah took her coat and stocking cap from the peg and stepped into her boots. As the door closed behind her, she could hear her father shouting at Maria.

Spinning the hat on one finger, Delilah crossed the yard to where the old play structure stood, and sat on one of its swings. Her father had built it, and even when she'd gotten too old for it, the grand wooden construction had remained. It had a castle-like tower, two regular swings, a gondola-swing, and a trapeze-bar. It was a monument, in Delilah's eyes, to how close she and her father had once been. Though Colonel Kelley had been nearly fifty when Delilah was born, they'd been like best friends. It stung her heart, thinking of how she now had to bribe him with sweets, as if he was a toddler.

Defenses worn down, she dropped her face into the hat in her hands and let herself cry, scrubbing the scratchy wool against her hot eyes and cheeks.

At the sound of a car's motor, Delilah looked up. Her hands wrapped around the swing's chains as she recognized Griffin's purple van. With a frown, she stood and turned away, combing her fingers through her hair and fanning her face with both hands. She heard the car turn into the driveway, and its door open.

"Morning!" he called out.

She took a bracing breath, tucked the hat in her pocket, and walked over.

"How did you find me?" she demanded.

"Are you in witness protection or something? Google Maps—your address is on tons of paperwork. And before you tear me a new one, I'm here because I brought you a present." He opened the back of the van and lifted out two familiar wooden chairs—one with lions' head finials, and the other with a mermaid carving—then set them on the ground. He swept a hand out like a promotional model at a trade show.

Delilah stared at them, gnawing the inside of her cheek.

"Your two favorites from the old bar furniture. I repaired them." He grasped the top of one and wiggled it to show its solidity.

Delilah chewed at a thumbnail and flicked a glance at his face.

"Hold on… have you been crying?" he asked.

She shook her head. "Allergies." Grabbing both chairs by the backs, she struggled toward the garage. "Thank you for this," she said over her shoulder as she shuffled away. "It was really thoughtful."

"Well, you're welcome and everything, but…"

Delilah heard the scuff of his black Converse as he jogged to catch up with her. He put a hand on her arm, and she set the chairs down on the cracked driveway with an impatient thud.

"Does this have anything to do with the message you accidentally sent last night?" he asked. "Because you never replied to my question. That thing about someone being sick… is it… you?"

"No." She carried the chairs to the garage's side door, twisting her shoulder to resist Griffin's attempt to help. The garage was scrupulously tidy inside, its shelves organized with labeled clear tubs containing fabric, patterns, and notions. Griffin stepped inside just as Delilah was about to close the door. She pushed away her exasperation and watched him inspect things.

Two huge tables stood parallel, one laid out with a rubbery cutting mat covered in measurements. The other had a long quilt-top draped over it, in a colorful log cabin design. A dehumidifier hummed in front of the shelves, and in the corner were two sewing machines, flanked by standing lamps.

Griffin touched the edge of the quilt. "This is amazing. Who's it for?"

"I don't know. Most of them go to a shelter. I don't know who ends up getting them." Through the door leading into the house, she heard her father shouting. Griffin caught her eye, and she looked away. "Let's go outside," she said. "We can walk, I guess."

Delilah peered at him sidelong as they crunched through the leaves in the yard, headed for the street.

"You look suspiciously radiant," she accused. "What have you been up to?"

"*Suspiciously* radiant? Huh. Just, uh, staying active." He lifted a low-hanging branch of a climbing rose bush as they passed under it, his smile a touch enigmatic. "Can't I be happy?"

"Have at it."

A gust of wind lifted Delilah's rose-gold hair. She took the hat from her pocket and pulled it on. Griffin's tumble of auburn locks—longer on top—danced into his eyes, and he raked it back. His hands were beautiful, Delilah had to admit. Large and strong, with the elegant length her mother had called "piano fingers."

A green pickup rounded the corner and stopped abreast of them. The window lowered, and a ruddy-faced older man leaned a freckled arm on the sill.

"Mornin', Lilah! I was gonna ask, you want me to tighten up the belt on your car? That baby screams like a sack full of cats when you start 'er up lately."

"Sorry about that..."

"Oh, it's not the noise. Maria said you're gonna be driving the Colonel to the dialysis center a few times a week, and I thought your car could use a tune-up before you start putting on all those miles." He smiled at Griffin and extended a hand to shake. "Ray Williams."

"Griffin Isaacs."

"Nice to meet you." He straightened his red cap, which had "Claymore Homes" stitched on the front. "Lilah, how's about Saturday for the tune-up?"

"I can't let you do all that work."

He scoffed. "I'd appreciate the chance to pay you back for the hours you spent teaching Madison to sew that dress for prom last year."

She gave a little flap of one hand. "You know I loved every minute of it."

"I'd feel better knowing you and the Colonel weren't going to break down on the highway..."

Delilah ducked her head. "All right. Thank you kindly, Ray. I'm much obliged. Tell Grace I said good morning."

"Will do." He touched the bill of his hat and drove off. Griffin and Delilah started walking again.

"So, uh… dialysis," he ventured. "That's what's wrong? Your dad?"

"Yep."

"I thought I was offering blood, not a kidney," he said with a mild laugh.

"I don't have plans to harvest your organs. Doc said he probably wouldn't make it through a transplant surgery anyway." She shoved her cold hands deeper into her coat pockets. "It's his time. Old man's had a good run of it." She sniffed. "Your dad alive?"

"Couldn't say. I've never met him."

Delilah looked up. "He and your ma didn't marry?"

"Nope. She married my stepdad when I was five, and they had my brother Byron."

They walked in silence for a minute, Delilah thinking about how different this was from what she'd imagined.

"Do you have… pictures of him at least?"

Griffin made both hands into L-shapes and framed his face. "Just this. My mom always claimed I look exactly like him except for eye color."

Delilah peeked at Griffin. "'Claimed'—past tense? So… your mom's gone."

"Ovarian cancer."

She nodded soberly. "Is your stepdad nice?"

"Dale's okay. Perpetually unemployed and depressive—Mom supported us waiting tables at a seafood place—but he's a decent enough guy."

"Have you tried to look for your dad online? Maybe you—"

Griffin's shoes barked against the asphalt as he stopped.

"Forgive me for sounding like a prick, but *you* never answer any questions. Christ, I asked you the other day if you like spicy food and you reacted like I was a stalker."

She gave a dismissive snort. "I did not."

"You absolutely did. And I've been assuming you're kind of a jerk, but apparently that couldn't be further from the truth—you're practically Mother Teresa around this town, albeit a short-tempered one. So what did I do wrong?"

Her mouth opened, then closed on a hundred things she wanted to say. She started walking back toward the house. "Thank you for the chairs."

***

Cross-legged on her bed late that night, Delilah tucked a section of hair behind one ear and stared down at her phone. Across the hall, she could hear her father snoring—a sound that she'd come to love, because it meant not only that she had time to relax, but that he wasn't dead.

Delilah: *Trust doesn't come easily for me, which is probably why I like living in Wylde – I already know what to expect from everyone here, good or bad.*

Delilah: *You asked about me, so here goes. I was a very late accident, and my dad was happy about it but I don't think my mom was. We weren't close. Dad always said "she's doing her best," which felt sad and not comforting.*

Delilah: *Sorry I walked away like that. Sometimes I'm not the best communicator. Believe it or not, I'm trying. (This is what trying looks like, haha – imagine if I wasn't)*

Delilah: *One last thing, and this is easier to say when I can't see you. Part of why you piss me off is that I'm sort of attracted to you sometimes. And that is confusing and stupid. Anyway, goodnight.*

The read-receipt came up just after she sent the last text. She held the phone expectantly for a few minutes, then set it aside with a sigh and shut off the bedside lamp. For a half hour she watched the leaping shadows of leaves on the ceiling, wondering what Griffin's childhood had actually been like. She'd been picturing him as a cool kid from an upper-middle-class family, living in some gorgeous Craftsman bungalow with a giant organic garden, drinking kale smoothies with his artsy parents, reading aloud to each other, taking rambling bohemian Europe trips.

Now it seemed more likely there'd been nights in childhood when they were both staring at the ceiling, three hundred miles apart, feeling alone.

Her phone vibrated on the bedside table, and she reached for it.

Griffin: ☺

chapter eleven

Halloween had gone surprisingly well, and had been a perfect opportunity to test out some of the new menu items Griffin had persuaded Delilah to allow.

"The stuffed mushrooms and those fritter-things sound fine," she'd said. "Anything people can eat with their hands. But so help me, Portland... if I see soup in my kitchen, you're going to wear it. No one goes to a bar for soup."

"Not even if we put toasted pumpkin seeds and basil oil on top?"

"*Especially* if you put crap like that on top. I know my customers."

It had been five weeks since he'd moved to Wylde. People were starting to recognize him, and aside from Shep Nash consistently calling him "Gavin," Griffin was now starting to feel more like a resident than a tourist.

On a morning in early November, after Hazel had slept over, she and Griffin stopped at Sweet Dreams to pick up coffee drinks before she dropped him at the saloon and drove back to Klamath Falls.

"You kids make the prettiest pair," Tammy said, grinning at them as she patted the side of the steam pitcher, heating the milk for lattes.

Hazel, who'd been feeding Griffin a bite of a raspberry bar, licked a bit of jam off her thumb and beamed. Her shoulders, draped in one of Griffin's thick sweaters, drew up shyly. "Awwwww, thanks!"

"You're like the two pups in *Lady and the Tramp,*" Tammy went on with a chuckle. "Sharing that ol' piece of spaghetti."

Griffin lifted his eyebrows at Hazel.

She raised a hand. "Dibs on being the Tramp. He had way more fun than Lady."

"There's a joke in there," Griffin said, "but I'm not touching it."

When they got to the saloon, they parked across the lot and listened to the stereo in Hazel's old red Subaru, sipping their drinks and passing Griffin's phone back and forth, looking at photos of a climbing area a few hours away.

"It might already be too late in the season for bouldering on Lassen," Hazel said, handing the phone back. "I'm a wuss once it gets cold. My hands would die."

"I'll keep you warm." His arms crept around her.

"You're... incredibly... cheesy," Hazel said between kisses.

The front door of the bar opened, and Delilah hauled trash bags toward the dumpster. She squinted at the car and then looked away.

"Duty calls," Griffin sighed. "I'll get my bike."

They both got out, and Griffin wrestled his bicycle from the car's cargo area, then closed the hatch. Hazel leaned against the driver's side door and twisted a handful of his shirt, pulling him down for another kiss. There was a moment of resistance as he realized that Delilah would see them, but the warmth of Hazel's chest against him swept away his self-consciousness. He rested his elbows on either side of her and gave himself up to her soft lips, faintly tasting of coffee and caramel.

The screech of the bar door opening again intruded on the moment. Griffin picked up one of Hazel's braids and brushed the tip of her nose with it. "All right, shortcake. I really do have to go."

Josie Juniper

"You know, I think I recognize her—your boss."

"She's *bossy*, but not technically my boss."

"She looks like a customer that comes into the shop sometimes. Buys mostly fabric."

"That sounds right—she sews a bunch."

"Tell her the girl from Bonny's Attic said 'Hi.'"

"You know, she's the one who told me about your store."

"No shit? In that case, tell her more than 'Hi'—tell her I also said 'Thanks for the boyfriend.'"

Griffin's stomach dropped. For the first time, it occurred to him that Hazel's feelings were out of his hands—separate, independent, and requiring interchange. He patted his pocket as if his phone had just vibrated, then took it out and glanced at the empty screen, feeling like a coward.

"See you this weekend?" Hazel asked, opening her car door.

"Absolutely."

As she drove away, he ambled across the lot and pushed the saloon door open, wheeling his bike inside.

"Park that dirty thing out front!" Delilah barked from behind the bar.

Griffin continued toward the office. "This 'dirty thing' is probably cleaner than I am, and it's carbon fiber. It cost more than my van. No way am I leaving it out there."

In the office, he moved a few things around to make space. He picked up a stack of mail from the desk and sorted through it. There was a scuffing noise behind him, and he pivoted. Delilah stood in the doorway, wiping her hands on a bar towel. She was wearing a tight plum colored shirt that wrapped around her small waist and tied over one hip. Her hair was coiled at the back of her head in a careless bun out of which a waterfall of strawberry blonde tresses escaped, and she had on earrings with dangling gold stars suspended from thready chains. A honey-pink shimmer accented her lips.

"Why do you look fancy?" he asked, returning his focus to the mail.

"Don't be ridiculous."

He opened one of the envelopes. "You know, you can't take a compliment."

"I can. But that wasn't one." Out of the corner of his eye, Griffin saw Delilah fold her arms, ankles crossed casually. "Got yourself a girlfriend? Noticed you outside with some short brunette."

Griffin scowled. "I don't know. Sort of. Maybe." He dropped the mail on the desk. "She works at that thrift shop over in Klamath Falls—Bonny's Attic. Her name's Hazel."

"Huh. Yeah, I think I've seen her. She looks about twelve."

"Because she's short? She's twenty-three."

"Too young for you."

"That's a matter of opinion."

Delilah snorted. "Well, I suppose I understand what you meant last week."

He pinned her with a bland gaze, but refused to take the bait, waiting.

"You said you were 'staying active,'" Delilah continued. "I get the joke now."

Griffin sat on the edge of the desk. "If there's a double entendre there, you're the one who… uh, doubled it."

"Either way, congratulations."

"Congratulations aren't in order—it's not like I'm engaged." He stood up. "Or is it just a miracle that someone will sleep with me?" He edged past her in the doorway, noting her herby scent, a little like fresh rosemary. He went and opened the register, pulling the tray from the cash drawer and gathering IOU slips. A minute later Delilah returned to her spot behind the bar, opening bottles of well liquor and corking spouts into them. Griffin noticed she wasn't wearing the earrings anymore.

After a minute of silence, she crossed to the jukebox and turned it on.

"God, no. *Why?*" Griffin asked when the first song began. "I can't stand this warmongering flag-fetishist creep. Can't you put on something good?"

"One of your sulky drug-addict bands, moaning about nothing?"

An indignant reply on his brother's behalf was on the tip of Griffin's tongue, until the conclusion of the unspoken exchange caught up with him.

Someone I love is an addict, he'd say in a huff.

And a lot of people I love are patriotic, she'd throw right back.

"Just something we can both stand," he said instead. "Johnny Cash maybe."

Delilah ignored him.

"Is this, like…" Griffin paused, then pressed on. "Are you being weird about Hazel? Because you're really in a shit mood."

She raised an eyebrow. "Your self-confidence is inspiring."

Annoyed, he dug a plastic coffee-stopper stick from his pocket, put it between his teeth, and went to the kitchen to start prepping vegetables. A few minutes later, Delilah came and took a knife from the rack, sharpening it and wordlessly joining in.

"That girl," she began. "Does she know you're only staying until January?"

"For the most part. Not everything has to be a *thing*. We can just enjoy each other's company." He glanced at the wall clock. "Where the hell are those brickwork guys? They were supposed to be here an hour ago."

A pained look crossed Delilah's face.

"What?" Griffin demanded.

"I told them we hired someone else."

Griffin looked down and grasped the edge of the counter, gaze locked on the white of his own knuckles.

"We have to stay local," Delilah continued. "Abe Ferguson's brother Noah is doing it."

"Some guy's brother dated you, so he gets the job?" Griffin gave a bitter laugh. "That's totally unprofessional. The people I hired have a five-star rating. You didn't even ask me."

"No, *you* didn't ask *me*. You just informed me that a bunch of strangers were doing the job. I'm trying to keep people around here from hating you, Portland."

Wylde Strangers

"People *don't* hate me. I'm a swell guy. You know who makes me feel like I don't belong in Wylde? *You.* And we lost a three-hundred-dollar deposit. Well done." He took his apron off, dropped it on the counter, and walked out of the kitchen.

He went to the jukebox and knelt down beside it, then pulled the plug from the outlet in the back. A hollow silence descended. Outside, Griffin heard Jack and Petra talking. He went and jerked the door open. They swiveled to look at him.

Griffin made a conscious effort to smooth his glare. "Sorry to startle you."

"No big," Jack said, lifting his shoe to stub his cigarette on the sole.

"Do you, uh... could I bum one of those?"

"A smoke? Sure." Jack shook one out of the pack and handed it over, then draped an arm around Petra's shoulder. "You need a light?"

"Please." Griffin drew in the acrid smoke, waving thanks as the two went inside. He paced slowly to the end of the walkway, his head rushing with the combination of caffeine and long-absent nicotine. He sat on the edge of the cement and surveyed the clouds. Behind him, the door opened, and he heard the unmistakable sound of Delilah's boots. She sat beside him.

"I should've asked," she said. "You're right."

"I know I'm right." He took a drag, not looking at her.

"Man, I suck at accepting a not-compliment, and you suck at accepting a not-apology."

He looked over with a weak grudging smile, then stared again at the clouds. "What a pair we are." Saying it out loud, he remembered Tammy at the coffee shop: *You kids make the prettiest pair.*

Delilah pointed at the cigarette. "I guess that's my fault."

"I'm just having one. I'm not going to start again. Probably."

Delilah leaned her elbows on her knees. Griffin surreptitiously watched her, sidelong—her regal nose with its minute scattering of golden freckles, her stubborn chin. In profile, her eyelashes were long, unadorned by makeup.

"I hate to be a dick about that deposit," Griffin said, "but I'm not actually flush with cash. I bought into your place with the buyout money from Velour, but all these renovations… it's on my credit line." He felt her look over with surprise. "So there's my big confession. I'm flying by the seat of my pants here." He inspected the glowing cherry on the cigarette and took another drag.

Delilah toyed with the topaz ring on her middle finger, twisting it. "Huh. So… I guess this is a labor of love for you."

He smiled dryly. "I'm not particularly loving it right now. I feel like I made a huge mistake."

Delilah was silent. An old blue Valiant drove by and tapped the horn, and she waved.

"Why did you do this?" she finally asked. "Decide to invest in Wylde?"

Griffin blew a jet of smoke from the corner of his mouth, away from Delilah. "It sounded like fun. Sadie and Weston are happy here, and the girl I thought I was going to marry dumped me, and… I mean, I liked you when we met."

Delilah emitted a wry note of laughter. "*Liked*."

He put an arm around her for a moment and squeezed her shoulders. "I guess I still like you. You're just a major pain." He felt her stiffen, and dropped his arm.

She stood and brushed off her pants, and Griffin tried not to follow the motion of her hands gliding over her curves. "Don't give up on the bar yet," she said gruffly. "We'll figure it out." She walked toward the door. "And for what it's worth, you're also a pain. But… I guess I like you too."

chapter twelve

"Do you want to hold the quilts on your lap?" Delilah asked her father as she buckled him into the front seat. "They'll keep you nice and warm…"

He shoved the folded log cabin quilt sideways off his lap, and she caught it just before it hit the wet driveway.

"I'll take that as a *no*." With a sigh, she set it on the roof of the car with the other two and checked for her father's fingers before closing the door. She opened the back hatch and transferred the quilts inside. Over the seats she could see him jabbing at the buttons on the stereo.

"No music!" he growled.

"The car's not on yet, Pop. The stereo isn't playing."

He continued his assault, cursing under his breath. Delilah heard a familiar engine and turned with one hand over her head, holding the hatch up. Abe's big blue truck with the white side-panels pulled in behind her car. He waved through the window and turned off the engine.

Josie Juniper

"Hey there, girl," he called out, hopping down.

"Abe," she returned with a nod.

"Glad I caught you. Heard you mention to Katie the other night at the saloon that you'd be dropping off blankets at the Gospel Mission when you take your dad to dialysis. I have a few things from my mom to send along." He reached into the truck bed and pulled out two deep storage tubs. Stacking them at Delilah's feet, he lifted the lid on the top one. "She told me to tell you it's two queen size, and six for babies."

Delilah unfolded a baby blanket—mint green with purple stars—and marveled over the tiny precise stitching on the hand-finished border. "Oh, Abe…" She looked over the edge of the blanket at him, and he ducked his head, dark hair dropping boyishly into his eyes. "These are beautiful," she told him. "Patty's such an amazing quilter. You let her know how much I appreciate this. There are gonna be some real happy babies at the women's shelter, I can tell you that." She refolded the star quilt and picked up the next one, yellow with pink tulips. "When did she find time to make all these?"

Abe rubbed at his jaw with the backs of his fingers, suddenly looking uncomfortable. His blue eyes skipped away from Delilah's gaze. "She, uh… she started working on 'em a few years ago."

Before he'd even gotten the sentence out, Delilah realized her mistake. Patty Ferguson had been clamoring for an engagement between Delilah and her son Abel from the first date, and had likely begun stuffing a hope chest with baby things the same day.

"Ah," she managed. She refolded the tulip quilt and set it on the ones she'd made, then scooped the others from the tub and added them. Her chest ached, recognizing that they were accessories to an alternate life. She tried not to look too closely at the cheerful patterns layered down the stack—pandas, foxes, bees, owls.

Abe set the empty tub in his truck bed, and Delilah opened the second one and lifted out the two queen size quilts. One was a traditional wedding ring pattern, the other linked hearts. Delilah's hands shook as she placed them in her car.

Wylde Strangers

She looked over the seats again at her father, whose head had tipped to one side in a spontaneous nap. Watching his shoulder for a moment, she could see it faintly rise and fall, and hear the whistle of his breathing. She closed the hatch silently, pushing her hip over the latch. Her eyes went cautiously to Abe's, afraid of what she might see. She fiddled with the key ring around her finger.

He took a step closer, and Delilah unconsciously stepped back, lips pressed together. A gust of mid-November chill ruffled his hair, and Delilah spied the tiny notch at the top of his right ear, from the time in sixth grade when Katie's little brother Lawson had shot him with a BB gun. She remembered Abe's hand over the wound, the blood between his fingers, and the tears in his eyes that he'd tried to hide from her. Mad as he was, he wouldn't hit Lawson, not even when Katie gave him permission.

"Lilah-girl," Abe began, reaching to brush aside a tendril of hair on her cheek, "I know it's over between us, but I wish we could be good friends again. I miss you."

His rough fingers smelled like Boraxo, and Delilah smiled at the simple homey scent. "I miss you too. I miss being young." She shook her head. "It seems so far away now, the time in my life when I thought anything could happen. Every day felt like opening a fresh page in a diary, being excited about what might get written."

He touched her chin. "Can I hold you for a minute?"

She watched his solemn blue eyes. "Sure, Abe. It'd be a comfort."

He pulled her into his arms. They were nearly the same height—Abe was an inch taller—and her head fit against his shoulder just as her body remembered. Delilah's eyes closed. She listened to the wind in the trees, the distant hum of an airplane, the even rhythm of Abe's breathing. He smoothed a tentative hand down her back and leaned away to look at her face.

"My birthday's next week," he said.

"It is."

"You know what I'd like? I want to go to the old four-plex theater that we all used to go to in high school and movie-hop. You and

Josie Juniper

Caleb, me and Georgia, Katie and Hunter, Savannah and Colt, sneaking from one theater to the other… even if the movies were terrible. It was fun just for the challenge."

Delilah laughed. "Oh, God, and the time Caleb brought the wine coolers and we were drunk as bedbugs in *Batman Begins,* and Georgia got sick in the popcorn bucket…"

"And that red-haired guy with the mustache who worked there, he threw us out, and you remember what he said?"

"Of course!" Delilah planted her hands on her hips and glowered, dropping her voice and executing a perfect impression. *"'This kind of behavior is unbecoming of young ladies…'"*

Their laughter apparently woke the Colonel, who shouted "Delilah Jane!" from inside the car.

She wiped the tears from her eyes and stole a glance at Abe.

"The whole time I was going with Georgia, I had a crush on you," Abe confessed.

"I knew." She smiled.

He took a deep breath. "What do you say to movie-hopping with me next week? Make a day of it. Red Vines and popcorn… we can even sneak in a little flask of something to go in our Cokes."

Delilah's residual laugh trailed off into a sigh. "You know I can't get away for a whole day ever. Between the bar and Pop…"

Abe offered a tight nod. "I understand."

"But…" She reached for his hand and gave it a quick squeeze. "I'd be game for one movie. I'll bring the Red Vines."

***

After Delilah had gotten her father settled in for his dialysis, she went back out to the car to make a quick trip to drop off the quilts and get coffee. As she pulled up the hood on her jacket against the rain now falling, she spotted a familiar face. Missy stood beside the blue Valiant she'd driven since long before Delilah was born. She wore a brown outback duster coat with a purple striped skirt showing beneath, and a khaki boonie hat with the cord drawn up under her chin. Glittery earrings shaped like open pea pods dangled from her ears.

"A little bird told me you've got about three hours to kill," Missy said with a smile. "I've got a cribbage board and two mochas with extra whip."

Delilah beamed. "What the heck are you doing here?"

"Oh, had to come into town to get a few things at a bigger hardware store—Travis didn't have the size of springs I needed. Saw you parked here, and I popped over to that café to get us a couple of drinks." She nodded sideways at her car. "Sit with me?"

They got in the Valiant and Missy ran the engine for a few minutes to heat up the inside. Delilah sipped the sweet drink, relishing the warm cup cradled in her hands. Missy swept her hat off and tossed it on the back seat, ruffling her wavy hair, still mostly golden blonde with streaks of silver.

"Don't take this the wrong way, but you look tired," she told Delilah. "Are you getting any sleep, since the Colonel took a turn for the worse?"

"I try for six hours. Don't always manage it though." Delilah licked a bit of whip cream off her lip. "I wake up a lot too. Just… worrying."

Missy reached and gave Delilah's elbow a squeeze. "I'm glad that kid invested in the bar, so at least the money issue isn't front and center anymore."

"Sometimes I think that actually makes it a little worse—now I'm afraid we're *both* going to lose our shirts."

"Don't let your imagination run away with you. I like the changes you two are making. That new patio is going to look great, and I have to admit… no offense to Howard, but the food's better now."

"Yeah, the city boy can cook," Delilah admitted. "I don't dare tell him. It'd go straight to his big dumb ego."

Missy chuckled. "I think he's got a good head on his shoulders. He came into the shop the other day—brought in a blender that needed fixing—and we got to talking, oh, must have been for over an hour. About books, and music… a whole lotta stuff."

"Hm. He can talk, that's for sure."

Leaning back as if to get a better view of Delilah, Missy squinted at her. "Now why exactly are you pretending you don't like him? I'll bet I know…"

Delilah gave a grumpy smile. "Hush, you."

Missy picked up her coffee and took a long drink, eyes laughing knowingly.

"Missy! No! Okay, sure, he's easy on the eyes. But he's also stubborn and snobby and kinda sarcastic. Not my type." Delilah took another sip of her mocha and tried changing the subject. "I'm going to a movie with Abe next week."

Missy's eyebrows shot upwards, then settled. "You know who isn't your type? Abel Ferguson."

Delilah frowned. "It's not a date. He just wants to be friends."

"He wants to be friends until he can sneak a ring onto your finger."

Slanting an uncertain look Missy's way, Delilah asked, "Would that really be so bad? I'm not getting any younger."

Missy's expression was suddenly grave. "It's always bad to run away from what you want and settle for something you don't." She looked toward the windshield, streaked with rain tinted red from a nearby neon sign. "I can promise you that. Don't end up with regrets. People regret the things they *didn't* do far more than the things they did. We regret the fears that stopped us from truly living."

In the silence that followed, Delilah studied Missy. Asking what was in her head seemed like an intrusion, but the look on the older woman's face spurred her to speak. "What did you run away from?" she asked quietly.

Missy flashed a brief sad smile. "I ran fast, but not far. That made it worse. Because I was still close enough to see what I'd missed out on."

Delilah furrowed her brow. "That's not really an answer."

Grasping Delilah's knee, Missy gave it a firm squeeze. "I know."

***

Before heading back to Wylde, Delilah stopped at the shelter to drop off the quilts. She gingerly opened the back hatch so as not to wake her father, asleep in the front seat, and grabbed an armload of blankets. She hoisted them and balanced the top of the stack with her chin. She'd gotten halfway to the door of the Gospel Mission when her footsteps stalled.

She stood for almost a minute, watching raindrops darken the polar bear crib quilt on top, before turning back. She put the stack down in the still-open cargo compartment and removed the six baby blankets, setting them aside to keep, just in case.

chapter thirteen

Griffin drew his arm carefully from under Hazel's neck and rolled over to pick up the buzzing phone. He blinked at Cleo's name, slid out of bed, and walked to the kitchen.

"What time is it?" he asked by way of greeting.

"Time for you to get your brother out of my life and my bar."

"*Our* bar. What did Byron do to piss you off now? And is it necessary to tell me at…" He glanced at the digital display on the stove, "three in the morning?"

"I'm not keeping him. He's lucky if I don't have him arrested."

"Whoa there, slugger." Griffin held up a hand Cleo couldn't see. "Slow down. What happened?"

"Four hundred dollars is missing from the till."

Silence fell between them. Finally Griffin prompted, "And you think Byron took it?"

"I *know* Byron took it."

Griffin's stomach twisted. "You looked at the tape, and it was definitely him?"

"The camera wasn't going. Anton turned it off."

"Uh, you understand that doesn't look so hot for Anton, right? Why the hell did he do that?"

"It's a privacy issue."

Griffin snorted. "Sounds more like an opportunity issue. I'm sure you haven't been able to resist shit-talking Byron to your boy-toy, calling him a junkie—"

"He *is* a junkie."

"—and suddenly Anton has a problem with the camera, and money disappears. It's a frame-up. Byron would never steal from the bar."

"That time he was crashing with us, he stole the goddamned cocktail ring I inherited from my grandmother, Griffin!"

"You *think* he took that ring."

Cleo let out a bark of laughter. "You're a delusional idiot, and your brother's a thief. He's been hanging out with Marco and Nix again, getting high as balls."

"He had *one* slip-up, weeks ago."

"He had one that he *admitted* to you."

Griffin raked a hand through his hair. "Dougie's been keeping an eye on him."

Cleo snorted. "He should have kept an eye on the till."

"We *did* have an eye on the till. Until your gigolo turned it off. Which is definitely a you-problem. I'm going back to bed." He was tempted to say something to let Cleo know the bed wasn't empty, but couldn't figure out a way to do it that wouldn't have sounded pointed, and therefore pathetic.

"Great. Stick your head in the sand. But just so you know, unless he's hustling dime-bags on the corner to support his habit, your brother's no longer employed—I'm not stocking Narcan in the office in case my goddamned dishwasher ODs."

Grimacing with distaste, Griffin recoiled from the phone. "Holy shit, Cleo… do you have to be such a cold bitch? Don't call me again unless the place is on fire." He tapped the screen and hung up, then tossed his phone onto the counter. Going to the kitchen sink, he turned on the tap and tipped his head sideways to drink from it before walking back to the bedroom.

Hazel was lying on her stomach with her chin propped on her folded arms. "Everything okay?"

He flopped down beside her. "Sorry about that. Not exactly flattering."

"It isn't great to hear you call someone a bitch—not gonna lie."

Griffin put a hand over his eyes. "I did, didn't I?"

"Yep."

His hand slid away, and he rolled his head toward her. "I swear I'm not that guy. I know even That Guy says he's not that guy, but... honestly."

"Okay." She chewed at a thumbnail, watching him.

"I could make excuses about how it wasn't an amicable breakup and we still have to own a business together, and she just said she'd cheerfully watch my brother die, but... it's better if I just apologize."

"To me?"

Griffin put both hands behind his head and looked over. "Well... yeah."

"I don't know if I'm the one who needs it."

"You want me to apologize to Cleo?"

Hazel shrugged. "That'd be weird, like I made you do it. It'd be meaningless."

Propping himself on an elbow, Griffin searched her face in the shadows, trying to get a better sense of her expression. The air around her felt tense.

"I mean, this is a situation where I can't win now," he said. "If I don't apologize to Cleo, I'm a dick... but if I do, it's fake, just because you implied that I should. And you apparently don't want me to apologize to *you*—which I think would be appropriate, because what I said was shitty and I'm sorry you had to hear it. So I do apologize. And not because you're pissed off."

"Fine. Good. Apology accepted."

He gave a slight laugh. "Doesn't sound accepted."

"It's close enough."

He sat up and leaned against the wall, tucking a pillow behind his back. "Are you saying you've never lost your temper and called someone a rude name?"

"It doesn't matter if I have. That's appeal to hypocrisy—a *tu quoque* fallacy."

Putting both hands over his face for a moment, Griffin sighed. "I didn't know we were in an Intro to Logic course. But you're right. I'm seriously going to shut up now, before I make it worse."

"Aaaaaaand you just did, with the sarcasm." Hazel got up and knelt beside the bed, stirring an arm in the darkness on the floor to find her clothes.

"Haze, wait." He scooted across the bed and sat on the edge near her. "Don't go, okay? I'll sleep on the sofa if you want, but don't drive home in the middle of the night because I put my foot in it."

She folded her arms, and Griffin could see that she was shivering. He pivoted and sprawled off the foot of the bed to reach for the space heater and switch it on. An orange glow from its on-light threw a hint of illumination across Hazel's face. He sat up again and reached for her, pulling her back into bed and under the covers.

Her limbs gradually relaxed. Griffin kissed her temple. "Who knew you had a peppery side? You're so mellow. It's nice to know you won't always take my bullshit."

Relieved as he was when Hazel softened in his arms, a small part of him was disappointed that she'd given in so quickly. When he fell asleep, he dreamed not of Hazel's forgiving brown eyes, but Delilah's fiery green ones.

***

He texted Dougie the minute Hazel had left the next morning.

Griffin: *Sry for the early msg, but call me as soon as you're up*

Dougie: *already awake*

Josie Juniper

The phone picked up on the first ring, and Griffin launched in immediately. "I need you to do me kind of a huge favor. I'll pay you. What are you getting at the bar, eighteen an hour? So let's say thirty an hour for this, plus gas."

"Plus… gas? Where am I going?"

"Bringing Byron to me. It's a six hour drive. I'll pay you for both ways. But it's gonna be tricky—he'll split if he figures out what you're up to."

"Jesus. Like taking a dog to the vet."

"Exactly. If your dog had thumbs and a taste for opiates. Cleo swears he's using again. Woke me up with some rant about how he supposedly pocketed cash from the till. She fired him."

"Dude, I was there for it. She lost her shit."

"Do you think he took the money? Or that he's back on junk?"

Dougie sucked his teeth. "Possibly yes on both?"

"Shit." Griffin poured himself more coffee. "Okay, here's the deal—I mean if you're willing."

"Of course."

"Get a full tank of gas first, some food, bottled water, so you don't have to make stops. Go to my place to check on Byron—tell him you're worried because of the shit that went down at the bar last night. When you're there, go in the bathroom. Under the sink is an old tooth-whitening kit, and inside there's a bag hidden with three ten-milligram oxys. I saved them after I took that bad fall at Smith Rock. Offer him one to get him in the car."

Dougie laughed. "What, hold it up and lure him outside like a cartoon?"

"Whatever works. Make up some bullshit—tell him you need help with something. Once you're a few miles down the freeway he'll know the score and freak out. *Do not stop,* okay? He won't be above pretending he has to take a leak and then giving you the slip and hitching back to Portland. Give him a goddamned Snapple bottle to piss in if you have to, but don't let him out of the car. Tell him he gets a second pill when you're halfway down. The third one I'll give him when you guys get here, so he doesn't swing on me."

Wylde Strangers

***

Griffin went into the bar early, working in silence without playing music. An hour into prep, his phone rang. Seeing Dougie's name, his arms tingled with a flush of adrenalin, sure he was going to say the mission had been a failure. He wiped his hands and grabbed the phone.

"We're on the road, boss," Dougie said in a tone of false cheer that implied it had been a trial. "Be there by late afternoon."

Griffin sagged with relief, one hand on his forehead. "Awesome. Thanks, man. Can't tell you how much I appreciate it."

"Hey, asshole!" Byron's voice piped up in the background.

Griffin sighed. "Can you put me on speaker, Dougie?"

"You know kidnapping's a crime, right?" Byron said.

"So's buying heroin."

"Up to three grams is a misdemeanor, bro. You're wasting everyone's time with your little shanghai surprise. And I left my phone in your apartment. I don't have anything but the clothes on my back. I think the stove's on too—your place is probably burning down as we speak."

"I checked the stove," Dougie cut in. "And the lights."

"See?" Griffin told Byron. "No worries. Enjoy the scenery, and we'll talk when you get here."

"The hell we will. I'm not talking to you, period. When I get there, I'm gonna kick you in the nuts."

"Aw, love you too, buddy. See you in a few hours."

When he left the bar at three o'clock, he realized he was disappointed that Delilah hadn't arrived yet. Most weeks he'd been relieved by the only slight overlap in their schedules. Griffin had always been a morning person, and working in an empty kitchen—music in the background and a triple-shot latte at hand—was a relaxing routine. But as he drove home along the High Road on this particular afternoon, he watched for Delilah's beat-up white hatchback. He was filled with anxiety over Byron's arrival, and for some reason, the thought of exchanging even a wave with Delilah in passing was encouraging.

To Griffin's surprise, Dougie's black Toyota was already parked in front of the tool-and-die works. Griffin parked and got out, walking over as Dougie rolled the window down. In the back seat, Byron slouched low, sunglasses on, arms folded, looking like a sullen teen in a movie. He ignored Griffin's wave.

"Hey, guys. Come on up. I'll get the heat going and make food." He threw another glance at Byron. "You too sick to be hungry?"

Byron maintained his silence and turned his head to look out the opposite window. Griffin raised his eyebrows at Dougie in question.

"He seems all right. We actually stopped in Eugene—he promised he wouldn't give me a hard time. Ate some fries, so he's functional."

Griffin opened the car's back door. "Come on, man. It's cold out here. Quit pouting like a goddamned kid."

"Nah, I'm good."

"How are you going to kick me in the nuts from there? At least stand up."

Dougie handed Griffin the plastic bag containing the final pill, and he held it up. "You want the last one now? Or do we break it in half and try to taper you?"

Byron looked at Griffin, his eyes sliding from the bag to Griffin's face. "One pill isn't enough to taper. I'm gonna feel like ass either way." He held his hand out.

"Nope. Gotta come upstairs for it."

Byron scooted across the seats, arching slowly like an old man, and got to his feet with a small grunt. "You know I hate you for doing this."

Griffin pulled him into a hug, and Byron resisted for a moment before settling, arms wooden at his sides.

"Wouldn't be the first time," Griffin said. "But maybe it'll be the last."

chapter fourteen

When Griffin appeared in the kitchen doorway, Delilah nearly jumped out of her skin. With a shriek she flinched just as her fingers had drawn perilously close to the end of the pepper she was chopping. The knife sank into her knuckle, and a rivulet of red bloomed onto the cutting board.

She set down the knife and turned on her heel to march toward the sink.

"Oh shit, Dee... are you okay?"

Wrenching the faucet on, she watched pink water trickle down the drain. "That's exactly why I asked you *not* to oil the hinges on the front door," she ground out. "Some businesses have bells, I have a squeaky door. It's been that way for years."

"I should've said something when I came in." He drew up beside her and pumped soap foam into his palm, taking Delilah's hand and lathering it.

Josie Juniper

"You should've left well enough alone," she shot back, smacking his hand away, spattering his shirt with red-tinted soap suds. "Knock it off—I'm not a child."

He looked down at the speckles, and undeterred, took her hand again and coaxed it under the water. "This is bleeding kind of a lot. Should you go over to Doctor Anand's and see if it needs stitches?"

"The first aid kit'll be fine."

Griffin's big hands glided over hers under the tap. He lifted her hand to inspect it, biting his lip in concentration in a way that made Delilah's pulse jump. She watched as the tiny pale dent from his teeth softened and filled in with color. She'd never stood close enough to inspect his lips in detail—a beautiful lusty shade, starfish pink with just a touch of darker bricky-red on the fuller bottom lip.

He looked up and apparently noticed her staring. "What?"

"Nothing," she said, jerking her hand from his grasp. "I just wondered if you should be breathing all over me like that. Out for five days nursing your sick brother? You're probably... teeming with disease." She grabbed a bar towel and looped it over the bleeding knuckle while reaching for the first aid kit. "And I can't afford to get sick."

He took the box from her hand. "He's not that kind of sick. It isn't contagious." Opening the lid, Griffin took out gauze and fabric tape, then a tube of antiseptic ointment. Delilah reached for it impatiently, and he pulled it toward his chest. "Will you let me help? Jesus Christ, you don't get special badass points for doing it yourself." He tore open the gauze. "Unless you happen to have a third hand, you're going to make a mess of it."

Delilah leaned on the edge of the counter and watched as Griffin bandaged up her finger. His wavy hair lay against his forehead in a way that looked both stylish and careless, and as he focused on the task at hand, she allowed herself to peruse the landscape of his face. Fine, straight nose; the kind of cheekbones that Delilah's mother had claimed meant Native American blood; strong jaw with a pale scar, shaped almost like the star-shaped crack a rock makes in glass.

"What happened there?" she asked, pointing at the spot.

Wylde Strangers

His gaze flicked to hold hers, then cut away. "Had a piton hit me in the face. It was my own fault. Just glad it didn't get my eye." He finished with the bandage, smoothing his hands over it before stepping back.

"Thanks," Delilah said reluctantly. She went to toss the blood-tainted peppers in the trash, then put the cutting board into the dishwashing rack. "What kind of sickness does your brother have?"

He took an apron off the stack and put it on. "Kind of a long story."

"I've got time." She glanced at the wall clock. "I don't have to be home to take Pop to K.F. for another forty-five minutes."

He grabbed a new cutting board and set it on a damp bar towel on the prep table to keep it from sliding, then took more peppers from the bag. "Thing is, I don't really want to talk about it. Not with you. I'm too tired to deal with someone being all… judgy and critical."

Her eyes narrowed. "Excuse me, Portland? I'm not like that."

He raised an eyebrow. "Seriously? Because yes you are."

She held the edge of the counter behind her, and felt the sting of the cut as her hands flexed. "You don't know me at all."

"Funny, you keep saying that. But I feel like I do. I see your patterns, your reactions. And you don't suffer a fool gladly."

"Only a fool *does*."

"Yeah, well. I think Byron might qualify in that department." The knife sailed through a pepper with quick perfectly spaced cuts. "And you're the one who doesn't know *me*."

"Really." The question was cynically flat.

"Really truly. Seven weeks, and you still haven't bothered trying. Because I think it's easier for you to act like I'm some stupid caricature. You still call me 'Portland' most of the time, for chrissakes. I'm not the hipster scene-kid you seem to think I am. I don't even have tattoos. Or drink PBR. Surprise surprise."

Delilah gave a crooked smile. "That actually does surprise me."

"Well, there ya go."

93

She boosted herself onto the counter between the sink and dishwasher. "I see your patterns too. You're just as bad as me. If I'm—what was it?—judgmental and negative—"

"Critical, I said. Not negative."

"Okay, you see that in me... and what I see in you is that you're a waffler."

The knife stopped, and he pinned her with a glare. "A *waffler?* Is that some sort of conservative buzzword for describing people who can recognize nuance?"

She pointed at him. "See? There's you pigeonholing *me*. You don't know how I vote just because I'm small-town."

"I'll bet I can guess."

"I'll bet you *can't*. And I just mean you spend a helluva lot of time analyzing and hand-wringing before you do a thing. Like how you sent me pictures of chairs for *hours* before you bought the new furniture for the dining room. I was ready to scream. It's probably the fault of that shitty music you listen to, but good lord, I've rarely seen a man spend as much time as you do overthinking every last detail."

Griffin stared at her. His eyes narrowed and he set the knife down. Delilah prepared herself for an indignant retort.

Instead he stepped around the prep table and closed the distance between them in four strides. With a flutter of panic, Delilah tried to push herself off the counter, but Griffin was too quick. He slotted his body between her parted knees, grabbing a handful of her loose ponytail as she tried to turn away. His grip was insistent but gentle, and before she had time to take in a breath to speak, his lips slanted over hers.

Her hands shot up and connected with his chest. She was about to push him away when the warmth of his skin through his shirt stopped her. Both of her palms slid down, and she opened her mouth to reciprocate the sweet pressure. A tiny sound drifted from her throat, and Griffin emitted a hint of a low moan in reply.

He loosened his grip on her hair, pulling the elastic tie out and combing his fingers through. Delilah leaned into the kiss as his tongue touched her lip. One of Griffin's arms hooked around her on the counter, and he pulled her toward himself. The contact as they crushed against each other was hot and almost bruising, and for a moment Delilah's legs wrapped around his waist to pull him closer before she realized what she was doing and relaxed her thighs.

Griffin pulled back, fixing Delilah with a lust-drunk scowl before swooping in again to claim her mouth. His fingers dug into her, and the pinch of it made her gasp. Her fists tangled in his shirt and pulled up the hem, bracing his sides with the Y of her thumbs and forefingers, trailing upward a few exploratory inches, sliding over the taut muscle.

"Stop, stopstopstop..." she managed against his mouth.

He drew back, watching her. He licked his lower lip—not provocatively, but in a contemplative way—and it took everything in her to turn her head aside and not kiss him again. She slowly returned her focus to his face. The pupils in his gray eyes were wide. Gradually, Delilah lowered his shirt and pushed him away, one hand covering the other as if she was administering CPR. Her breath was trembling and shallow, and her heartbeat hammered in her chest.

"I don't always overthink it before acting," he said, his breath just touching her cheek. He took two steps back, studying her like the map that might keep a sailor from falling off the world's edge.

Delilah's hands gripped the counter again. She realized her knees were still apart, and she pulled them together slowly, not wanting to draw attention to the obvious fact that she needed him between them again. Her hands tangled in her lap. She looked down and saw that blood had soaked through the bandage, and she hopped off the counter.

"No," she replied. "But... maybe you should have, this time."

He pressed his lips together, discreetly licking them again, as if he tasted her there still. "Is that what you really want?"

She paused for a long time, thinking through a half-dozen replies, and, as she'd accused Griffin of doing, inspecting each possible outcome. She remembered the goodnight kiss she'd allowed Abe to give her after the movie the previous week. The tiny stitches on the baby quilts. The little diamond and peridot ring Abe had shown her—insisting it was "in case you're curious what it looks like, no pressure."

Then she thought of Griffin getting back into that ridiculous purple van, possibly in as little as six weeks, and driving away. Text messages, paperwork faxed, maybe the occasional in-person visit. A silent partner.

If Griffin Isaacs was going to be a silent partner, Delilah's heart would need to be silent too.

She crossed to where her coat and purse hung on a peg. Taking them down, she stuffed her arms into the coat.

"Yes. That's what I really want," she said, her voice rough. She jerked the purse strap across her body like an ammo belt. "Mistakes happen."

She walked to the front door and yanked it open, grateful this time that it made no sound.

chapter fifteen

The hollow *tap-pok, tap-pok, tap-pok* of the ball was punctuated with an occasional laugh or insult as Byron and Weston played table tennis. Across the room, Sadie and Griffin lounged on the overstuffed sofa, their thick-socked feet on the coffee table. A Guided by Voices album played on the stereo, and a fire snapped and murmured in the big natural-stone hearth.

"Byron seems like he's doing well," Sadie said, leaning toward Griffin and lowering her voice. "He looks happy."

"Sure. He's in the 'pink cloud.' Just like the last half-dozen times." He took a sip of his beer, watching Byron clowning around, trying to execute a 360 spin before the next hit, and failing. "It's only been eight days. If I can get him past six months, it'll actually start to mean something."

Sadie lifted her red hair off her neck and dropped her head against the sofa, studying Griffin. "That's a lot to put on yourself—'If *I* can get him past...' Byron has to make the change."

"I'm not confident he *wants* to. He needs a reason." Griffin sighed. "I don't know. Fingers crossed."

"If he goes back to school and finishes the music degree, maybe he could teach. Do something with music that actually makes a living."

Griffin pulled a wry smile. "Would *you* hire Byron as a teacher? The idiot has an arrest record now. That ship's sailed. He practically has 'Bad Risk' stenciled across his forehead." Griffin tipped back the rest of his drink. "Which is probably why women love him—the allure of the chronic unrepentant fuckup."

"Doesn't hurt that he's got that pretty face."

"Great. Maybe he can find a nice horny fifty-something sugar-mama."

"My mom thinks he's adorable."

"Perfect."

Across the room, Weston crowed with victory and dropped his paddle on the table. "In your face, Averill," he told Byron.

Griffin's brother tossed his own paddle in the air with resignation and caught it. "Sadie," he called out. "Your husband cheats." He picked up his bottle of Pellegrino and sauntered over to the sofa to join them.

"Cheats?" she joked. "How do you know we don't have an open relationship?"

Byron flopped down beside her and draped an arm over her shoulders. He nuzzled her neck with a growl, and Sadie retreated with a squeal of laughter.

"Bloom, I'm moving in on your wife," Byron warned.

"You couldn't handle her."

Sadie edged out of Byron's mock-amorous clutches, stood and picked up Griffin's empty bottle. "Another?"

He shook his head. "No, thanks. But I'd take a seltzer."

"Done." She padded off to the kitchen.

Weston poked at the fire and set another log on, then collapsed onto the sofa, scratching at his beard. "How long are you planning on staying?" he asked Byron.

Byron replied "a few days" at the same time Griffin said "until I go back." The two locked eyes, then Byron's gaze skidded away and he took a sip of his seltzer.

"Dude, you're not leaving in 'a few days,'" Griffin told his brother. "I didn't pay Dougie four hundred fifty bucks to bring you for a visit. You live here as long as I do."

"I can't stay that long. I'd miss Christmas with Dad."

Griffin rolled his eyes. "Are you ten years old? Dale's fine."

"Don't be a dick." Byron picked at the edge of the label on his bottle. "I can't stay."

"Shut it. You're not leaving."

"There's nothing to do in this shithole town." Byron threw a glance at Weston. "No offense."

"None taken," Weston replied with amusement, sloshing back a drink of his beer.

Pointing an accusing finger at Griffin, Byron appealed to Wes. "Tell him to at least stop locking me in when he goes to the bar. The top deadbolt's keyed on both sides, and if there was a fire or something, I'd be screwed."

Wes looked at Griffin. "He has a point."

"I'll make sure to unplug the toaster when I leave in the mornings," Griffin said to Byron, his voice flat with sarcasm. "I don't trust you yet. Work for it."

"See?" Byron protested indignantly. He settled back into the deep cushions. "I don't have my phone or my guitar, and I'm stuck wearing your clothes."

"Fortunately I have excellent taste and we're the same size. And I'll buy you a harmonica."

"Like any prisoner," Byron grumbled. "And your fashion sense is 'hobo with a thing for indie bands.'"

Griffin's phone rang, and he rose in his seat and dug it out of a pocket. Seeing Hazel's name, he stood and walked toward the hallway leading to the bedrooms.

"Hey, shortcake. What's up?"

"Wondering what you're doing later. I haven't seen you in over a week, and I thought maybe if your brother's doing okay, you could drive out to my place."

Griffin chewed at his lip. "I think it's too soon. The guy'd be halfway up I-5 the second I turned my back."

Sadie came into the hallway and handed Griffin the open seltzer, then retreated.

"It feels a tiny bit like you're avoiding me," Hazel said tentatively.

"What? Nonono, definitely not. I'd love to see you. The timing's just bad."

"Like, I get that you were stressed out when he was detoxing, but the past few days you seem... stand-offish, maybe?"

"Haze, I'm just tired." He slowly paced the length of the hallway and saw Sadie beckon to Wes on one of his return circuits. The couple went into the kitchen, heads together in low conversation.

"I'm not trying to be clingy or whatever." Hazel gave a hum of laughter. "I'm climbing the walls a little without sex, if you want the truth."

The image flashed in Griffin's mind: Delilah's eyes closing for a kiss, the plump curve of her lips, peachy-golden hair soft in Griffin's hands. That incredible moment when he'd felt her legs clasp around him for a mere second and imagined what it would be like to push inside of her, to feel her arch against him.

For three days they'd effectively avoided each other—business information in passing, lukewarm pleasantries, both avoiding eye-contact. The wake of Delilah's woodsy-green scent brought the memory of the kiss back every time, viscerally. His hands tightened even now, thinking of the smell of her, and the heat of her skin.

His mind clouded with Delilah, Griffin offered the next words without realizing how they'd land. "We're not exclusive or anything—if you want to call someone else to come over, I'd understand."

A long silence followed, and Griffin ran a hand over his face, wishing he could retract the words.

Hazel's tense sigh gusted into the phone. "Wow. That's... a lot."

"That probably didn't come out right."

"Sounds like it came out *exactly* right. I just... um, it's news to me. The not-exclusive thing. I know it's dumb to assume, but I guess I assumed. Like, I earned a nickname, but not... y'know, monogamy?"

Griffin opened the door to Weston's office and went inside, sitting in the big leather computer chair. "I mean, monogamy is kind of huge. Right? It's been, what, six weeks? Do you really think we're there?"

"I'm *already* there, personally. But apparently that's one-sided. Should we have been being more careful?"

"Things are already pretty careful. You've got the birth control thing in your arm, and we use condoms."

"Like four-out-of-five times, sure. Now I feel like a fool."

"Haze, I'm not sleeping with anyone else," he said, doing his best not to sound exasperated. "I'm literally not. I swear."

"But you're throwing me at some hypothetical other guy tonight. Are you just being kinky, or trying to blow me off?"

"I would've thought you'd be happy to have the freedom."

"Doesn't feel much like freedom. It feels like you're a commitment-phobic jerk who's farming me out."

Sadie peeked around the doorway, and Griffin shot her a wince, pointing at the phone. She stepped over to the desk and wrote *Do you need rescuing?* on a sticky-note. He tipped his head uncertainly, then shook *No*. Sadie nodded and retreated.

"Listen," Griffin said, "I do want to have a conversation about this. But I can't *now*—I'm at my friends' cabin with Byron. Trying to make him do healthy social stuff. Music, food, games."

There was another long pause, and Griffin remembered that the issue of meeting his friends had come up before. He could almost hear the question she was holding back: *Why wasn't I invited?* He rushed on, anxious to dig himself out of the hole.

"I'm going to make it up to you. Tomorrow, all right? Hell, if I have to hire a goddamned bodyguard to babysit my brother, I will.

101

I'll take you out for a real dinner and then stay over at your place and not move from that bed."

"Hm. As long as you move when you're *in* it." Her voice held a smile.

"It's a date." He heard laughter in the next room, and the stereo changing to an Interpol album. "I've gotta go, shortcake. I'll call in the morning."

"Fine. But you're lucky I don't take you up on your offer and go right-swiping on a bunch of dick-pic randos. Goodnight, ya big jerk."

Griffin set his phone down and leaned back in the chair, staring at the dark beams across the ceiling. The sound of another game of table tennis started up in the living room.

He wondered what Delilah was doing right now. She was at the bar, but where was she standing? What was she wearing? Was her hair up or down? With a frown, he grabbed his phone and opened their text thread, typing *How's the place look tonight?* just to have something to say. He deleted the words unsent and stuffed the phone in his pocket.

Sadie returned. "Am I intruding?"

"No. It's more like *I* am, on our evening. Sorry about that."

"Don't stress," she said with a wave, perching on the desk. "So, Wes and I had an idea just now. We think Byron should stay with us. We both work from home, so he won't be alone. Wes is even thinking maybe he can get Byron interested in coding, teach him the basics, hook him up with an online class."

Griffin's expression froze, and he watched Sadie with his mouth half open. Finally he smiled and shook his head. "You guys are amazing to offer, but I can't do that to you. He's my responsibility."

Sadie put her hand on top of Griffin's head from her higher vantage point on the desk. "Byron is his *own* responsibility. The rest of us just love him."

"But… wouldn't it be an invasion of your privacy?"

"Silly boy, we're married—we don't have sex anymore!" She laughed. "Okay, kidding. But, uh… from what I overheard—not that

I was trying—it sounds like you're having the same privacy dilemma. Let him crash with us for a while. Just a few weeks maybe, see how it goes."

Griffin gnawed at the inside of his cheek, thinking. "Did you ask Byron?"

"Not yet. I wanted to check with you first. But I'm guessing he'll say yes—we're a lot more fun than a grumpy old man like you."

"You're probably right." He stood up and put his fists in his lower back, stretching. "I could use a break—it's true. If you really mean it, thank you."

"We definitely mean it." She put an arm around Griffin and gave him a sideways hug. "Besides, it'll be good practice for me, keeping an eagle-eye on someone young, loud, and hungry…"

Hearing the tone in Sadie's voice, Griffin searched her face. "Wait," he breathed. "Are you…?"

She nodded, beaming. "Four months along. We had an ultrasound, and this little man looks great already." She patted Griffin's cheek. "By the end of April, he's gonna knock you and Byron out for title of Prettiest Boy in Oregon."

chapter sixteen

The ballerina's skirt had been in tatters for the past fifteen years, since the day that Delilah's old cat Bluebell had chewed on it, but the pink-and-white music box had always reliably played "You Are My Sunshine." That was, until the morning that the Colonel had started yelling about "that damned racket" and knocked the hinge-lidded box off the shelf. Now it remained wound up, its tension unreleased by song, and the diamond-shaped mirror nestled in the pink velvet had cracked.

It had been a monumental test of patience not to scream at the old man, so hurt was Delilah when she'd picked up the damaged sentimental treasure. Turning on him where he sat in his wheelchair, her teeth had clenched in rage. Then she'd seen his face, eyes awash in unshed tears, and her own eyes had brimmed up, the living room taking on an uncertain oceanic sheen.

"Oh, Pop..." she'd sighed with resignation. "You know better. It's all I have from her."

Wylde Strangers

The weary assertion wasn't quite true. She'd gotten plenty of gifts from her late mother as a child. But they'd been unfailingly practical: clothing, a backpack for school, an alarm clock. The music box she'd been given for her thirteenth birthday had been the only frivolous and feminine gift Delilah had received from Wanda.

The bells above the door of Mayor Missy's fix-it shop jingled when Delilah walked in, reminding her of the music box's song. Missy looked up from an old wind-up kitchen timer she was repairing at the counter. She swept off the magnifying goggles she was wearing.

"If it isn't Miss Delilah," she greeted. Glancing at the white box cradled against Delilah's chest, her smile seemed to falter, then rallied. "Whatcha got there?"

Delilah held it up. "The music won't play—I think it's stuck." She handed it to Missy, who opened the lid and inspected. "I know it's just a silly childish thing, but my mother gave it to me, and… well, Ma wasn't usually big on mushy stuff."

Missy paused, eyes unfocused as if looking through the item for a moment. She touched the cracked mirror and the ragged skirt. "Your mom gave you this, huh?" she said conversationally. She plucked the velvet from the side of the interior and peered in with a small flashlight. "Did it come with jewelry?"

Delilah leaned on the counter, her chin resting on a palm. "No, nothing like that. Why?"

Missy chuckled. "Oh, I think I've heard of that before—a jewelry box shouldn't be empty when you give it as a gift." She shrugged. "Probably saw it in some corny old film." She closed the box and turned it over, patting the bottom. "No problem. I can have her back to you in a few days. The movement—the music part—won't take long to fix. I'll cut a new piece of mirror for inside too, and give this gal a new skirt."

"Really? That'd be amazing. Thank you. I knew you could do it—I always tell new people when they come into town, 'Missy Owen can fix anything.'"

Missy gave an indelicate snort. "Anything with gears."

Something in her tone brought to Delilah's mind the regret she'd alluded to that day in the Valiant when they'd shared coffee drinks in the rain. She covertly studied the older woman's expression, but there was nothing telling in it—just her usual genial no-nonsense smile. Remembering the advice Missy had given, Delilah folded her hands together, covering the backs of her fingers.

Missy's eyes zeroed in on Delilah's right hand. She reached for it and turned it over, then pinned Delilah with a stern look. The little diamond-and-peridot ring glinted in the glare from the nearby craft light.

"Is this what I think it is?" she drawled.

"Yes and no," Delilah replied, feeling the heat of something close to shame creep over her face. "It's Abe's but... we're not engaged. It's not even on that hand."

"I see that. I also see that you don't have the expression of a woman who's excited to be wearing someone's ring. As much as I think Abel Ferguson is a poor match for you, I'd be congratulating you if I thought you were happy about it." She set the music box aside gently. "But you've got the embarrassed look of a woman who was just caught digging through the trash because she thought there might be a chocolate bar at the bottom." She dropped Delilah's hand. "So, what happened?"

A tangle of images rose in Delilah's mind like a fever dream. She tried to sort them and present them honestly, knowing that Missy could spot false coin when she saw it. She tucked a section of hair behind one ear, staring down at the counter.

"Abe just said... you know, try it on for size, wear it around and see if you like the feel of it."

Missy emitted a sniff of cynical laughter. "That's real romantic. He said it like that? Don't tell me—this is Abe. I can all but hear it."

Delilah met Missy's eyes. "Yeah. That was about the size of it." She twisted her wrist to inspect the ring. "I have to admit, it wasn't the moment a girl dreams of, having him say it like a hardware store clerk sending me home with paint samples. 'Check that out, li'l

Wylde Strangers

lady,'" Delilah joked, dropping into a pitch-perfect impression of Abe's voice, "'and come on back when ya make up yer mind.'"

Missy cracked up, her eyes crinkling into fine taut lines. "Oh, that Ferguson boy... bless his heart. Doesn't have the sense to make a proper marriage proposal."

Delilah winced. "It's better that he didn't. The way I was feeling that day, if Abe had swept me off my feet, taken me into town for dinner, a romantic walk at sunset, dropped down on one knee, told me he loved me... I might've said yes."

Missy leaned on her folded arms. "But he *didn't* say he loves you."

Delilah flipped a dismissive wave. "I already know he does. Nobody needs to say hokey crap like that. We've known each other forever-and-a-day."

Missy's eyebrows raised knowingly. "I think you'd love a bit of that hokey crap, Delilah Jane Kelley—for the right man to grab you in his arms like something from a movie and kiss you silly, murmur some sweet nothings."

The blush that overtook Delilah's face in a fiery wave nearly panicked her, knowing Missy would get the truth out of her. She turned and began digging in her purse as if looking for something. She took out a piece of gum and started to unwrap it, then gathered the courage to glance at Missy from the corner of her eye. The narrow-eyed smile she saw made her arm drift slowly down and replace the gum.

"All right, out with it—what happened?" Missy coaxed in her smooth way.

Delilah sighed, pushing her hair out of her eyes. "The night when Abe offered me the ring—four days ago—Griffin... kissed me earlier that day."

"My my my. I'll just bet he did." Missy chuckled. "That look on your face tells me it tipped your apple cart right over."

Delilah's lips bloomed into a relieved smile, glad she was finally able to talk about it. Her words rushed out like smitten teen girls chasing down a heartthrob's autograph. "Oh, Missy... it was a kiss

Josie Juniper

that makes you *stay* kissed. I thought I'd about lose my mind when that frustrating handsome idiot put his lips on mine. If I'd been standing, my knees wouldn't have held me up."

Missy's eyes widened in shock. "Mercy, girl. You weren't standing up? That *was* quite a kiss."

Delilah laughed. "No, I don't mean it like that. I was sitting on the counter in the kitchen."

"All right then," Missy said with a smirk. "You had me worried there. I was about to march the two of you to the altar."

Delilah's smile wilted slowly. "There's no future in it, and it's best if I try to forget. It'd never work."

Missy leaned on a hand. "Hm. Convince me."

"He's my business partner. Getting involved could be dangerous. Just months ago he was in that situation with someone who's his ex now—they can't stand each other."

"Maybe they can't, but it doesn't mean *that's* why. But go on."

"He's dating someone."

"Irrelevant, unless they're committed."

"We're too different! We don't like any of the same things."

"Aside from each other," Missy said.

Delilah scowled. "That doesn't count."

"I'd say it's the *only* thing that counts. Hell, do you seriously think love hinges on whether or not you agree about sushi and foreign films, nonsense like that?"

"It means there'd be bickering, all the time."

"If you do it right, it just means there'd be *compromising* all the time. And that you'd both come to like some *new* things."

"Okay, you seem to have an answer to everything—"

Missy's laughter rang out. "Oh, Miss Delilah! I wish. Look at me… I'm an old spinster who tinkers with broken toasters. I didn't have the right answers for my own life. Maybe that's why I can see it so clearly, what a mistake you're making in not following your heart."

Delilah shot Missy a grumpy look and chewed at the inside of her cheek. "Well, I haven't gotten to the most important thing, and that's the fact that he's leaving. Back to Portland, in just weeks."

Missy reached for Delilah's hand. "If you care for that boy, don't let him go."

Delilah pulled her hand away. "I did that with Caleb, and it killed him. You know how he wanted to escape this town—had his sights set on Los Angeles, wanted to be a stunt man... he had *dreams*. But I was still in school and he stayed for me, and... now he'll never leave. He's in that graveyard forever."

"Wylde didn't kill that reckless boy. You know what did? The fact that he never met a bottle he didn't like. Or a powder or pill, for that matter. Hanging out with those speed-freaks with their little dime-store motorcycle club? He was headed down a bad road. I loved Caleb, but he didn't deserve a wife as good as you would've been to him. Whether he was here or in L.A., he was going to make a beeline for trouble. He may have broken your heart by dying, but believe me... he would've broken it one way or the other."

Delilah didn't realize she was crying until two tears dropped onto the back of her hand. She swiped at her face and sniffed. "Sometimes I think that too. But it feels unfair to him. And I can't help but think about how happy we might've been."

"It's not unfair—it's honest. Don't make Caleb Walsh into a saint just because he wrapped himself around a telephone pole."

Delilah winced. With anyone else, she would have barked at them for the harsh image, but she couldn't fault Missy.

"And as for 'how happy you might have been'," Missy continued, "I can use that same argument now, for you ignoring how you feel about Griffin. And I'm not above doing it." She softened her words by pointing at Delilah with a smile, one eye squinted like a sea captain surveying the waves. "I've got your number, little gal. You've never been able to hide anything from me."

Delilah looked away from Missy's steady green eyes, going back to the ring on her finger. "I'll think about it. I'm just not sure whether one bite of a perfect dessert is better than the whole grocery store sheet-cake I *know* I can have."

Missy delivered a wink. "See, that's where I think you're wrong. I believe you can have the *whole* perfect dessert, if you're just willing to order it."

chapter seventeen

The long miles up the interstate spooled by in reverse as Griffin got closer to Portland. He'd only been able to sleep three fitful hours at Hazel's—the second sleepover that week—and had crept out of her bed at four in the morning to hit the road north. As he'd bent down to smooth her hair aside and kiss her temple before leaving, she'd awakened, looking at the clock and sitting up.

"Why are you going now?" she'd asked, shrugging the blanket to cover one shoulder in the cold bedroom. "Are you feeling weird about last night?"

"No, no. Of course not."

"Because it's not like it was your fault. You were doing all the… you know, the right things. I don't know why it wasn't working. I think I was just tense."

"It's fine—I was tired too. We were both off."

Hazel had reached out and glided a hand up his thigh, the invitation to try again clear as she touched his zipper, but he'd caught her hand and, taking a step back as if to execute a bow, leaned over and pressed a kiss to her knuckles.

"I'll text you later today. Should be there by eleven at the latest."

Hazel had lain back down, letting the blanket fall away to expose her breasts. The motion was engineered to look accidental, but Griffin knew she'd done it to punish him a little, to show him what he'd be missing.

"Are you seeing *her* while you're there?"

"I have to," he'd said. "It's not social—it's business."

He'd said it casually, but now, an hour away from Portland, his gut twisted with apprehension for the meeting. There'd been another phone call between them when Byron had been four days into withdrawal and at his worst. Cleo had screamed at Griffin and he'd had to walk downstairs out of the apartment, pacing the dirty floors of the empty tool-and-die shop, shivering, so as not to upset his brother. Since then, there'd been only two texts—one to set the day to meet, and another from a rest stop just outside of Salem once he was nearly there.

Griffin: *I want someplace neutral, not GL. Noon, Java Genie?*

Cleo: *12:30*
Cleo: *And you're being a drama queen*

She was sitting in her favorite corner spot when he arrived, with what he already knew was her usual café breve. He acknowledged her with a lift of the chin and proceeded to the counter to order, buying a savory scone—the kind he knew Cleo hated—to go with his latte, and went to sit across from her. She pointedly finished the text she was writing, not looking up. In the thumbnail photo at the top of the screen, Griffin could make out what was unmistakably Anton's suave grin.

She set the phone down and darkened the screen with a squeeze, then lifted her gaze with stagey leisure, eyes bland.

"Why the 'neutral meeting place'? Are we in an episode of *The Sopranos*?"

"Just didn't feel like being someplace where we've spent that much time fighting. Also didn't want people underfoot."

"You mean Anton."

Griffin broke off a piece of the scone and ate it, shaking his head with a little laugh. "I'd love to flatter you by saying yes, but that's not it. People there *like me*, so I'd be fielding questions every few minutes while I'm trying to talk business with you."

She smirked as if she didn't believe him. "Okay, Griff." Taking a sip, she licked foam carefully from her upper lip. She was wearing silver lipstick and eye shadow, and her hair—freshly tipped in a new color, pale periwinkle—was pulled back in barrettes. Earrings shaped like green plastic babies dangled from her earlobes. She looked effortlessly cool, and, as usual, knew it.

"I want you to buy me out of Gold Lizard. I'm done."

Cleo's cup stalled halfway to the saucer, then completed its journey with a *tink!* She sat back and assessed him. "You didn't have to drive all the way up here for that. An email would have worked. Even a text." She placed her silver-polish-tipped hands flat on the table and leaned forward, lowering her voice in mocking sympathy. "Or…did you just want to see me?"

"Hate to disappoint you there, but no. I'm here in person because if you pass on buying my half, I have someone else interested. I'm calling them right after, for another meeting."

"You can't just do that," she shot out.

He pulled his head back. "Uh, obviously yes I can."

"I don't mean legally. I mean ethically. The right thing to do would be to speak to me before talking to anyone else—"

"Which I'm doing right now," he interjected.

"—and tell me who you're considering. Don't ambush me with a surprise-new-partner. It might be someone I don't approve of."

"Okay, but that's a moot point if you take the offer."

Her nostrils flared, and Griffin remembered how the involuntary expression of frustration had charmed him when they were first together. It'd been ages since the last time he'd called her by the nickname that had come out of it—"Mopsy," one of Peter Rabbit's sisters.

"You're bullying me," she accused.

Griffin ran a hand over his face. "I assumed you'd jump at the chance to get rid of me. Christ, your parents have the money and would fork it over in a second. The other person is just a backup plan, because I want this done quickly."

Her head turned slightly, like a suspicious bird. "Why the hurry? Is it something to do with Byron?"

"No. But thanks for your concern."

"I didn't say I was concerned."

His eyes closed. He absolutely didn't miss her strictly literal manner. No sense of humor, bottom-line conversational style… little patience with foreplay, for that matter. Once it had felt like honesty. Refreshing and bold.

"Yeah, that was sarcasm." Steeling himself before wading back into the sensitive subject, he ventured, "And I know it's not a ton of dough compared to the overall value of my share, but I'm happy to give you a four-hundred-dollar discount for what Byron might have done."

She picked up her cup and swirled it, suddenly finding the contents enormously engaging. "The money was returned."

The news hit him like the sudden smack of a branch in the dark. He struggled to get the words out. "Why didn't you say anything? When did it show up?"

She shrugged, not meeting his eyes. "The next day."

"The next goddamned *day?*" His voice raised enough that people at nearby tables glanced at him before uncomfortably turning away. He fought to control his tone. "And you didn't tell me?" He crossed his arms, stunned. "Dougie didn't say anything about it either."

"I didn't make a general announcement. I was just glad to have the money back."

A rare caustic burn of slow-moving fury inched through him. "You didn't tell people because you wanted them to keep thinking it was Byron." He huffed in disgust. "You've done a lot of shitty things, but this is right up there. Beautiful."

Her dark blue eyes snapped up. "Your brother did a lot of shitty things too. He's basically the reason we broke up."

Griffin had always worried that was the case, but felt ashamed for thinking it. The confirmation gave him a sensation like a fast-falling elevator. Immediately he wondered if Cleo was just preying on the fear she knew Griffin had, playing that card to shift blame for her own actions. The suspicious detail of Anton having turned off the camera swam back to his mind.

He leaned on his folded arms and pinned her with what he hoped was the most resolute stare he'd ever delivered.

"There was a time when I thought your candor was your greatest virtue. So don't bullshit me when I ask this: did you let Byron take the fall because it was Anton, and you didn't want to fire your boyfriend after he confessed? Because right now I'm so confident that's what happened that I'd bet you my half of the bar." He waited, as Cleo played with the handle on her cup. "Am I right?" he prodded.

She looked up, her silvery lips compressed in a stubborn line. "Byron didn't do it, and I got the money back. That's all that matters."

Griffin reclined in his chair with a sigh of forced laughter. "Good luck with that guy, Cleo. For real. You're going to need it." He picked up his latte and finally took a drink—lukewarm, with stiff bubbles beginning to crust the edge. He lifted the cup in a sort of toast. "Maybe I should offer my half to Anton. He's a keeper."

They sat in silence for a minute, and eventually Cleo's hand crept to Griffin's plate and broke off a piece of the scone. They both knew she hated sunflower seeds, and the olive-branch symbolism in her sharing a bite was apparent. She put it between her lips like a penance and offered Griffin a glance that was closer to humility than he was prepared for.

He wanted so much to be furious with her, but suddenly he saw her current state with clarity: alone, entangled with a good-looking but unscrupulous douchebag, overseeing two bars solo since late

September when Griffin had left. Most likely overwhelmed, uncomforted by her family's money or her superficial and competitive girlfriends. He remembered her patterns so distinctly, and knew she was most likely living off Sobranie Cocktail cigarettes and the occasional handful of pretzels. Examining her more attentively, he noticed that she'd definitely lost weight, and not in a healthy way.

"Are you dating anyone?" she ventured, her voice faux-light and breezy.

It jolted Griffin that the first thing that came to mind was Delilah laughing while talking to a customer as she poured a drink—the way her head moved in a little twist, the bright musical tone, the flash of her teeth peeking from her full lips. On the heels of the image Hazel caught up, her warm eyes, the crimped pattern her hair retained when she shook out her braids, the Marilyn Monroe voice, the way she looked at him—a bashful smile, as if asking permission—before initiating the trail of kisses that headed below his navel.

"Uh, yeah. A girl I met over in Klamath Falls—like a half-hour from where I'm living. Hazel. She does some rock climbing too. We have stuff in common." The last sentence came out as if he was justifying to himself why he should be seeing her, he realized.

"That's nice." One corner of Cleo's mouth tilted up in something more like ruefulness than an actual smile. "Got any pictures?"

"Sure." He swiped his phone open and sorted through a few. "Not that one..." he murmured more to himself as he looked for the right thing to display.

"Oho! She sent you nudes?" Cleo asked with a light laugh.

"She's twenty-three—she was raised on Snapchat. So yeah, I've gotten a few." He found something flattering—Hazel sitting at the kitchen island at Griffin's apartment, holding a glass of wine—and set the phone down, rotating it.

Cleo leaned over to examine it. "She's pretty. Do people tell her she looks like Jennifer Lawrence?"

"Constantly." He took the phone back and pocketed it.

Wylde Strangers

A teasing smile unfurled on Cleo's face. "Twenty-three, huh? You officially can't give me shit anymore about Anton being twenty-six."

"I can still give you shit about him being an asshole poser, and a thief."

Cleo's gaze cut away, then edged back. "Touché."

They watched each other, the ambient sounds of the café pressing in around them. Cleo opened her bag and took out her MAC lipstick and reapplied it, using the back of a spoon as a mirror. Griffin knew this meant they were done.

"You should finish that," he said, flicking a finger toward her breve. "You need the calories. You haven't been eating."

She tilted the cup to look inside, then shook her head. "I'm okay. Thanks." Suddenly her tone was all business again, the moment of connection having evaporated when exposed to light. "And yes to the buyout. I'll call my dad. Does this mean you're not planning to come back to Portland? Are you going to join the ranks of the Millennial homesteading eccentrics, get some goats and chickens?"

"I was thinking llamas," he joked, trying to reel back some of the comfortable vibe they'd had only minutes before, but it was gone. His smile eased away, and he continued, "Yeah but seriously, I don't know. I have some ideas, and they'll take money. But I'm not positive yet that I'm a good fit for Wylde."

Cleo met his gaze, concealed again behind her cool façade. "I'm glad you found someone who's tempting you to give it a shot. I mean that." Her tone said she didn't, but knew it was the socially appropriate closure. The moment solidified between them like names scratched in cement—the end of not only the relationship, but the partnership. Soon there'd no longer be any pretense for contact.

He knew Cleo was referring to Hazel, but didn't bother correcting her. Instead he put out a hand to shake. Cleo stared at it for a second, a brief ripple of something like a curled lip drifting across her expression, as if insulted to be treated like the business associate she was. She took his hand and delivered a negligible squeeze, then stood up.

"I'll fax you the papers," she said in parting.

It wasn't until she pulled the café door open and walked out that he recognized the crack in her voice, the hallmark of incipient tears. He stared after her, and as she passed the window and disappeared, he too felt their sting.

chapter eighteen

The person standing in the dish pit was clearly not Petra.

Lanky-but-muscular shoulders in a clinging t-shirt, tapering to a trim waist, long legs in gray jeans that looked like Griffin's... except this person was not Griffin. Jet black hair—a little too long—hung past the collar of his t-shirt, and his bare lean arms, wet from dishwater spray, were liberally decorated with tattoos.

Delilah paused in the kitchen doorway, one hand frozen on her purse strap. As the music coming from the nearby portable speaker swelled, the man in front of the sink broke into a comically off-key falsetto *"Goin' down, goin' down..."* along with Led Zeppelin.

She went and turned the speaker off, and the man's voice strangled into a squeak as he whipped around to face her. He immediately grinned.

"Holy shit, Griff wasn't kidding—you're hot as a three-dollar pistol." He extended a hand, appeared to realize it was wet, and dried it on the back of his pants before re-offering it. "I'm Byron."

Josie Juniper

She scowled, derailed by the compliment, then cautiously shook his hand. "All right," she said gruffly. "Delilah Kelley. What are you doing in my kitchen?"

"Dishes," he replied, hooking a thumb over his shoulder to point at the sink.

"I get that part." Taking her purse and coat off and hanging them on a peg, she added, "I mean *why*."

"Oh. Right." He picked up a glass bottle of Coca-Cola and took a long drink. "Uh, did your parents ever send you snipe hunting when you were a kid? Y'know, to keep you busy and out of their hair? I think it's a little like that." With a boyish, manic energy, he reached out and turned Delilah by the shoulders, toward the light. "Daaaaaaaamn, look at those eyes. You're like a special effect. Those aren't contact lenses?"

Something about his absolute lack of a filter reminded Delilah of Caleb, but in a way that made her feel protective rather than attracted. She rolled her eyes and allowed a tiny indulgent smile. "Nope. The real McCoy."

"Sweet." He returned to the task of slotting dishes into a rack with the lightning precision of an old pro.

"Where's Petra?" Delilah asked as she put on an apron.

"Who's that? Cool name. Is she cute?"

"Her boyfriend thinks so," Delilah returned. "And she's my dishwasher."

He glanced over his shoulder, hands still engaged, hosing off a platter with the spray-arm as accurately as if he'd been looking at it. "I don't know where she is. Griff just shoved me back here and told me to get to work. He's in the office. Hey, do you like milkshakes? That's what we need back here—a milkshake blender. I could go for one big time. No, *a malt*—we should get malt powder. Hell yeah."

Delilah slowly rolled up her sleeves, charmed despite herself. "Do you just say everything that pops into your head?"

"Pretty much, yup." As if to illustrate Delilah's observation, he asked, "Did you know your hair is sorta the color of those marshmallow circus peanuts? It's possible I might just be hungry though."

She laughed and slid a knife from the rack, sharpening it. "Are you, uh... feeling better? From your illness?"

Byron shoved the rack into the dishwasher and dragged the arm down to lock the doors and start the cycle, his wiry biceps taut. He leaned back against the counter holding the edge, elbows out like wings, fingertips drumming. With a laugh that displayed a straight white smile with slightly pointed eye-teeth, he said, "That's a super tactful way to put it."

Delilah pressed her lips together, debating whether to ask for clarification or let it go. She still wasn't sure what had been wrong with Griffin's brother—it obviously wasn't anything terminal, as he now appeared to be rosy-cheeked with health. "You had... the flu?" she ventured, trying to sound casual.

He flipped a spatula into the air and caught it behind his back. "Well, junk-flu, yeah. I was high as the International Space Station the night before I came down here. Feeling pretty good now though."

She managed an easygoing nod, the knife's rhythm against the sharpening steel remaining consistent. Suddenly the similarity to Caleb made more sense—the walking-party magnetism of a born hedonist, the raw chatty candor.

She took a few onions from a box on the counter. Byron opened the doors on the dishwasher and came over to the prep table.

"Here, lemme do that for you—it'll give the dishes a few minutes to dry." He pointed at the band-aid on her knuckle. "Heard about your battle wound there."

A ripple of anxiety went through Delilah, wondering if he'd also heard about the circumstances surrounding it. When she sneaked a sideways glance, his expression was friendly, open, neutral. She handed over the knife wordlessly.

Byron stripped the onion with ease, and the knife whispered across it with surgical symmetry. He hummed "When the Levee Breaks" to himself, seemingly just as happy to listen to it inside his head.

Josie Juniper

"You're good at that," Delilah remarked, nodding at the flashing knife. "Are you a professional chef?"

"I'm not really a professional anything—except possibly junkie," he joked, just touching Delilah's side with an elbow. "I've worked in a lot of kitchens, 'cause they don't typically drug-test." With the knife-edge he scraped the perfectly diced first onion into a one-sixth-size hotel pan. "Was a music major before I crashed and burned. Might go back to school some time."

"What instrument do you play?"

"Tons of stuff, with varying degrees of shittiness," he admitted with a crooked smile. "I'm actually decent at guitar, piano, bass. I can play drums if I have to. Violin and clarinet as a kid. Oh, and trumpet. Short attention span. Theremin is fun, but it's mostly assholes who are into it."

"I don't even know what that is."

"It's got antennas, and you don't touch it—you just move your hands near it. Some magical-looking Harry Potter shit."

"Dee, can I talk with you?" Griffin called out from the office at the other side of the bar, standing in the rectangle of light.

"Sure." She gave Byron a smile. "Nice meeting you."

"You're not getting rid of me that easily," he said, closing one eye rakishly and wagging a finger. "I'm your new favorite employee."

Something about having Griffin watch her approach made Delilah especially self-conscious. For over a week now they'd given each other a wide berth. But as she wove between the empty tables, her hips tipping right and left around the obstacles, Delilah had the distinct sense that Griffin's focus was on her curves.

He stepped back from the doorway and waved her inside, which annoyed her on more than one level. First, because the simple gesture seemed to imply that it was *his* office. And second, because his stiff posture hinted at Something Serious, and after that morning at Doc Anand's with her father, Delilah wasn't sure she could take more grave news.

Wylde Strangers

He closed the door behind her. "Sounds like you met Byron. Didn't realize you'd be here so early. I should've made the introductions."

"Didn't need your help, but thanks."

"I caught the tail end of him letting the cat out of the bag about his, uh… problem."

Delilah sat in the padded office chair with the stuffing erupting from various cracks. "'Cat out of the bag'? There's no reason he should have to hide it."

Griffin was apparently so startled by her reaction that, in the act of sitting on the desk's edge, he nearly missed it.

"Oh, I remember…" Delilah continued. "You said I was going to be judgmental about it. Because small-town equals small-minded, right?"

Griffin lifted his hands. "Okay, you got me. I didn't think you'd be cool with it—no."

"We used to have a doctor here in town who threw around pain pills like rice at a damned wedding. I've known plenty of folks with problems. People are not their problems. Your brother's a nice guy. Way funnier than you—handsome too, for what it's worth."

Griffin's brow furrowed. "Yeah, I suppose he's more your type," he said, almost to himself.

"Were you hoping to catch me being a close-minded jerk, so you could get up on your high horse and set me straight?"

"No!"

"I'm glad you brought him in to meet people, gave him something to do for the afternoon."

Griffin took a slow breath as if gearing up. "That's what I wanted to talk to you about. I'd like to make a change—"

"Another one?" she cut in.

"—that'd benefit everyone. I know you're exhausted taking care of your dad and bartending, and Byron needs a job. I'd like to make him the dishwasher and have you train Petra to bartend. Start her on the basics next week when we're closed to do the windows, then she can shadow you and barback when we reopen. She could be up to speed and working alone by Christmas. She's cute and friendly and would make great tips. You'd still draw your same salary. But... with a leave of absence to take care of family. You could get out of here, once Petra's solid."

The look on his face was equal parts earnest and... apologetic? There was a pained quality Delilah couldn't quite read. She stared at him in silence. In the kitchen, Led Zeppelin started up again. Suddenly she felt like a stranger in her own bar. Riding on a wave of shame, the possible reason for Griffin's 'generous offer' caught up to her.

"You don't want me here," she murmured. "You're trying to push me out—the dusty cowboy-bar relic who's dragging her feet and hobbling your plans."

Locking his hands on top of his head in frustration, Griffin tipped his head to the ceiling. "Dee, *no*. Jesus Christ, don't be like that. The numbers are up. The changes we've made are already paying off. You and I are—"

"Then you lost your damned mind and kissed me, and the embarrassment is killing you." Her voice was a near-whisper, as if they'd be overheard. "You can't stand to look at me after almost stooping to that level—a tacky country girl."

His gray eyes flashed like a tossed coin. "Don't talk about yourself like that!"

She'd known she was going too far even while speaking—it sounded self-pitying and bitter. Worn down, still reeling from the grief of what Doctor Anand had told her that morning, she had nothing left to insulate herself against the longing she felt every time she looked at Griffin... and the humiliation of knowing he couldn't possibly care for her. He belonged in a different world. His kiss had been a lark, an experiment, like ordering a weird foreign dish with friends, to take one bite and laugh about how strange it was.

Caught between either looking pitiable or angry, she went with angry, despite knowing she was in the wrong. She watched Griffin's breathing through the thin black fabric of his shirt. Her hands were hot and trembling with the need to put one palm on his chest and feel the movement.

"If you want the truth," he said, "I *can't* stand to look at you anymore. Because every time I do now, I want to take you to my bed. I want to undress you with the rain beating down on my roof. I want to taste every part of you."

His words spread out and went still, settling into the silence like the white foam edge of a wave.

Delilah stood. She saw Griffin straighten almost imperceptibly. His hands turned palms up. She took a step closer, and realized that their positions were reversed from that day in the kitchen. It would have been the most natural thing in the world to walk into the V between his knees—to let him hold her, kiss her, make love to her.

Her fingertips just brushed his palms, then slid away. Everything in her seemed to pulse with a rhythm. Her elated and terrified heart kicked wildly. There was an aching throb of lust at her center in response to the images his words conjured. But louder than either was the pounding refrain in her head which told her: *You know how this would end. Walk away before it destroys you both.*

And that was the one she listened to.

chapter nineteen

Delilah had put on the Colonel's favorite film, *Bullitt*, and tucked him into the old maroon recliner with a blanket. For the past few years, she'd either neglected to decorate the house for Christmas, or made a feeble nod to the season with days to go. But this year she'd gone all out, and early. It was only December 2nd, but there were already lights around the windows, a lavishly trimmed tree, and festive wreaths and swags.

Sitting at the kitchen table with Maria, Delilah nibbled at a candy-cane-shaped butter cookie, staring out the window at the Williams kids making snowballs across the street.

"I feel so helpless, just... bringing him home to die," Delilah said, her voice low, though she knew her father couldn't hear her over the car-chase screech of the TV.

"You're not," Maria asserted sternly. "You're bringing him home to *live*. You've made the house beautiful, so he can enjoy his last Christmas. Focus on the positive, *mija*."

"If he even *makes* it to Christmas. The other day I was standing in Bixby's drugstore looking at the gift display, and I realized I'm not sure about buying a present for Pop this year. If he's not here on Christmas Day, that package'll break my heart..." She smiled sadly as a memory came up. "When I was little, Pop and I loved trying to fool each other with the wrapping—putting a tiny thing in a big box, or nested boxes, or a note inside an empty one, sending each other on treasure hunts to find the gift." She leaned her chin on a hand. "We had so much fun. It drove Ma crazy. 'All that wrapping paper, wasted!' she'd holler. But we loved it." She popped the last bend of the cookie into her mouth, chewing meditatively, lost in reminiscence.

Maria covered Delilah's hand with her own. "There now, see? You think about those happy things. Get him a gift, and do your crazy wrapping."

Delilah's gaze swung back to the living room, where her father stared at the movie. She hoped he would whistle when Jacqueline Bisset arrived onscreen. When he did that, she always felt comforted that he was still in there, still himself.

"Doc Anand told me the same thing—act like everything's normal, enjoy our time. He said taking Pop to a hospital would just be a sad end. He always loses it at the hospital, and then they have to give him sedatives. I'd rather have him here and alert than doped up in Sky Lakes, when there's nothing more they can do about his heart. 'Continue the routine,' Doc said."

Maria got up and squeezed Delilah's shoulder in passing as she went to the sink and started washing a cookie sheet.

"You don't have to do that—let me," Delilah said, pushing to her feet.

"I don't mind. You should rest while you can."

"I'm fine," Delilah dismissed with a wave. "It's been quiet, since the bar's closed to put in the new windows. Petra's training herself until we can get back in there and start her on customers. She's made a million of these little flash cards with cocktail recipes. She's so excited—it's kind of cute."

Josie Juniper

As much as Delilah hated to admit it, Griffin's idea about the staffing alteration was a smart one. Byron was already a customer favorite—especially with the women—and even Jack had warmed up to him once he realized Byron didn't plan to put the moves on Petra.

Stung as Delilah had been at the suspicion she was being pushed out of the bar by Griffin, she now saw the merit of taking time off until he went back to Portland. His plan was now to stay until February, to help during the remodeling... and being around him was too hard. The level of awkwardness, barely manageable after the kiss, was now suffocating in the wake of Griffin's declaration. Delilah knew that embarrassing a man was the worst kind of assault on his ego, and she was sure the day she'd walked out of the office without a word, she'd done just that. Since then, exchanges between them had been brief and brittle.

"You want me to stay until bedtime?" Maria asked.

"I can handle it. But thank you." She hugged Maria. "I don't know what I'll do without you, after he's... gone. I've seen you almost every day for the last ten years. This house will be so quiet."

"We will still see each other," Maria assured her. She stepped back and took both Delilah's hands. "Maybe in another year, you'll need me again, for a nanny, yes?" She lifted the hand with Abe's ring.

Delilah tried to smile, but the ring sent a twist of dread through her stomach. Rather than creating the effect Abe had desired, the glittering token on her finger felt increasingly like a tiny noose.

"I don't think so," Delilah said, shaking her golden waves. "We're just friends now. We've known each other forever."

A knowing smile curled on Maria's face as she took her jacket off the back of a chair and shrugged it on. "Luis and I grew up together too. He lived two houses down from me. And we've been married thirty-eight years. Maybe it's never been shining armor and castles, but we're content. We understand each other."

Delilah politely acknowledged this, smiling as she walked Maria to the door. "You're right. There's more than one kind of fairy tale."

Wylde Strangers

She'd meant to say *more than one type of happy ending*, but felt the mistake was fitting—after all, some fairy tales were full of monsters and madness rather than true love's kiss.

Since the day Griffin had confessed his feelings, Delilah no longer thought she could settle for "content" with Abe. The problem was, she couldn't have Griffin either—because she was the one wearing the armor. And exhausted as she felt, she didn't remember how to take it off anymore.

***

Usually the Colonel was agitated just before bed, and getting him to comply with the many steps in the process took well over an hour. Tonight he was oddly quiet, his button-black eyes far away. Sometimes when he got that look, Delilah knew it meant he was remembering the war. His teeth clenched when that was the case, and Delilah knew not to talk. Other times the faraway stare was wistful, and she'd gently ask what was thinking about.

"Her," he'd always say.

Wanda, her mother—Delilah knew.

When Delilah was a little girl, Wanda and Moses Kelley had certainly seemed to be anything but a love match. There was silence or bickering, but rarely loving words. She couldn't remember ever seeing them kiss. They'd slept in parallel twin beds, like a giant equals-sign, announcing them as equally miserable.

But long familiarity must have bonded them, because every few weeks, that shadow of grief—missing the woman he'd spent forty-three years with—crept across the Colonel's gaze.

Tonight he wore a similar look, but rather than being distant and withdrawn, he watched Delilah. His eyes rested on her as she helped him to brush his teeth, put on his pajamas, and arranged the blinds the way he liked. The first few times she noticed, she gave him a reassuring smile. Was it Christmas nostalgia, making him sentimental? She was glad she'd decorated the house, and had even let him have an extra cookie. He must have been recalling, as she'd been, those happy days of her childhood.

So often her father was out of touch now, lost in his own world. A frightened part of her wondered if deep down he knew he didn't have much time left, and being close to the end was giving him a burst of clarity.

She helped him into bed and drew up the side-rails, then settled the covers around him. His eyes still followed her. Finally she let out a small laugh, unnerved.

"*What big eyes you have*, said Little Red Riding Hood!" she joked, patting him on the arm. "You sure are staring tonight, Pop."

His eyes closed slowly, and she switched off the lamp on the bedside table, then studied him in the dim room, her heart aching with the knowledge that she might only be doing this a handful of times more. Suddenly his voice—more lucid than she'd heard it in ages—cut through the darkness.

"The day you came to us was the best day of my life and the worst day of your mother's," he said.

She froze. Her knees felt weak, purely from the eeriness of hearing a fully constructed sentence from him. She crept back to the bed and perched near the foot. The tone of the statement was so odd—full of tenderness and pride, but also hints of anger and sorrow. Delilah's breath caught in her throat, afraid to speak, afraid to break the spell.

Finally, she emitted a whisper of a laugh, and replied, "Well, I reckon that's true. Childbirth isn't exactly a picnic, from what I hear. The happiness part probably starts the next day."

As if he hadn't heard her, the Colonel continued. "Thought Wanda would change. Hurt 'em both."

A shiver inched up the back of Delilah's neck. She sat in silence for several minutes, considering what he might mean, and what to ask. The blue nightlight and moving shadows from the tree outside the window created an underwater sensation, and for a moment, Delilah felt as if she and her father were the only two people on Earth.

"Who do you mean by 'both'?" she asked, just above a whisper. The silence dragged out. She touched his ankle and he flinched. "Is that... me and Ma?"

His even breathing said he'd fallen asleep. Delilah sat for a long time, hands clasped in her lap, staring at the stain of red light on the white walls of the hallway, a reflection from the Christmas tree.

Next year, she'd be an orphan.

Was it still an orphan if you weren't a child?

No parents. No siblings. The bar was a second home to her, the customers and employees like family, but... would that be enough?

Griffin's declaration came back to her.

Surely he'd only said it because he was caught up in the moment. There was no way for him to understand that if they tried to be together, he'd soon be unhappy. Trapped. Like Caleb had been. Like her parents had been.

Delilah wanted to go to Griffin, to fall into his arms and hide. To test out the promise of their lust, if only for a few hours. But one time in his bed would be too many, because a thousand times wouldn't be enough. If Griffin stayed in Wylde, he'd suffer. But if he *didn't* stay... Delilah would suffer.

With a sigh she rose and stretched. Walking to the door, she heard her father's voice again, but this time only a sleepy mumble:

"Melissa was wrong. Too late, too late."

This time, Delilah didn't pause to hear more. She rushed out the door, chased by the same feeling a child has when they leap onto a bed from feet away, afraid something will grab their ankles.

Who the hell was Melissa?

chapter twenty

The first few taps went mostly unnoticed over the sound of the stereo and the tumbling of laundry—Griffin assumed it was a zipper hitting the sides of the dryer. A louder *crack!* shot through the room and he realized it was coming from the window. He went to look, and saw Delilah standing in the swirl of tiny gritty snowflakes below, her hair uncharacteristically hanging loose, no coat, shoulders shrugged against the cold in a long aqua sweater. She saw him and lifted a hand, more like an acknowledgment of responsibility than a wave. Griffin cranked the lock aside and pushed the casement window open.

"You're officially the only person other than Al Cudahy who's used the acorns," he called down.

"I forgot my phone."

"And your coat. Come up before you freeze."

When Delilah preceded Griffin through the door he held open, she took in an audible breath through her nose. "Are you baking? It smells amazing in here."

"Muffins—they're almost done. I had a shitload of neglected bananas." He went to the two space heaters and turned them up higher. "I, uh… was getting a lot of 'em for a while because Hazel likes them. But we haven't hung out lately."

"Ah." Delilah hugged her upper arms and rubbed them to warm up, standing near the space heater by the sofa. "Should I ask why?"

Griffin fiddled with the zipper on his hoodie, running it up and down a few inches. "Probably not. Doesn't make me look too great." He wandered to the stove and turned on the burner under the kettle. The next words came out despite his better judgment. "I don't need to hand you more ammunition for thinking I'm an asshole." Immediately wishing he hadn't said it, he added, "Do you want tea? I'm out of coffee."

"No thanks."

He clicked the burner back off. "I don't want to make things weirder by sounding unfriendly, but why are you here?"

She lowered herself sideways onto the sofa. Her voice was very small as she said, "Katie's out of town and something upsetting happened, and… I needed a friend."

They watched each other, Griffin unsure of the proper response. He longed to go to her, to pull her into his arms, but the thought of having her run out the door again—as she had after both the kiss and the talk in the office—stopped him. The rejection was an unignorable pain that had plagued him for a week, and he held back not because he wanted her to feel that pain too, but because he didn't think he could carry more himself.

"You have tons of friends," he finally said, shooting for a light delivery that hopefully wouldn't sound petulant. But if he'd managed to achieve the correct tone, it collapsed under the weight of his next words. "Why aren't you talking to Abel?" He pointed at Delilah's hand. "I heard you tell Petra he gave you that ring."

She glanced down at it. "This doesn't mean… *that*. It's not a promise."

"Not a promise from *your* side, or from his?"

Josie Juniper

In the silence that followed, Griffin kept his gaze on Delilah like a loose handhold—warm and certain, but unaggressive. She braved one quick glance and looked away. The stove timer shrilled, making them both flinch. Griffin slipped on an oven mitt and took out the muffin tin, setting it on the cold burners.

Delilah nudged her boots off and twisted around on the sofa, watching Griffin over the back, leaning on her folded arms. "I'm willing to look like an asshole if you are too—fair's fair." She nibbled at her lower lip. "I don't... feel that way about Abe. I don't think I ever did. But he asked if I'd wear this for a while and think about switching it to the other hand. To let him know if the answer is Yes. But..." She rotated the ring absently. "It's not going to be a yes, no matter how long I keep this thing on. And I'm too chicken to tell him." She finally met Griffin's eyes. "So there's *me* being a jerk. What did *you* do?"

Griffin put two hot muffins on a plate and went to the sofa. He set the plate on the coffee table and sprawled against the jumble of mismatched throw-pillows in the sofa's opposite corner. With a diffident shrug, he said, "She called my bluff."

"What do you mean?"

The album changed on the stereo, and the bashful warble of Joanna Newsom's *Ys* started up, just as the dryer slowed to silence. At the windows, a hiss of hard icy snowflakes blew against the glass.

"A few weeks ago, Hazel and I had an uncomfortable talk about whether or not things were exclusive. I sort of encouraged her not to put her eggs all in one basket." With a sigh he scooted down further, folding his arms. "Then after you let me know how you felt—or, uh... *didn't* feel—I thought, *Okay, Hazel's nice and cute and we have a ton of stuff in common.* Like, on paper I should be really into her. So I told her 'If you still want to do the boyfriend-girlfriend thing, I'm game.'" He chuckled. "And then she told me she had this opportunity to go backpacking in Oaxaca with a guy-friend, and said 'He's into me and stuff will probably happen.' So... irony."

Delilah winced. "I guess."

"Yeah. I was a cliché dickhead. Natural consequences, right?" He sat up and reached for a muffin, started to peel off the paper but set it down again with a snort when the cake stuck and began to tear. "Can't even keep a muffin from falling apart, let alone my life. Gotta love the symbolism."

"You're rushing it," Delilah said.

"How so?"

With an exhalation of laughter, Delilah clarified, "The muffin. It's too hot."

Griffin gave a reluctant smile. "Gotcha."

The childlike rawness of the music soothed him, and for a moment everything felt nicely aligned—he was more at ease with Delilah than he'd been since before the kiss. The room was warm, deflecting the storm outside, and he could just catch the piquant scent of her hair. He extended his leg and poked her foot with his own.

"Tell me about the upsetting thing that happened. I'm sitting here being a whiney little bitch and you actually came over for a reason."

The smile faded from her lips. "It's my dad. He's not in good shape. Doc Anand said he may not make it to Christmas—"

"For real? Less than three weeks?"

Delilah nodded. "And the other night, he said some cryptic things. I think he's been… hiding something."

Griffin chewed at the inside of his cheek. "You said he's not all there though, right?"

"Usually, yes. But this was the opposite—for a minute he was crystal clear. And he said what a horrible day it was for my mom when I 'came to them'," she explained, making finger-quotes. "Not when I was *born*, which is what I initially thought. Then he said something about how he'd hurt people, and the most mysterious part: he said 'Melissa was wrong.'"

"Who's Melissa?"

Delilah lifted her angular shoulders in an exaggerated shrug. "I wish I knew. I tried to get more out of him the next day, but it was like it never happened. I'd almost think I dreamt the whole thing."

Josie Juniper

She leaned to get a muffin and began painstakingly easing the paper off with tiny tugs.

"I have this sick feeling that I might be adopted," she continued. "Remember when I accidentally sent you that text that was meant for Maria, and it mentioned my blood type? My dad's A-positive—I think my mom was too, though I might be remembering that wrong—and I'm type B. I looked it up and that isn't possible, if they're both A's."

Griffin thought for a minute, pinching at his lower lip with his fingertips, eyes narrowed. "Huh. I know I wasn't there or anything, and you think he was in his right mind, but... it really sounds like stream-of-consciousness territory. They don't even sound connected. I mean, probably everyone talks about the people they've hurt, the mistakes they've made, stuff like that, when they're—" He stopped himself.

"About to die," Delilah said calmly.

"Well, yeah. And Melissa could be anybody. It could be some kid he knew back in 1950, who knows? Or from a TV show—you said he watches a ton of TV." He took a slow breath through his nose. "And as for saying it was a bad day for your mom when you were born—"

"No, when I *came to them*."

"That might've just been clumsy phrasing. If you were adopted, that'd mean they were dying to have a baby, so you coming home *wouldn't* be a bad day. A bad day for your mother would be childbirth."

Delilah set the muffin back on the plate and covered her mouth, slowly.

"What is it?" Griffin asked.

She peeled her fingers away. "Unless my mother—the one who had the horrible day—was someone else. Not Ma. Not Wanda Kelley. She *was* forty-four, after all. And there was one other comment he made. He said *I thought Wanda would'*...*"* She shook her head. "'*Learn*'? No, '*change.*' *I thought Wanda would change.* Or was it *'change her mind'*?" A tear quivered on her lower lashes,

136

then dropped straight onto her jeans, bypassing her face. She glanced at Griffin, apparently embarrassed.

He opened his arms. "Come here."

Delilah's eyebrows tugged together in alarm, and she made an almost imperceptible shake of the head.

Griffin closed his eyes for a moment. "I'm not going to try anything, I promise. I learned my lesson. No creepy ambush-kissing, no impassioned speech that probably bordered on sexual harassment." He beckoned with both hands. "I've been a shitty friend. You said you needed a friend today. I can do better."

She watched him soberly for a moment, then scooted across the sofa toward him. She pivoted and reclined against his chest, her head easing back a centimeter at a time until it made contact with his shoulder.

He enclosed her in his arms. The scent of her so close sent a jolt of arousal through him, and he breathed smoothly, focused on mastering his response so he wouldn't seem like an oversexed twelve-year-old having to carry a notebook in front of his pants. He shifted slightly on the sofa, as if to uncramp his leg.

Delilah's hands settled inside of his, palm to palm. Her thumbs stroked the sides of his hands from wrists to pinkies, over the calluses. He lowered his head, laying his cheek on the soft fragrant waves of Delilah's hair. He caressed her forearms through the soft knit of the thin sweater, and Delilah sighed, nestling deeper against him.

"Thank you," she whispered.

He lifted his head, and dared to drop a subtle kiss on her hair. "For what?"

"I told you I needed a friend. And it's true that I have plenty of them in Wylde." Her arms bent and curled, capturing his hands and pulling them against her. He tried not to think of the round softness of her breasts, warm beneath his wrists. "But what I really meant, I think," she said, "was… I need *you*."

***

Josie Juniper

Abe's fourteen-year-old Australian shepherd, Mickey, was gray-muzzled and slow, but still had enough energy to stand in the front window of Abe's rental house and lick the glass when Delilah parked in the driveway. She smiled as she got out of the car and walked up, watching the blue-eyed elderly dog. Abe opened the door before Delilah knocked, and pulled her into a hug on the cement doorstep.

He seemed to notice how she delivered a consoling pat and leaned away from his attempt at a kiss, so his lips landed awkwardly on her temple. He tilted a stiff smile at her and ushered her inside the warm house. Mickey paced an arthritic circuit around Delilah's legs, tailless behind wriggling. She leaned and ruffled the dog's fluffy ears, then took off her knit hat and stuffed it into her coat pocket.

"Something to warm you up?" Abe offered. "Coffee? Or I think I have some tea 'round here—though you were likely the one who left it. So I reckon it's mighty stale."

"I'm all right." She followed him into the living room. "I can't stay long. Should be at the saloon by four o'clock."

The huge TV was on, showing a football game, and Abe grabbed the remote and muted it. Delilah couldn't help but think that the ever-present sports in the background would be her life, had she chosen to marry him. He'd mute it out of courtesy, but he couldn't bring himself to turn it off entirely and miss a good play. Even now, his gaze flicked to the screen as they displayed the score.

She was relieved that his attention was drawn away long enough for her to take the ring from her pocket. Something about having him see her remove it was too sad. He flashed an apologetic smile after checking the football score.

"Abe…" she began. Her hand was closed over the ring, and his gaze slid to her fist as if he suddenly knew what was hidden inside.

He took a step back and sat on the striped sofa. She followed and perched beside him. Mickey walked up to Abe and inserted his muzzle into Abe's hand in intuitive comfort.

"It means so much to me that you trusted me to wear this," Delilah began, unable to make eye contact. She laid the ring inside of a cork coaster on the coffee table. "It's going to look beautiful on the woman who deserves it." She was tempted to go on, but instinct told her it was best to be simple and direct—like Abe himself.

He eyed the ring. The whine from the muted TV was oppressive, and a similar whine from Mickey floated over the top as the dog picked up his master's distress.

Abe gave Delilah a half-hearted smile. "Figured it was a longshot."

"I'm sorry," she managed. "I just—"

He held up a hand, and Delilah was surprised at the tension in the gesture, something akin to anger in a man who was almost cartoonishly good-natured. She bit her lip and looked down.

"I don't need much, Lilah—I'm a straightforward guy. I would've been over the moon to marry you, have a few little rugrats with those pretty green eyes of yours, and fix up this place together... You know, I'm buying it off my landlady. Made her an offer the day I got the promotion."

"That's wonderful. It's such a sweet house," Delilah said, touching Abe's knee. He glanced at her hand, and she removed it.

"But what I *really* don't need is for you to explain why. I don't want to hear that part. Whether it's that we've known each other too long, or you're wiped out from dealing with work and your dad, or..." He threw a glance at the TV again, but this time—Delilah could tell—it was because he was nervous. "...or you've got a bad case of that city boy you supposedly can't stand. I'd like you to keep it to yourself."

She nodded, looking into her lap again. "I'll skip the 'let's please be friends' part too. That's what scares me the most though—the idea of losing your friendship. You're as natural and constant a part of my life as..." She trailed off.

Abe chuckled. "As any of the other scenery in town. I know, girl."

Josie Juniper

She sniffled and looked up. "As scenery goes, you're not hard on the eyes. You know the ladies love you." She gave a small exhalation of laughter. "Hell, Katie told me the other day that Georgia was asking about you. Still holding a candle, since high school."

"She's moving back to Wylde, you know," Abe said, his voice light and casual.

"Georgia? Huh. Katie didn't mention. Guess Boston got too cold."

Abe shrugged. "Winters are cold as hell here too. But home always feels warmer, somehow." He picked up Delilah's hand and dropped a kiss on it, then put it back on her lap with a pat. "We'll never stop being friends. Holding a grudge is a helluva lot of work."

"True." She exchanged a relieved smile with him.

"It may sting, but I do thank you for being honest. Worst thing woulda been for you to marry me and then we both end up miserable—maybe making some kids miserable too."

Delilah thought of her own parents' chilly union, and wondered who they each might have been genuinely happy with, had they been given the chance. She looked up at Abe, his shy smile and notched ear, all the tiny details that made him so uniquely himself. Some woman—maybe Georgia?—would treasure every one of them. Suddenly, she remembered something she'd left in the car. "Hold on—I'll be back in a flash."

She went out and came back with an armload of bright pillowy fabric: the baby quilts Abe's mother had sewn.

"The wedding quilts were for a specific couple," she said softly, not quite able to meet his eyes. "But these crib quilts are for a baby who hasn't been born yet. That little one'll be so lucky to have Patty's fine work." Abe's eyes lit up as she passed the stack to him. "You'll be a good dad, Abel Ferguson."

chapter twenty-one

It was the first time Delilah's best friend Katie had been in the Wylde Saloon since returning from a two-week trip to visit her grandmother. She'd been a mess since the breakup of her engagement with Eli, and Delilah had coaxed her down with the promise of free rum-and-Cokes and some girl-chat. Wednesday nights were generally quiet, and Delilah knew they'd have plenty of time to talk.

Everything might have gone marvelously if Byron had stayed in the kitchen. But he was too social to be trapped in the dish pit, and had taken to busing tables so he could wander. No more than ten minutes after Katie had arrived, he waltzed out to make a circuit of the bar, then headed back balancing a stack of platters and a few empty pint glasses. He was wearing faded jeans and one of Griffin's black band t-shirts turned inside out. His dark hair was pushed behind his ears, and a late-night shadow of stubble accented his jaw.

He nodded at Delilah in acknowledgment as he slipped behind the bar with his burden of plates and cups. His gaze lit on Katie, who was prodding the cherry in her drink with a slender red straw. He froze. She looked up, and their expressions of shock were mirrored. For a moment, Delilah wondered if they somehow already knew each other—the reaction was so striking. A smile swept across Byron's face, and he walked over with the measured steps of a sleepwalker.

"Is it something in the water here?" he asked Delilah. "How does this town grow such beautiful women?"

Delilah and Katie both rolled their eyes, but Katie's scoffing held the hint of a smile. Byron set down the plates and wiped his hands off, extending the right.

"Byron Averill—part-time musician, full-time dish-drudge, and with any luck your future husband." His white grin flashed again. "Christ almighty, you look like you stepped out of a movie. I can't believe you're just walking around with that face, like a regular person."

Staring at his open palm, one corner of her mouth dimpled with an indulgent smile. She shook hands with him. "Katie MacNair. You must be Griffin's brother. You're... exactly what I've heard."

He leaned on the bar on his folded arms, focused on Katie with the hopeful delight of a shipwrecked sailor spying land from a raft. "Ah, you can't believe everything you hear. Unless it was great. In which case, it's all true—I'm America's Sweetheart." He winked and shifted to rest his chin on one palm.

"Oh good lord," Katie said with a laugh. "Did you seriously wink at me?" She took a sip of her drink through the straw. "A wink is acceptable on almost nobody. Grandfathers. Members of the Rat Pack. Cartoon product-mascots."

Delilah was torn between being overjoyed to see Katie relaxed and smiling—flirting even—and worried that she'd end up liking Byron, who was one big charming puppy draped in red flags. Not to mention the fact that he'd only be in Wylde for about six more weeks. The last thing Katie needed was an impossible crush.

"Don't you have work to do?" Delilah prompted him. "Or are you just going to stand around leering?"

"God, I hope that's a real question," he breathed, "so I can choose the second option."

"It was rhetorical. Now get back in the kitchen."

He sighed and straightened to his feet. "Gotcha, *jefe*." Giving Katie a mournful head-tilt, he stage-whispered, "Don't go anywhere—your next drink's on me."

He hoisted the stack of plates and headed around the corner into the kitchen, whistling "Volare." Delilah squinted at Katie, who stood up on the crossbar of her stool to stare after Byron, unsubtly checking out his ass.

"Katie," she warned, her voice flat.

"Delilah."

"Katie-bear."

"Lilah-bunny."

Delilah covered her eyes with one hand, peeking at her best friend through the fingers. "I know he's adorable. But don't."

"Don't what?" Katie dragged her glossy curtain of black hair around to one side of her neck, wrinkling her nose. "I can look, can't I?"

"He's leaving in like six weeks."

Katie's shoulders, clad in a shimmery bronze off-the-shoulder blouse, drew up in affected casualness. "Why can't I have fun? Do you know how long it's been since I had a first date? Five years."

"You and Eli only started dating *four* years ago."

Katie lifted her manicured hands. "Exactly! I never even *had* a real first date with him. He just appeared and then persisted. Like a plantar wart."

"That's the best description of Eli Armstrong I've heard since the time Savannah called him 'a walking pair of cheap sunglasses.'"

They both cracked up. A group came in and settled at the other end of the bar, and Delilah went to help Petra make their blended drinks. She talked with them for a few minutes, and by the time she turned around, Byron had installed himself across the bar from Katie.

Josie Juniper

As Delilah walked up, he reached to sweep aside Katie's hair under the pretense of inspecting one of her earrings. Katie leaned just enough into his touch that Delilah knew immediately that she'd invited the contact.

"You're right—it *is* turned around backwards," Byron said. "I'll get that…" He gingerly twisted the kinked metal joint in the earring and let it go. "There. Perfect." He smoothed Katie's hair over her ear. "You should show those off. They're pretty."

"These?" Katie asked, pinching the bottom of one earring. "They're nothing special…"

"I meant your ears," Byron said with a sly smile.

Delilah cleared her throat behind him, and he and Katie both swiveled to meet her glare.

"You know that joke you told me yesterday," Delilah asked Byron, "about the guy who tells the duck 'I'm going to nail your feet to the floor'? That'll be *you*, if I see your skinny butt out here bird-dogging Katie again."

He scrunched his mouth to one side. "I'm caught up on dishes."

"If you've got time to lean, you've got time to clean," Delilah intoned.

"Roger. Break over." His gaze swung back to Katie, and he remained very much still leaning, the two of them mere inches away.

"You know, this is on inside out," Katie giggled, hooking a finger into the neck of his t-shirt.

Once again, the newly oiled hinges on the front door betrayed Delilah. Without warning, Eli Armstrong slid into her peripheral vision, taking the stool beside Katie's. The glare in his icy blue eyes was half sarcastic amusement, half murder. Katie's hand yanked away from Byron's collar.

"It sure is, string bean," Eli said, addressing Byron in response to Katie's observation. "Don't you know how to dress yourself yet?"

Byron pushed himself upright, hands flat against the bar, assessing the newcomer. Delilah tried to get a read on Eli's threat-level. Some days the muscular crew-cut blond was all talk, and other times Delilah had to "hook" his keys and call Officer Gribble to calm him down and drive him home.

"Yeah," Byron said, conspicuously relaxed. "Had to turn it inside-out after I got blood on it from the last guy who gave me shit."

Delilah sucked in a breath. She and Katie exchanged a look.

Eli chuckled. "You talk big, pretty-boy. I'd warn you against bothering the ladies, but you look like you play for the other team, so…" He strangled open the beer he must have gotten from Petra before walking over. "…no worries." He took a leisurely drink, eyes never leaving Byron's. "Maybe you can paint each other's nails."

Byron made a slow shrug, smiling. "I *am* good with my hands."

Eli smirked. "You wouldn't be if I broke 'em. Why don't you buzz off before I lose my temper?" He draped a brawny arm around Katie, who cringed away and then settled, as if resigned to his possessive embrace. His grip tightened in a squeeze that made her wince. She smiled reassuringly at Delilah and Byron.

"Are you okay with that?" Byron asked Katie, gesturing at Eli's arm as if it was an inanimate thing, and not attached to two hundred forty pounds of irascible truck driver.

"Mind your own damned business!" Eli snapped. "Me and the lady are engaged." He peered into Katie's half-empty glass. "What are you drinking there, babygirl? I'll get the next round."

"No, thank you," she told him. "And we're *not* engaged anymore." Turning to Byron, she reassured him, "I'm fine."

Apparently enraged that Katie's attention had shifted, Eli grabbed her chin and wrenched her head around.

"Hey!" Delilah barked.

No sooner than the word had left her mouth, Byron snatched Eli's thumb from the air as it slid away from Katie's face. The strike was as lightning-fast and precise as someone catching a fly, and he bent the digit toward Eli's forearm, locking it against the wrist in his long-fingered grasp. Eli jumped to his feet with a yell, the barstool tipping over and skidding across the wood floor like a sled. His other arm rose, the hand fisted and threatening a punch. Byron must have crushed the thumb harder against Eli's arm in response, because the menacing fist dropped away, and Eli let out a tight grunt of pain.

"I think you should apologize to Katie," Byron said simply.

"Let go of me with that pussy thumb-wrestling shit," Eli managed from between clenched teeth, "and trade like a real man."

Byron shrugged. "You were rude," he said, his voice light and easy. "But it won't have to come to a fistfight unless you keep running your goddamned mouth, saying things that aren't apologies."

Talk in the bar had gone silent as onlookers watched, the only sound the Waylon Jennings drifting from the jukebox and the ragged catch of Eli's breathing. As tempted as Delilah was to step in, part of her rejoiced at the sight of famed bully Eli Armstrong on the receiving end of humiliation for a change. She'd spent years consoling Katie over the misery he caused.

She met the eyes of men in the crowd, and seeing that no one was in a hurry to interfere, concluded that they felt the same way.

Byron's focus shifted for just a second as he glanced questioningly at Katie, and Eli saw his opening. He grabbed Byron's shirt by the front, then got his trapped hand loose and took a second handful of fabric. Throwing his considerable weight into the move, he hauled Byron over the bar top and onto the floor. Mugs and glasses went flying, women screamed, and glass shattered. Byron bounced to his feet as naturally as if he'd been a rubber ball. He ducked under the right hook that came flying at him and sprang back up, laughing.

Unfortunately, he didn't realize that Eli was just as good with the left, and the next swing caught him at the corner of his mouth. He dropped as if felled by the blow, but a second later it became clear that it was a ruse, as he hooked Eli's ankles with one leg and knocked him down. Eli grabbed for the nearby stools as he fell and sent two of them spinning away. In an instant Byron was on top of him, his right fist smacking a neat rhythm with three good punches to the face before Eli bucked him off and lunged at him with a growl like a wounded bear.

"Enough, enough!" Delilah yelled at them. "Danny, Richie, get in there and pull these fools apart!"

The two men Delilah had tasked with the job strode over and grabbed Eli and Byron. Eli kicked and thrashed in Richie's grip, blood running from his nose in a crooked diagonal. Byron settled down immediately when Danny's pudgy arms threaded through his. He turned his head and wiped the bleeding corner of his mouth on the shoulder of his shirt.

"I'm okay," he said to Danny. "I swear." Danny released Byron, who put both hands up in surrender. He smiled and touched his bleeding lip. "Holy shit, that was a solid punch, lefty." He ran his tongue across his teeth to check them.

As Delilah stepped into the space between the two combatants, Richie cautiously let Eli go.

"Are you idiots done smashing up my damned bar?" she demanded, swiveling from one to the other, hands on her hips. Nearby, someone righted the barstools. Petra started sweeping up the broken glass. "You both got in at least one good hit. Shake and call it a night, or you're fired—" She pointed at Byron, "—and you're eighty-sixed." She jabbed a finger at Eli.

Byron extended a hand immediately. "Sorry, man. Are we good?"

"No, we're not good, you sneaky little queer," Eli said sullenly, ignoring the peace offering and pinching his nose with a handful of napkins someone gave him. "You kicked my legs out from under me like a girl."

"Is that... a girl thing?" Byron asked, touching the blood at the corner of his mouth with his tongue. "Good for the girls, then. Only a sucker won't fight dirty when it's called for."

Eli took a step toward Byron, and Delilah's hand shot out to brace his chest. "I said knock it the hell off!"

From Delilah's pocket, Maria's text tone chimed. She took her phone out and swiped it open, wondering what the older woman could be texting about this late. Her stomach dropped like lead as she saw the message.

147

Maria: *911*
Maria: *pick up*

Delilah took a step back, her arm stirring the air behind her for a place to sit. The phone rang and she opened the call.

"*Mija*, come home. It's your father." Maria pulled in a ragged breath and sniffled. "He's gone, honey. He... died."

Delilah's hand felt numb, fat, like meat. The phone dropped away. She took a step forward.

"Lilah?" Katie asked, reaching for her.

Byron stood in front of Delilah. His hands lifted, and she dimly wondered why. The room pitched, and the air hissed with a white silence. As everything tilted, Delilah tried to figure out how she'd managed to step into a hole of some sort in this nice newly refinished floor. Her last thought was the realization that Byron's arms were up to catch her as she fell.

chapter twenty-two

It didn't matter to Delilah that the closets looked exactly like what they were—gutted symbols of grief, contents piled in front of the open doors. The Christmas tree had been dark for the past three days since Colonel Kelley had died. There was no point. Everything about the holiday now seemed to mock Delilah. The doors were open on the closets and closed on her heart.

She had to keep searching. It must be here somewhere—the clue, the smoking gun. When and if she found it, would she even recognize it?

She'd almost managed to forget the strange things her father had said that night the week before. Almost. It had become just a secondhand puzzle with missing pieces, returned to the shelf. Then she'd overheard Mayor Missy at the funeral, just hours before:

You really did take it to your grave, you stubborn old man.

Delilah wanted to ask Missy what the muttered declaration had meant, but first she hadn't been sure she'd heard it right, then she'd been perpetually surrounded by well-wishers. To her surprise, Missy had slipped away at the end of the service. Part of Delilah had expected support—Missy's trademark gruff-yet-jovial words of comfort, her reassuring height and sinewy arms, which had so ably provided consolation and strength to Delilah years ago when Caleb had died. But both her lifelong friend and the powder blue Valiant had been nowhere to be seen.

On the drive home, Delilah had reflected on what she'd overheard, and the oddness of Missy's disappearance. Tires whispering against the asphalt as she approached the house, she'd resolved to tear 119 Larkspur Road down to the studs if necessary, to discover the secret Moses Kelley had been guarding.

The little farmhouse had neither basement nor attic, but it did have a triangular crawlspace under the west-side eaves. When the closets yielded nothing, Delilah shimmied out the paneled crawlspace door—breaking two fingernails in the process—and crept inside, waving a flashlight in front of herself to avoid cobwebs.

The first thing she found was a crate filled with magazines: copies of a 1973 true-crime mag in which her father had apparently published a piece: a "Moses Fortune" was mentioned on the cover for the short story "Dangerous Girls of Midnight." Delilah chuckled to herself, skimming it. A little naughty, but hardly a scandalous secret worthy of taking to the grave.

Next she found dusty camping supplies, which was perplexing since her family had never gone camping.

Third, what looked to be a sewing basket. She almost set it aside, knowing it was her mother's, but then decided to check if something inside might be useful—an old seam-ripper or set of pinking shears might be a nice keepsake from Wanda.

Delilah flipped back the hinged lid. For a second, she thought it was empty. Then she noticed weight inside the satin side-pocket. She reached in and felt the cool shift of something lithe and metal. She drew out a short chunky gold chain, and pointed the flashlight's beam at it.

Wylde Strangers

It was a bracelet with one swaying charm, delicate and slender—a ballerina *en pointe*. Threaded on the clasp with a scrap of faded pink ribbon was a brittle and curled note:

For my beautiful baby on her 13th birthday.
Love forever from your mother.

It was not Wanda Kelley's handwriting.

***

The bar was closed for the day out of respect for Colonel Kelley's funeral, so Delilah drove straight to Griffin's apartment. He'd asked if he could attend the service, but Delilah had told him he shouldn't—"in case something goes wrong at the saloon."

"Such as what?" he'd questioned skeptically.

"I don't know. Flood. Fire. Tree falls on the roof."

The look he'd given her said he knew he was being excluded, and though Delilah could tell that it made him feel like an outsider again, she couldn't bear the thought of having him see her break down. It had been bad enough, the few tears he'd witnessed the previous week. The irony was that she'd been dry-eyed throughout the funeral, her lips a grim line.

As she parked now outside of the tool-and-die works, she wrenched the rearview mirror down to inspect herself. She'd never looked more pale, plain, and tired. The bun she'd worn to the funeral was crooked and mussed. She steeled herself and got out of the car. Before closing the door, she leaned to honk the horn.

He looked out the window, held up a finger, and disappeared. A minute later he pushed open the heavy downstairs door. He stood in the entrance, wearing a t-shirt and plaid flannel pajama bottoms. The pair wordlessly studied each other.

"It's over?" he asked.

She nodded and walked toward him, her legs stiff in a knee-length black skirt. She'd already taken off the tights she'd been wearing earlier, after they'd torn while she was edging out of the crawlspace. Her feet in black satin flats were freezing, and she clutched her black blazer closed over the thin gray blouse beneath it.

Griffin put an arm around her shoulders as he shut the door behind them. "Are you okay?"

Delilah shook her head. She mounted the first of the metal steps leading to the apartment, and stumbled. Defeated, she started to turn around to sit down. Griffin caught her gently by the elbow.

"Let's get you warm upstairs."

The ugly gold sofa beckoned like a life-raft, and Delilah walked straight to it and lay down. The TV was on, showing some old black-and-white film. Griffin shut it off. He took an afghan from the back of the sofa and opened it over Delilah.

"It's not fancy like one of your quilts, but it'll work," he joked, settling into the matching armchair at right angles to the sofa. "Are you hungry? Thirsty?"

She shook her head again, feeling her hair tugging further out of the bun in fuzzy disarray against the pillows. Working a hand into the tiny pocket of the blazer and then out from beneath the covers, she held her fist out. Griffin sat forward and put his palm beneath it, and she dropped the bracelet. He held it up, examining the charm and tag.

"What's this?"

She gave a weary smile. "The smoking gun." Seeing his confusion, she went on, her voice a quiet rasp. "It's from my mother. Not Wanda Kelley—someone else. Looks like my adoption theory was right."

Griffin rested his fist against his mouth, brow furrowing with concern.

"And Missy knows who it is—I'm sure of it. Everything is starting to make sense now. I took a ballerina music box to her a while back to be repaired—one I got for my thirteenth birthday—and she asked me if it originally had jewelry inside. Then she said something at the funeral today about Pop taking a secret to his grave." Delilah rolled onto her back, staring at the metal ceiling beams. "Of course she would've helped them. You know she does everything around here. She's the one with solutions. Miss Fix-it. 'A river to her people,' like that guy in *Lawrence of Arabia*. Those old Kelleys need a baby? No problem—I'll find them one." Delilah pantomimed checking something off a list. "The thing I don't understand is how no one in town let it slip, all these years."

"Unless they don't know." Griffin adjusted in the chair, warming to the subject. "Assuming you're right, here's a thought: didn't you say, about your mom, that she was really reclusive? And also sort of... a bigger woman?"

"Sure."

"So she already doesn't get out much, and she's big around the middle, then she says 'Oh, I had a baby.' If you were adopted but brought to your parents discreetly, no one would question her having had you naturally."

"The town doctor would know."

"You told me Doctor Anand is new, and that the doctor Wylde used to have was pretty unethical. A guy like that might be easy to buy off."

Delilah pulled the afghan up under her chin. "This is all too much. I'm so depleted." She rubbed her eyes. "I can't sleep at home. I stayed with Katie the first night and Maria's family the second, then last night I just stared at the walls."

Griffin stretched his legs to rest on the coffee table, chewing at his lower lip. "You, uh, could stay here. It's almost dark out anyway. I'd take the sofa."

She sighed with relief. "Just one night. I don't want to impose."

"I'm glad I can help." He smiled, and Delilah admired the dimples Tammy at Sweet Dreams always raved about.

"You sure your girlfriend won't mind?"

He eased deeper into the chair. "Hazel's still in Mexico. Also she's not my girlfriend. A few days ago I sent her a text, just to be friendly and see how her trip was going, and her reply wasn't even in words—just a selfie of her and what's-his-face. Aiden, I think.

Jayden? But yeah. I think she might have been trying to rub my face in it a little. Which is fine."

"Okay." Her eyes closed, then opened. "Do you have an extra toothbrush?"

"You're in luck. I bought a two-pack when Byron got here, and the second one is in a drawer."

She yawned. "Prepared. Must've been a Boy Scout."

He laughed. "Hardly. We couldn't afford the uniform. But I was in any group that was essentially free after-school childcare—chess club, track and field."

The next thing Delilah was aware of, it was dark and she could make out the faint white angles of the ceiling beams. She realized she was being carried, and with a gasp threw her arms around Griffin's neck.

"Sorry," he said, just above a whisper. "I wasn't sure if it was worse to wake you up when you looked so peaceful, or pick you up like a caveman."

"You could've left me on the sofa," she said, her knees drawing in. "Put me down—"

"Almost there." He set her on the king-sized bed. "And trust me, that sofa's crap."

Delilah looked around the bedroom—the neatly arranged bookshelf beside the huge bed, a butterfly chair in the corner mounded with laundry, a tall dresser with a mirror, which had an old-fashioned globe standing in front, reflected. Two worlds.

Griffin took a few things off the top of the clean laundry. "Here. Long-sleeved t-shirt, and these pajama pants have a drawstring so they won't fall off you. Toothbrush is in the package, on the bathroom counter. Hope you don't mind clove toothpaste."

"So *that's* what you smell like!" Delilah said. Immediately she was embarrassed at having admitted that she'd noticed.

He smiled and took a few steps back, out of the doorway. "Yep. And yours is cinnamon. I, uh… tasted it on you once."

She felt heat rise to her face despite the cold of the room. "Hey, Portland?" she called after him.

He ducked back around the doorway.

"If the sofa's crap, it's fine with me if you sleep in here," she told him. "This bed is enormous. Just... stay on your side."

His eyebrows raised. "If you're sure, it's a deal. Slumber party it is."

***

The blue of a phone screen shone in the dark, and Delilah turned over. "What time is it?" she asked.

"A little after midnight."

She sat up, headachy and dehydrated. "You sound funny. What's wrong?" She took a glass of water from the bedside table and drank some, feeling like she'd never had anything as delicious as that cool liquid in the glass jelly jar.

He rolled his head to look at her. The light shadowed his face in a way that made him look unfamiliar—both young and old. For a moment she could see who he'd been twenty years before, and who he'd be twenty years in the future.

"Had an idea and looked it up. The name you said your dad mentioned—Melissa. Do you know what the nickname for it is?"

She set the glass down. "I don't know. Mel?"

"And Lisa. And... Missy."

Delilah drew up her knees and wrapped her arms around them.

"That seems to imply that Missy *was* involved in some way, like you thought," Griffin went on. "But then I discovered something else. Looked up her business license for the fix-it shop. Her full name's Melissa Jane Owen."

"Jane is my middle name too," Delilah breathed.

"I remember. So now I'm wondering... what if Missy didn't just *find* your mom, but... she *is* your mom?"

chapter twenty-three

They'd been talking for an hour when the rain started. Remembering the scenario he'd described to Delilah that day in the office—making love to the sound of rain on the roof—Griffin felt a pinch of embarrassment, wondering if she'd think of it too. Every time the rain pounded overhead since his unabashed declaration, he longed for Delilah. His lips would unconsciously press together in an echo of the feel of her mouth, his fingertips moved slightly as if tangled in her hair, and the blood fled his brain for a stampeding migration south.

"I'll just have to talk to Missy," Delilah said in conclusion to their discussion of the adoption bombshell. "But I'm going to wait until I'm not upset. There's no rush at this point—Pop isn't going to be any less... gone. If I go into the fix-it shop guns blazing, as emotional as I'm feeling, it'll come out accusingly. What if I scare her off, and she *never* gives me the answers I need?"

Trailing off, she glanced up at the roof as the rain built to a roar. She eyed Griffin cautiously, both of them snared in the silent indisputable awareness that they were thinking the same thing.

Delilah looked away first, lying down again, turned on her side toward him. With a frown, she said, "You, uh… smell really nice for some reason."

The plain statement sent a tremor of arousal through him. Its guileless physicality immediately made him imagine their skin touching, which led to a vivid picture of his lips against the crook of her shoulder, the skin damp with the hot exertion of mutual lust. His mind tried to scramble away from both the thought and her words, and he was mentally assembling a joking reply when he heard himself say something very different than what he'd intended.

"You always smell amazing. Like an herb garden in the sun. It's such a summer smell—it reminds me of being a teenager, getting minute-long crushes on beautiful strangers as I passed by them. You smell like… wishes."

Delilah's lips—which were slightly dry and oddly the sexiest he'd ever seen them—parted. Her unpainted mouth had a vulnerability that drew him like a magnet, and he wanted to touch her lips with his tongue and feel the texture, the fullness, feel her open to accept him, to draw him closer. He tore his gaze away.

"*Like wishes*—that's one of the nicest things anyone's ever said to me," she told him. She tucked both hands under her cheek on the pillow. "You can be sort of charming. I hope you haven't used that line before."

He scooted down and lay beside her, their postures mirrored. "It's not a line. And I haven't." His own lips suddenly felt dry, and as he moistened them, he saw her eyes shift to watch. "I think this is my cue to move to the sofa," he said quietly.

She adjusted her elbow, edging closer, then stopped as if to gauge his response. "I don't think I want you to leave."

He tugged the blanket up to her shoulder, and the warmth of her skin was almost too much. Touching her was natural, inevitable. It was like all the things he'd mistaken for magic as a child, which—

once he'd learned about how they worked—became *better* than magic: surface tension, air pressure systems, photosynthesis. He let his palm mold to the curve of Delilah's shoulder. She closed her eyes and put her bare feet against his shin.

"I really should go," he asserted. "Before mistakes are made."

Her eyes opened, and the felty-black ring around her bright green irises trapped him as surely as manacles. "Would it be a mistake?"

He ran the backs of his knuckles up her shoulder, unable to resist, following a path to her neck, grazing along her jaw, and stopping to touch her lower lip with his thumb. "You said so after I kissed you: 'mistakes happen.' And—" He drew his hand away, securing it beneath the covers. "I'm worried that what you need isn't... um, isn't what your eyes seem to be saying—"

"And my feet," she interjected with a smile, stroking his shin with her toes.

"And your feet. You're fragile right now. This is a distraction, and that makes sense—I'm not criticizing the impulse. But I'd be an asshole to take advantage of it."

Her arm wriggled into the space between his head and shoulder until they were inches apart. "I'm the one who'd be taking advantage. But that isn't talking me out of wanting you."

She aligned her body against his. Griffin's heart yanked in his chest. She was so close that he could track the downy perimeter of her eyebrows, down to the last toffee-gold hair. He tipped his head back to marvel at this small personal detail. His hand sneaked above the covers again and he smoothed her left eyebrow with his fingertips. It was softer than he'd expected.

Delilah rested her wrist against his waist, as if too nervous to let her actual hand make the first contact. She surveyed his face before pressing her forehead to his shoulder, and stayed there for a moment, hiding, in apparent private conference with herself. With a flick she pulled up Griffin's shirt hem and slotted a tentative grip above his hipbone.

"Dee," Griffin whispered. "Are you sure?"

Wylde Strangers

In response, she arched to kiss his collarbone, his throat, his jaw. One of her legs swung up to lock over his hip, and with an impulsive scramble she pushed herself upright, rolling Griffin onto his back and settling over his hips. The blanket dropped away. The light from the window behind Griffin painted her face in silver and black. His hands roamed to her hips and clasped them.

"I did *not* expect to see you here," he admitted, a smile overtaking his face with the languor of a stretch.

She put her hands flat on his chest. "I didn't expect to *be* here."

Griffin edged back toward the headboard, raising himself on his hands. He noted Delilah's troubled frown and realized she must be thinking he was trying to get away—to climb out of the big bed and go to the living room. Reassuringly he pulled her tight against his lap. "I'm not going—I'm taking you with me."

Her hips tilted to position herself against the evidence of his need through the layers of fabric separating them. His hands glided beneath the hem of the oversized shirt Delilah had borrowed. He swept it up and over her head, only realizing when his fingertips passed her ribs that she wasn't wearing a bra.

She watched his reaction soberly. Her arms went behind her back, bracing herself on Griffin's thighs to display herself without reserve.

Her exquisite form was everything he'd fantasized about—lush teardrop breasts with delicate areolae, tipped with perfect coral-bead nipples. The hint of her ribs feathered down her torso like ripples in a pond. Her flat stomach was a velvet plane above the womanly curve of her lower belly. Her slim waist nipped in with contours seemingly made for spanning with eager fingers. Griffin lurched against her body, wanting to hold that waist and move inside of her.

He took his own shirt off and hauled her closer in the crook of one elbow, the other hand tracing from neck to shoulder to breast as their lips met, gingerly for a moment before hunger pushed them together hard, like an unforeseen wave. If he'd thought he remembered the taste of her, the feel of her tongue sweeping his with urgency, the surprising touch of her teeth as the two of them glanced off each other, he was wrong—this was nothing like he remembered. It was a thousand times better. He willed his hands to be gentle as one dug into the groove of her spine and the other cupped the weight of her breast. His thumb caressed the nipple in exploratory passes, mindful of the subtle shift in the pressure of her thighs and the grip of her hands in his hair as she responded.

She rose on her knees and reached between her legs to touch him, cradling the outline of his sex before tauntingly stroking the length, and he drew in a quick breath through his nose. Her nails scraped his angular hipbones as she quickly dragged his loose pajama bottoms down by the elastic. She threw herself back into a kiss after stripping him. Every nerve in Griffin's body seemed to be standing at attention, poised for a command that might push him over the edge.

She sat up and fixed him with a lurid smile, then slid back until she was kneeling over his knees, leaning forward so her long loose hair pooled in his lap. She straightened and swept it around her neck out of the way, then grasped him with confidence.

"We look good like this," she said, her voice a husky whisper.

"It's pretty incredible from this angle too."

She bit her lip almost shyly before bending to take him in her mouth. He didn't know where to rest his eyes—it was all sublime. He watched the silhouette of her in the low light, every curve, the smooth motion, her muscles gliding like velvet. His eyes drowsed shut and his head dropped back against the headboard. The rain drummed overhead, thundering like the blood in his veins.

"God, Dee… you're killing me," he managed. In response he felt her laughter vibrate against his hot hard flesh, and the sensation, paired with her wicked tone, nearly unmanned him. He took a handful of her hair and coaxed her up, the action taking every bit of will. He slid her along his body back up to his lips. "I want to be inside you," he murmured.

"Yes, *please.*"

He flipped them both over in a lazy roll, and before he could even reach for the pajama bottoms Delilah wore, she shimmied out of them and kicked them away with a youthful enthusiasm that spurred a renewed swell of need. His mouth sampled every inch of her as he worked his way down her body. When he got to her belly, he smoothed a hand up her thigh and in between, teasing her with feather-light strokes. After a few minutes he bent her knee and placed one of her legs to rest on his shoulder, then ducked to replace the ministrations of his hands with his mouth.

Delilah reached for his arm and dug her nails in, edging away. "Wait, not that—not yet," she pleaded in a whisper. She urged him back up to her mouth and kissed him hard. "I need you. *Now*. Don't tease me."

Griffin swept both hands along her arms to capture her wrists lightly above her head on the pillow. He settled his weight on her incrementally, watching her eyes.

"Am I too heavy?" he asked almost inaudibly.

She shook her head, wrists moving restlessly in his grasp, and pushed her hips up to encourage him, cocking one leg aside. "I like it. You're the perfect kind of heavy. It's… touching everything just right." She shifted in a slow fretful rhythm and shut her eyes hard. "I need more…"

He kissed her, moving against her heat, sliding enticingly, greedy for her as he felt how ready she was. His lips sketched a trail to her ear. "You're so beautiful," he whispered. "Open your eyes." His hands squeezed hers as he pushed inside her, and she clasped around him as if she would never let him go.

chapter twenty-four

After brushing her teeth and getting dressed, Delilah sat on the edge of the bathtub and propped her forehead on her palm, elbow on one knee. She stared at Griffin's bathroom floor, her eyes wide and heart aching.

He'd said so many beautiful things. *Damn him.* Somehow he knew exactly what to say, as if he could see inside her mind and knew when to be tender, or funny, or just the right amount of dirty. She could have lain in his arms forever, feeling his body inside and out of her own, his hands, slow and patient or rough and bold.

The third time they hadn't even finished, just content to be joined, curled together in the faint glow of dawn. *You were made to be seen in this light—at sunrise*, he'd whispered against the back of her neck, his fingers tracing Delilah's curves. *This is the reason the sun comes up,* he'd said. *To touch you.*

She could admit to herself unreservedly that she'd never made love with someone like that. She'd been so hot for Caleb that he hadn't needed to do much more than show up and give her that smile, and her clothes were on the floor. There'd been awkward interludes with two boys in college, always with an obligatory feeling, knowing she was supposed to "move on" from Caleb's loss. The name of one of them had even eroded away over time, like a sandcastle, until he'd just become The Blond with the Jeep—either James or Jake, she wasn't sure.

And Abe, of course. Two years of perfectly pleasant sex. He stuck to a routine, and occasionally Delilah had wondered if he was following steps he'd read in some men's magazine or website. He tried. Abel Ferguson was nothing if not courteous. But he seemed to have no ability to read the feedback he was getting.

Griffin had been Delilah's first inkling of What All the Fuss Was About. It was hot, surprising, effortless. Every touch and kiss, every detail of communication—both verbal and nonverbal—instantly understood. Her heart pounded now, just thinking of it. She hadn't showered, not only because of the noise, but because she loved having his scent all over her and wasn't ready to let it go. Her feet on the bathroom floor were bare and cold, and she stared at them, afraid to move, afraid to make some sound that might wake Griffin before she slipped out.

It was impossible. It was stupid and selfish, the idea of being with him, of walling him off from his life, like that poor bastard in "The Cask of Amontillado." Immurement, a sacrifice to Delilah's need. And she *did* need him, physically and emotionally—she knew it now.

Her shoes were next to the sofa, she remembered. She opened the bathroom door slowly. Griffin stood at the kitchen island, in pajama pants and his black hoodie, chest bare without a shirt beneath. He held up the kettle amiably. "Coffee?"

After a pause, frozen in the doorway, she shook her head. "No thank you. I didn't know you were up."

"I'm a morning person—not super into sleeping in. But, uh… a few hours were nice after dawn, I've gotta admit." He smiled, and his dimples made Delilah's pulse stumble even more than usual, now that she'd felt them with her fingertips.

She went to the sofa and sat, wordlessly reaching for her satin flats. She was easing her heel into the second one when Griffin's hand lit on her shoulder, from where he stood behind the sofa. He drew her hair aside and kissed her neck just below the ear. She closed her eyes, hands stalled at her task. He stepped over the back of the sofa and sat beside her. Touching her chin, he turned her head and kissed her. She responded mechanically, a beat too late, and his eyes were troubled when they parted. Immediately she turned away, unable to witness his confusion. She wriggled into the shoe.

"Are you leaving?" he asked, touching her knee. "I mean, it's fine if you have things to do, but… it doesn't feel like that's why you're putting your shoes on."

"The 'walk of shame,'" she said with a wry smile. "You caught me."

He drew his head back as if evading a slap. "Whoa, *wait*. Dee, this isn't a 'walk of shame' situation." He waited, as if hoping for a reaction. "At least not for me."

"Well, sure," she joked. "It's your apartment—you don't have to walk anywhere." She stood up, and he reached for her hand.

"That's not what I meant, and you know it." The hurt in his voice was well masked, but Delilah knew him enough now, after eleven weeks, to recognize it.

Instinct told her this was the moment. She was either going to fall into his arms and drag him into the quagmire of her life, or don her best bitch-face and let him escape. Now, with her father gone, agonized over a childhood hijacked by a loveless mother, and cut off from the one who hadn't cared enough to keep her, she knew the risk was too great that she'd make Griffin into *everything*.

She fixed him with a pointedly bland look, clasping her hands in front of herself to hide their trembling, but making it look casual, careless.

"I appreciate you letting me stay. And, what happened… happened. It was really nice—I'm not saying it wasn't." She glanced at her shoes to give her throat a moment to relax before her voice cracked. "But I don't need a boyfriend. We're adults. Let's just…

act like it." She shrugged. "Years from now when you come to Wylde to check on the business, if we both stay in this thing, it'll just be... y'know, something we know about each other. Maybe we'll even laugh about it."

His mouth was a grim line. "No. I won't ever do that."

She peeked at him and had to remind herself to keep her face neutral. "Won't... come to Wylde to check on the bar?"

"Won't laugh about it."

They watched each other.

Griffin stood, and Delilah took a step back, bumping the coffee table.

"Don't you hide from me now," he demanded. "If your mind's already made up, I've got nothing to lose in wearing my heart on my sleeve—this *means* something to me." He looked away for a moment. "And I know you're grieving, so I'm not going to act like a wounded sad-bastard, like it's all about me." His hands slid around her waist and he drew her close, then combed both hands through her hair, holding her head gently, thumbs brushing her temples. "Delilah," he intoned, just above a whisper. He kissed her forehead. "*Delilah*. I love your name. I've always been half afraid to say it, like an incantation." He kissed her nose, then her lips. "You're a sorceress. I had to nickname you just to save myself."

She knew he meant it in the sweetest way, loving and playful, but the words reminded her of exactly why she could never be with him. Her hands drifted up to push his off, dreamlike and slow. She sidestepped away from the coffee table, trying to ignore the cramp in her chest when his expression went dark, as if a storm cloud had rolled over it.

"Thank you for... distracting me," she managed, fighting to keep her mouth firm as her lower lip threatened to tremble and give her away.

He held her gaze for a long moment, then sank his hands into the pockets of his plaid pajama bottoms. "Sure," he said. "Happy to have helped." His casual tone skirted the border of sarcasm, but with no note of hostility. That would have been easier to take. Instead he just sounded tired.

She sneaked one quick glance at his beautiful gray eyes with their long dark lashes, remembering them inches from her own. "What... shift do you want today? I can... I can do either, now that Petra's bartending." She pivoted toward the door and went to it, resting her hand on the doorknob.

He exhaled a small bitter laugh. "I suppose we wouldn't want to be there at the same time, right?"

Her fingers tightened. "More efficient that way."

"Gotcha." He sighed. "Well, I can't be here all day, thinking about this. I'll shower and head in to do prep. You go home and... get some sleep, I suppose."

"Yep." She opened the door, head down. Two tears dropped off her lashes and hit the cement floor. Her feet smeared them as she passed.

chapter twenty-five

Facedown on the bed, her face crushed against the pillow, Delilah heard Maria's voice sing out.

"*Mija!* You're here?" The front door closed, the bells on the knob jangling.

Delilah struggled through layers of sleep and squinted at the bright early-afternoon sun knifing around the edges of the blinds in her father's bedroom. She pushed herself upright, not wanting to be caught sleeping in his room, but Maria was already headed up the hallway.

"*Dios mío*," Maria muttered as she apparently passed the gutted hall closets. "What are you up to with this?" Maria peeked into the bedroom across the hall, then turned around to check Colonel Kelley's room. "Oh, honey…" She walked in and held out a hand. Delilah took it, then dropped her face to Maria's warm knuckles, the plump crepey skin smelling faintly of cornmeal. She felt hot tears starting again. She'd already cried herself to sleep and hadn't thought there was anything left.

"Just doing some spring cleaning," she sniffled, to explain the closets.

"It's not springtime." Maria sat on the edge of the bed and wrapped an arm around Delilah's shoulders. "Come to the kitchen—I brought chilaquiles. You eat, and I'll fix the closets."

Delilah swiped at her face with a sleeve. "I should take a shower first."

Maria nodded, peering at Delilah sidelong, as if she knew.

Delilah realized she must smell like sweat and sex, and her cheeks burned. She crawled backwards off the bed and stood up.

"Do you need a bath?" Maria asked. "A very hot one... with pennies?" Maria's careful tone recalled to Delilah the fact that Maria believed hot baths with pennies somehow prevented pregnancy.

"I don't, um... no," Delilah assured her. "I have the, uh..." She shook her head, unsure where Maria stood on IUDs. "Thanks, but the stew will be plenty."

A half hour later, she sat at the kitchen table with a bowl of steaming chilaquiles, which Maria had topped with a fried egg. Delilah's hair was damp, affixed to the top of her head with a tortoiseshell butterfly clip, and a gel ice pack sat beside her plate. Periodically she held it to her face to try to alleviate the redness around her eyes.

Maria pulled out a chair across from Delilah and sat down.

"You don't have to come in anymore," Delilah told her quietly.

"You paid me for December already... but I'd be here anyway, just as your friend. I'll come in January too if you want. For as long as you need me."

Delilah gave her a weak smile. "I really don't deserve you."

Maria flicked a dismissive wave. "Of course you do. Tonight when you go to the bar, I'll fix the other closets too, and bake you a pie. You're too thin."

Delilah snorted. "Hardly."

Maria sat back, buttoning her cardigan and assessing Delilah. "You're trying to be skinny for some boy?" She pointed at the naked finger where Abe's ring used to be. "Not Abel—another one."

Avoiding Maria's eyes, Delilah shrugged, concentrating on scooping up bites of the spicy chicken.

"I think I know who it is…" Maria said in a gentle singsong.

Delilah looked up, her spoon arrested in transit.

"Mister Isaacs *is* very handsome," Maria went on. "Is he the one who… made you so tired?"

In answer, Delilah picked up the ice pack again and pressed it to her face.

"I thought so," Maria declared. "You want to talk about it?"

Delilah shook her head, hiding behind the cold compress. She pulled it away and considered Maria carefully. "Do you know if my father had secrets?" She asked it as simply as someone requesting the time, hoping to catch the older woman off guard.

Maria's dark eyebrows drew up. "Every man has secrets."

Stretching her arms across the table, Delilah took Maria's hand in both of hers. "It's about my mother. And… Mayor Missy. Have you heard anything?"

Looking evenly into Delilah's eyes, Maria told her, "I am telling you honestly, *mija,* no—I haven't heard anything. But it sounds like *you* have." She patted Delilah's hands. "Your father and mother are gone. Don't look too hard for these answers. Your parents are not here to defend themselves, to explain, if you find out something you don't like. Your father loved you, and you had a good life with him. Be happy for that…" She pushed the stew bowl a little closer to Delilah. "…and eat."

***

The purple van—which Delilah had been calling "Barney" since the week Griffin moved to Wylde—was in the saloon's parking lot, along with Jack's pickup. Delilah parked her battered hatchback and turned off the engine, staring at the van and wondering whether to drive the few blocks down to Sweet Dreams to pick up a mocha, and stall for a while. She didn't want to see Griffin.

Except… *she wanted to see Griffin.*

Recklessly. Maybe stupidly.

She wanted to look at his hands—the strong square palms, long fingers, stepping-stone calluses, and even the tiny white crescent moons on his fingernails—and feel the thrill she knew would shiver through her, remembering where those hands had been. It was the kind of impulse that made a person look straight down while standing at the edge of a cliff... one daring peek to set the blood racing.

She checked her watch. Four o'clock. Maybe he'd come out any second now and leave? Then she could look at him from a distance, without getting close enough to smell him, or hear that smooth coffee-dark voice, or argue with herself over whether she was relieved or disappointed if he didn't touch her.

She got out of the car and strode across the lot, her boots crunching the gravel. When she pushed through the door, Griffin was sitting on the floor in front of the jukebox with the hatch open, apparently initializing a batch of new CDs which were stacked beside him. Jack and Petra were in the kitchen, horsing around.

Delilah hung up her coat and purse, then walked to the jukebox. Griffin's head turned only slightly, acknowledging the boots and faded jeans beside him.

"I'm almost done—a few more minutes," he said without looking up.

He wore ragged black jeans and a NASA tee with a thermal beneath, pushed to the elbows. His arms and shoulders looked heart-stopping when he was shirtless, Delilah now knew—he had a strict and involved routine of chin-ups, pull-ups, and weights during the off-season for climbing, to keep himself toned. She stared at the fine hair on his arms, annoyed.

"Why are you messing with my damned jukebox again?"

Griffin grabbed a handful of CDs from the stack and handed them up to Delilah, still without eye-contact. She shuffled them in her hands—Florida Georgia Line, an early Taylor Swift country album, Luke Combs. All country. She noticed a bit of cellophane clinging to one of the cases and realized the CDs were brand new. Her arm dropped waxy-slow. Almost as slowly, Griffin looked up at her.

"Well, *I* feel like an idiot," Delilah admitted.

He stood and brushed his pants off, then picked up the empty cases and loose alternative CDs he'd removed. He walked toward the office, Delilah following.

"Why the switch?" she asked.

He put everything in the top drawer of a metal cabinet and rattled it shut. "It's wrong to change the feel of this place. We should stick with it being what it is. The patio is going to be great, and I'm glad to have done the windows and the floor, and gotten good furniture. But no more weird food, trendy cocktails, or indie music. And definitely no name-change." He hooked a thumb at the cabinet. "New music is fine, but it should be new *country*. I admit defeat."

Delilah's stomach dropped. "*Defeat?* Are you... going back to Portland early?" An even worse thought occurred to her. "Or selling your half to someone else?"

He leaned on the desk. "Would you prefer that?"

She told herself to stop looking at his lips—he'd definitely notice.

Stop looking at them. Oh my god, the eyes aren't much safer...

Every part of him now seemed like communal property that had been newly surrounded by electric fencing. Just hours before, she'd touched him wherever she wanted, without hesitation. Knowing every contour of his body, and not allowing herself access, was far worse than when it had been a mystery. The memory of the telltale shift in his breathing before climax materialized, and Delilah felt herself blush. She turned away.

"No," she managed. "I'd prefer that you stay. It wouldn't be right to... to give up." She focused on the old calendar on the wall—a farm supply store freebie from 2012. "A man should always stick with a thing. Not run away."

Delilah felt Griffin step up behind her, close enough that she could sense his warmth against her back.

"True. But so should women."

She silently willed him to touch her shoulders, to kiss her, but he just continued to stand maddeningly close.

Finally Delilah cracked. She turned around and looked straight up at him, then braced both hands on his chest and backed him toward the big office chair. When she gave him a small shove, he sat down with a hint of a triumphant smirk.

She went to the office door and locked it, then flicked the light off. It was nearly black in the windowless room, with one thin yellow line of light at the bottom of the door. She pulled her boots off as she walked back, dropping them.

"Only for today," she said firmly. "It hasn't been twenty-four hours yet." She unzipped her jeans and stepped out of them, then straddled Griffin's lap on the chair.

His fingers immediately teased at the lace edging of her underwear. "I can't promise that."

Rising up, Delilah reached for his fly, jerking the button open and clawing the zipper down. She hooked a finger into the silky fabric between her legs and pulled it aside, unwilling to wait another second before lowering herself onto Griffin—who was ready so fast that she half wondered if he'd been walking around like that all day. She sighed deeply, her suspended breath releasing in a tight moan, then dropped her forehead to his shoulder. He dragged the barrette from her soft waves and fanned his hands through them.

"One day only," she insisted in a husky rasp, her hips swaying with a languid friction. She tightened on him possessively. "But this isn't the last time. I'm going to need it again."

He gripped a handful of her hair, holding her hard enough that she let out a little hiss through her teeth and stopped moving. He pulled her mouth to his and kissed her with a coy and agonizing restraint. "Did I say you get to make rules?"

The devilish smile she heard in his voice sent a rush of heat through her. She pulled her shirt off, and felt Griffin twist the clasp of her bra open with one hand, as neatly as brushing away a mosquito. She shrugged it off and dropped it, crushing against his chest to graze her nipples on the fabric of his shirt as she renewed her rocking motion. "Twenty-four hours," she gasped, barely able to get the words out, her skin was so sensitive in the black room, every nerve laser-focused.

He slid a hand into the back of her underwear, cupping the full round curve of her ass. His other hand explored the front with slow adept thumb-strokes.

"I love the position you're in," he whispered near her ear, "but I don't know if it's one for negotiating."

chapter twenty-six

When Griffin pushed open the big downstairs door, Byron held up an overstuffed white plastic handle-bag which hung off one lanky tattooed arm, and a mint-green appliance of some sort in the other, cord dangling.

"Look what I found!" he crowed, his voice high with childlike giddiness, as he thrust the metal appliance at Griffin.

"What is it?"

"The White Whale. The Holy Grail. The Fountain of Youth. The, uh… what's another thing people search for?"

Griffin cradled the machine against his chest and followed his brother up the steps into the apartment. "A Grand Unified Theory? The meaning of life? Dunno."

Byron flung the door open as if making a hero's entrance. "It's a milkshake machine, bro. I told Delilah the day I met her that we need one at the bar. Found it for six bucks at that thrift shop in Klamath Falls—the one you told me about, where your girlfriend works." He threw both himself and the brimming bag onto the sofa and kicked his shoes off. "You didn't tell me she was back from Mexico, by the way."

Griffin set the milkshake machine on the coffee table and bent to pick up the discarded shoes, shooting Byron a disapproving frown. He went to put them on the rack next to the door. "I didn't know she was back. And she's not my girlfriend."

Byron paused in his digging through the bag and looked up. "For real? That sucks, man—she's cute as hell." He started layering shirts over the back of the sofa, after popping the tags off. "Guess I shouldn't have hugged her. Wait, was she the asshole, or were you?"

Griffin settled into the perpendicular chair with a sigh. "No one was the asshole. No hard feelings—it just didn't work out."

Flapping the wrinkles out of a red plaid flannel shirt, Byron said, "She gave me her employee discount. Maybe she felt guilty about something."

"Or she's just a nice person. Which she is."

"Guess so. Anyway, I'll bring your clothes into the bar tomorrow, now that I have my own. And I'll get ice cream and make milkshakes. Ooh, with those cheap candy canes! Christmas and all that crap. What do you think Delilah's favorite ice cream flavor is?"

"It's rum raisin," Griffin said without hesitation.

Byron made a face. "Gross. She's crazy." He chuckled. "No wonder she's always checking you out behind your back—she obviously has no taste." He paused halfway through removing a tag. "How'd you know that? About the rum raisin?"

Griffin took his phone out and connected to the Bluetooth speakers, then scrolled through his music, avoiding Byron's eyes. "I pay attention to details." He put on FKA Twigs and set his phone down. "I know a lot of things she likes."

He thought of the twenty-four hours they'd shared two days before—starting at the apartment, then at the bar, next in the van, and finally back at her house, on the sofa with the Christmas lights flickering. Learning to read her body, her expressions, the tiny sounds she made. The way she'd been mad at him for a second the first time she came—her eyes awash in what looked like angry tears—then immediately wanted to do it again. The second time, she'd laughed, a pure involuntary staccato moan of joy, and Griffin had thought he'd never heard anything so beautiful.

The next day, there'd been radio-silence. Griffin had waited until halfway through the afternoon so as not to look pushy, then had sent a simple *Thinking of you* text, to which there'd been no reply.

This morning, he'd had a glint of hope when her text-tone chimed, but was quickly disappointed.

Delilah: *What did you do with the produce order receipt?*

Griffin: *Might have left it in the walk-in when I was putting things away. Sry.*
Griffin: *Are we going to talk about it?*

Delilah: *The produce order?*

Griffin: *No. You know what I mean.*

Twenty minutes later, her reply had come:

Delilah: *We already did talk about it.*

So. She was standing firm on her assertion: twenty-four hours only, clean break, never to be mentioned again.

Byron reached for Griffin's phone. "Jesus Christ, not this eerie space alien shit." He opened the music app. "Can't we listen to something good? Whoa, check out your Top Artists list. No wonder you always look grouchy." He flicked the screen, scrolling. "Here we go—Tom Petty. No one can be in a bad mood listening to *Damn the Torpedoes*."

"At least turn it down so I can keep being—what was it?—'grouchy'."

"Hilarious." Byron tossed the phone onto a stack of *New York Times* sections. "Is this about Hazel?"

Wylde Strangers

"Definitely not."

"*Definitely* not, eh?" Byron began rolling the shirts up like he was packing for summer camp, then putting them back into the bag. "Is it… something about Delilah?"

Griffin rubbed a hand over his face. "I kind of, uh… slept with her."

Byron froze, his mouth an amused O, then flopped back on the sofa cushions, laughing. "The hell you did. Wait… did you? Oh my god—*you did.* Holy shit!" He raked a hand through his dark hair. "You're the only person I know who could bang a girl that hot and look bummed about it afterwards. Was it terrible or something?"

Griffin sank down in the chair. "No. But that'd make things a lot easier."

"Ah. Okay, I get it—you're into her now, but you already screwed it up."

"Normally I'm the first person to admit I'm a piece of shit, but *no*. She just doesn't want anything to do with me. It was great, but she was like, 'one day only, then it's done.' Essentially said she needed to be distracted because she's all messed up over her dad dying, and some… uh, other family stuff."

Byron gave a dismissive wave. "Is that all?" He got up and went to the refrigerator to drink some orange juice straight out of the bottle, despite Griffin's glare. "She'll come around. Give it a while, then remind her what you've got."

"Yeah, that's a terrible idea. I'm not gonna be some manipulative douchebag about it. She knows where to find me."

Byron came and sat down with the orange juice bottle in hand. "I guess that's for the best anyway, since you're going back to Portland in a few weeks."

Griffin eyed his brother. "What do you mean *I'm* going back? Not *we're* going back?"

With a shrug, Byron took another drink. "Thinking of hanging out here a while. The coding thing with Wes is going okay, and… I dunno, might get to know Katie a little more. I *did* win a duel over her honor, after all. I'm basically owed." He gave an impish smile.

"You're owed jack-shit. And your maturity level is about twelve years old compared to Katie."

"She's got *one* year one me—she's twenty-nine. And I have my charms."

"You're as charming as a sack full of rabid monkeys."

"Hey, monkeys are awesome."

Griffin was afraid to say what he was thinking—that he was delighted his brother was voluntarily taking more time away from Marco and Nix and city life. Instead he made an indirect show of support by telling Byron a little about the plans he himself had been considering.

"I was thinking of staying longer too. The old guy who owns this building might be willing to sell. There's a lot of cool shit I could do with a space like this. Might be a good investment with the money from Gold Lizard. I think I'd have enough even after paying off the repairs I did on credit for the saloon."

Byron smacked the orange juice container down in a parody of resolve. "In that case, it's settled—you don't blow off the thing with Delilah if you're staying in Wylde. Make it work. Quit being a little bitch about it."

Griffin rolled his eyes, slumping into the chair cushions. "She's depressed right now. I'm not gonna take advantage of that and bully her into a relationship."

"Or even tell her how you feel."

"I did tell her! Belaboring the point just gets… embarrassing."

Byron snorted. "For a smart guy, you're dumb as hell." He poked at a molar with his tongue, lost in thought, then looked at Griffin sidelong. "I never told you where I went, that time I bailed on rehab."

Griffin's eyebrows went up. He leaned his chin on one hand against the chair's arm. "True."

Byron combed a hand absently back and forth through his hair, his eyes far away. "I left with a girl I met there. Laurel. The place had this 'no physical contact' rule, and we thought that was bullshit, plus… y'know, we both wanted to get high. So we hopped the fence one night and hitched to Seattle." His eyes cut away, and he scowled.

"We stayed with friends of hers, ran out of money, did some sketchy shit to stay high... then she got sick. She had huge abscesses—" Byron pointed at his own arms, "—and I figured that was why she had a fever. Get her some antibiotics, boom. Fixed, right? But it was actually this blood infection that did a number on her heart."

He turned sideways on the sofa and put his feet up, like someone on a therapist's couch, and folded his arms.

"I visited her every day. I was sleeping rough. Wake up, do a little panhandling for an Egg McMuffin and a shower at the Y, then back to the hospital. We'd watch TV, and I'd read to her. Her favorite book—*The Little Prince*. We got through it five times. And every time..." He turned for a moment and looked at Griffin. "Have you read it?"

"Years ago, sure."

"Okay, so every time, I'd get to the part where the Prince was trying to explain how he felt about that flower, how it was defenseless, and he'd lose his shit and start crying, and... *I'd* almost cry. I got these bruises, because I'd have to pinch my leg hard to not cry and look like a dumbass. *That's* how bad I wanted to tell Laurel—" His voice cracked. After a pause he cleared his throat. "I wanted to tell her I... loved her. But I was all, 'Nah, be cool. She's got shit to deal with already. It's the last thing she needs to hear right now.'"

Byron got up and walked the long way around the sofa. He went to the bathroom and blew his nose, then returned. Griffin was very still, afraid to move and have Byron stop talking.

"Then one morning I show up, and they said Laurel had a stroke. Her brain's wiped out. There were these two nurses—we'd always called them Jekyll and Hyde, a nice one and a mean one. The bitchy nurse said I wasn't family and I couldn't go in anymore. The nice nurse said—" He took a slow breath and cleared his throat again. "She said Laurel's family in Coeur d'Alene—they never even came to visit her—decided to DNR. Pull the plug. When the bitch was on break, the nice one let me go in and say goodbye."

Byron swiped at his face with a sleeve.

"So, I told her then. I don't know if she heard me. I should've said it sooner. I'd been telling myself, 'Oh, it's the last thing she needs to hear…' but maybe it was *exactly* what she needed. And I was too chickenshit." He rubbed a hand up and down his face like he was resetting it. "Anyway, not to be all dramatic, but the moral of our story today, boys and girls, is *don't be a stupid dickhead and not take a chance on saying how you feel*. Even if you have to do it loud, or more than once, or if you feel like a pussy. Because it's still better than realizing it's too late to say it at all."

The weight of Byron's confession settled between them like the silent aftermath of a mudslide. After a minute, Griffin spoke up.

"Christ almighty, dude. Why didn't you ever tell me? I can't believe you've been carrying this around for three years." He gave an exhalation of bitter laughter through his nose. "I don't really know what you went through. I've always just seen the outside—the relapses and… irresponsible bullshit."

Byron gave a careless shrug, still turned away on the sofa. "Yeah, well. No big. You're forgiven."

Griffin took a deep breath. "I don't know how you do it. You're so happy-go-lucky. 'That crazy bastard's always smiling,' Dougie says. Joking and clowning. And you've… seen shit like that." He shook his head.

Byron offered a weary grin. "Gotta keep smiling, brother. You know why? Because the gods hate it when you laugh at their punishments." He stood up and walked toward the bathroom again. "It's the only way you can get back at them for the shit they do to us."

chapter twenty-seven

The powder blue Valiant was parked unevenly on the shoulder. Delilah slowed down, and seeing that the car was empty, scanned the jungle-wet expanse of the cemetery beyond the sagging cyclone fence. Missy stood in her long coat and a yellow felt hat, hands shoved deep in the coat's pockets.

Thinking it over, Delilah went another half mile before looping around a block to drive back. She parked across the street from the Valiant and walked over, slipping easily between the gap in the crooked gate without having to move it and give herself away. The bitter late-December wind—cold enough to suggest the possibility of a white Christmas a week from then—moved through the rough grass in eddies that made it appear the turf was winking. Tentacles of a bare willow tree shrugged beyond Missy, framing her in a tangle of black.

Delilah's steps slowed as she neared Colonel Kelley's grave—denoted with a temporary marker while the VA worked on a headstone. She watched her old heart-pattern boots parting the wet clinging grass, the leather darkening with damp. The left boot had a crack in the sole, and she felt water seeping into her sock already.

She felt that chill inside all the time now. Since the day she'd walked into her empty house, knowing nothing would ever be the same. Since the moment the little metal ballerina charm had twirled in her grasp, tracing out a mocking dance that hinted at a stolen childhood. And especially since the morning she'd awakened alone, body still deliciously aching from her acrobatics with Griffin, and told herself she had to stand firm and never touch him again.

Delilah let her feet swish the grass on the last few steps so she wouldn't startle Missy. The older woman half-pivoted in response, but didn't turn around. The temporarily peeled turf had been flopped back over the grave like a lumpy comb-over. Delilah recalled Missy's nearly inaudible words the previous week: *You really did take it to your grave, you stubborn old man.*

Stopping beside Missy, Delilah thrust her own hands into the pockets of her sky-blue wool coat. The silence told her everything she needed to know. It would have been so easy for Missy to turn to her with a hearty greeting, hooking her into a sideways embrace and offering a few quips. The sustained lull, in the place of false cheer, was as good as a confession. For minutes they stayed in that knowledge together, as the willow flicked up and down as if it was fly-fishing for the truth.

"You wouldn't have said it out loud—about Pop's secret—if you hadn't wanted me to go looking," Delilah finally said.

"I know." Missy gave a sad smile, still looking down at the little wooden marker. "Did you find anything?"

By way of reply, Delilah pulled her left hand from her pocket and held it up. The ballerina charm swayed and glinted on her wrist in a gust of wind. After she was sure Missy had taken a good look, she pocketed her hand again.

"You must have questions," Missy offered quietly.

"Sure I do. But I hardly think it's fair to make me do all the work. You don't have any idea how much I know—so I guess this is a test.

Wylde Strangers

If I catch you lying, we'll never talk about this again." She cinched her scarf closer around her neck. "Or anything else."

Missy chuckled. "Man alive, you are Mose's daughter. You sound just like him."

Delilah skewered Missy with a look. "*Am* I his daughter?" As soon as she'd said it, she realized she'd shown her hand, and wished she could take it back. She turned away. "I don't have his blood type—the doctor told me."

"No. You probably have mine. Is it B?"

Nodding, Delilah dug the toe of her boot into the seam in the sod.

"Alrighty," Missy said with a resigned sigh. "Let's talk, kiddo. Mose Kelley *is* your father—"

"Biologically?"

"Yes."

"But not Wanda."

Missy shook her head. "Mose always said she did her best."

Delilah snorted. "That's what he told me too. She treated me with the polite tolerance you'd offer someone *else's* child. Which makes sense now. She acted like a stranger. I'm not saying she didn't do right by me—she taught me to cook, to sew, made me clean my room, get good grades. But always with a lukewarm distance."

Missy opened her mouth as if to reply, then pushed a fluttering strand of gold-and-silver hair beneath her hat and went silent.

"Does anyone else know?" Delilah demanded.

"Old Doc Roberts knew. He died last year, retired in Grant's Pass, at his son's place. Your dad gave him five thousand dollars' worth of gold Liberty Head coins—a lot of money in those days—to say Wanda gave birth to you. Then an engraved nine-millimeter Browning for the birth certificate."

A memory came up, of going to the gun show with her father one year when she'd been about thirteen years old. He'd shown Delilah an ivory-gripped pistol with a filigree pattern, and said, *I used to own one of these.* She'd asked why he didn't have it anymore—it was so pretty—and he'd tickled her under the chin and said, *I got something I wanted a lot more.*

Josie Juniper

An airplane went by far overhead, the falling drone sounding like a disappointed bee.

Delilah forced the words out. "Why did you give me up?"

Missy sighed again. "I was afraid. Thirty-five years old. And a homewrecker! Went back to my ma's house in Little Rock when I realized... what had happened. She said, 'Melissa Jane, you don't know the first thing about babies. No man will want you with someone's bastard in tow, after you behaved like a perfect harlot.'" She emitted a rueful shred of laughter. "I told her everything, thinking maybe if I humbled myself—Mama always accused me of being stiff-necked and uppity—she'd take pity on me. Instead she looked me dead in the eye and said 'The best thing for everyone would be for you to take the brat to its pa, make like Hagar giving Abraham's baby to ol' Sarah.' I was out of money and out of ideas. I called Mose at the bar and we talked it over. When you were three weeks old, I rode the Greyhound back to Medford, and your pa picked us up. His face lit up like he'd seen the face of God Almighty when he laid eyes on you."

Missy paused, then took a breath as if she was about to continue, before her lips shut with a tight frown. Delilah wondered if she was talking herself out of a further confession. She touched Missy's sleeve.

"What else?" she prompted.

A watercolor wash of emotions drifted across Missy's face, blending until they had no distinction. She smoothed her expression with a mild smile. "*Nothing* else. I stayed in town so I could watch over you. Your father and I were careful never to speak unless there was a plausible reason and plenty of witnesses. No one suspected."

Delilah's eyes stung with frustrated tears that would have felt better falling, but refused to do so. "I want to know so many things. How did it happen? Were you happy together? For how long? What did Wanda think of you? Did you ever—"

"None of that matters," Missy insisted. "Let the dead bury the dead."

"No," Delilah snapped. "You don't get to do that! If you didn't ever want to have this conversation, you should have..." Her voice snagged roughly. "You should've *stayed gone*," she managed, the last word strangling off. A gust of wind pushed Delilah from behind, sending her golden hair dancing around her face. She swiped it aside with an impatient hand.

Missy took her hat off and removed the twisted pink bandana that served as a hat band. Gently she gathered Delilah's hair and tied the bandana around it in a low ponytail.

"I know this changes everything," she said. "More'n likely *ruins* everything." She touched Delilah's cheek with the backs of her knuckles. "It's been a privilege watching you grow up, and being your friend. The one bright spot in that horrible year, when both Caleb and then Wanda died, was that... I finally felt like I had a useful role. I wasn't just that quirky lady—'Mayor Missy'... I was a real comfort. I knew it was the closest I'd ever get to being your mother."

"I couldn't have gotten through it without you," Delilah croaked out.

Missy looked at her feet with a little laugh. "Yes, you could have. You're tough as nails, girl. You're Colonel Kelley's daughter, and don't you ever forget it."

Delilah's brow furrowed. "Did you... did you name me?"

Missy nodded. "It was the only thing I asked for, for myself—that when they got the new birth certificate from Doc Roberts, they keep the name Delilah Jane." She gave a crooked grin. "Wanda wanted to name you Amy Ethyl."

Delilah grimaced. "Oh, God! Thanks for sticking to your guns."

They both laughed.

Missy looked up with an expression more shy and tentative than anything Delilah had ever seen on the tall brassy woman. "So... *does* it ruin everything?"

Delilah's face fell, the smile wilting. "I wish I could say *no*, but... I don't know yet. I still have a lot of questions. And I don't think I'll ever be able to *not* wonder how my life could have been different. I think I'm angry."

Missy took a step back and returned her hands to her pockets. "You can't be angrier at me than I am at myself, and no mistake."

"I want to know what happened. I want to believe in something! Soul mates. Fairy tales. Thwarted tragic romance. Something bigger than me and bigger than this town."

Missy shrugged. "The truth is that people are foolish and cowardly and screw up. I don't know if I can give you a bigger better story—heroes and villains and True Love's Kiss, all that claptrap. Maybe all I can give you is a lesson: don't make the same mistakes."

"The ones *you* made, or the ones I've already made?"

"Both." She smiled. "If you want a fairy tale, go find your prince and write one. Just remember, princes aren't necessarily perfect."

Delilah thought of Griffin, that lavishly flawed, adorable, maddening, pretentious, irritating, talented, smart, sexy jerk. The way he alphabetized his books, but left his clothes in a ridiculous wrinkled jumble. His incessant chewing on those stupid green plastic sticks. The way he got the hiccups when he ate bread, then would spend the next twenty minutes cursing after every hiccup rather than stopping to get a glass of water. The fact that he conspicuously pronounced the first r in "February" and the second t in "twenty," like a teacher's pet.

So annoying.

Driving toward home, Delilah thought over the conversation she'd had with Missy. Before they'd left the cemetery, Missy had set a tiny bottle of Dr. Bronner's soap on the Colonel's grave in offering, saying simply, *We used to go camping together. He'd understand.* Something about it was so specific and tender that before Delilah realized where she was going, she'd parked in front of Griffin's apartment, wondering if she was walking into a disaster, or away from one.

chapter twenty-eight

Fumbling for the towel hanging off the shower curtain bar, Griffin wiped his eyes and leaned to look at the buzzing text.

Delilah: *Are you here? I'm out front*

He dried his hands and stood with a foot each inside and outside of the old claw-foot tub, writing back a quick: *shower – down in a sec*

He hurried into jeans without bothering with his boxers, then pulled a cuff-frayed forest green sweater over his head as he made his way across the living room. He stuffed his feet into mashed-down shoes without socks and descended the steps to throw open the big door, the shoes shifting awkwardly like flip-flops.

Delilah sat in her car, arms wrapped around herself in a pale blue coat that made her rose-gold hair look like a sunrise over water. She pushed her door wide with a metallic creak and pop, climbing out slowly, almost reluctantly. Standing behind the open door, she worried at the top of it, picking at the cracked rubber seal. "Are you busy?"

"No. But I am kind of freezing my ass off." He beckoned with a head-tilt. "Get in here before my hair ices over."

Back in the apartment, he nudged his shoes off by the door and watched as Delilah stepped out of her boots and circled the room nervously, one hand dragging along the back of the sofa, the kitchen island, the front of a bookshelf.

"Do you want to take your coat off?" he asked, sitting on the sofa.

She nodded, but kept the coat on, continuing her circuit. "And maybe more," she said quietly.

He let out a small skeptical laugh. "You know, there was a time when you gave me a raft of shit for... 'waffling,' I think you called it? But every time you come over here, you pace like a lost soul, like you're waiting for me to talk you into something. Not exactly on-brand for someone so fiery."

She stopped with her fingertips resting on the spine of a dictionary, staring at her feet. "I'm upset. I need someone to talk to."

He nodded. "Funny you're not calling Katie."

"She's at work."

"Okay, cool. Glad I'm convenient."

Delilah looked up, her hand dropping away from the books, a glassy sheen of tears in her eyes.

Griffin shook his head. "No, don't do that—seriously, Dee. I'm sorry if your day sucks, but I'm not going to be your distraction again. You're the one who's hurting *my* feelings. Because there are only two things that could be going on here: either you don't give a shit about me, but you're fine with using me to fuck the unhappy out of you from time to time, or... you *do* care, but you're too much of a coward to own it, and you're manufacturing excuses to have allegedly-therapeutic sex. Both options make me feel shitty, to be honest."

Her lip curled. "Don't use that term."

"What? *'Fuck'?*" He shrugged. "You won't let it be anything else."

Forehead crumpling, Delilah moaned, "Why are you making this difficult?"

"*You're* the one making things difficult. I'm being plain as hell, and you're the goddamned Oracle at Delphi. I don't want riddles. You shoot from the hip in every other context. But with this? You and me?" He pointed a finger back and forth between them. "You make it weird, and then you make me guess *why* it's weird. If you have a strategy, I can't figure it out."

Delilah folded her arms and looked away. "I don't have a damned strategy! I'm just confused." She crossed to the sofa and sat beside him.

"About what?" He waited. "Abe?"

"No. I… gave him the ring back." She made a little sniff of laughter. "I think he's probably relieved. An old friend of ours, Georgia, moved back to town, and he's sniffing around her now. Obviously he wasn't pining for me *too* much."

Griffin stretched an arm along the back of the sofa and rested his head on it, watching Delilah for a long minute. His eyes narrowed as he finally spoke up. "I don't buy it—the confusion thing. You're not confused."

She stretched her own arm out and laced her fingers through his, steepling their hands. "No?"

He squeezed her fingers and shook his head. "Nope. People usually know exactly what they want to do. Most of our time in life is taken up trying to figure out how to justify it."

"All right, smartass. What do I want?"

Griffin scooted closer. "Your pupils, and the color in your cheeks, and the way you just licked your lips… that tells me you want me to lead you into the bedroom, take your clothes off slowly enough to make you crazy, and touch you everywhere. But the little wrinkle between your eyebrows tells a different story. It says that five minutes after we're done, you'd be out the door—all business again, no eye contact."

Delilah rolled her eyes. "Nine guys out of ten would be tickled pink by that arrangement."

He gave a tiny sideways shrug. "The tenth guy's a different story."

Edging closer and curling one of her legs into Griffin's lap, Delilah let go of his hand and ran her fingers up his arm, over his shoulder, and down his chest. She leaned in and kissed him, slow and deep. Griffin pulled back a moment, then rested his forehead against hers, eyes closed. "I thought you needed to talk to someone."

She angled her head to kiss him again. "You talk enough in bed for both of us."

***

They lay at right angles on the blanket-rumpled mattress, Delilah's head on Griffin's chest, her feet hanging over the bed's side. He combed his fingertips through her hair, spreading it out in a lacy cloak that draped his torso.

"It's like Rumpelstiltskin's gold," he murmured, holding a lock between his fingers and brushing Delilah's nose with it.

She smiled and batted his hand away. "No tickling." She sat up and curled her arms around her bent knees. "I should text Petra and tell her why I'm late."

Griffin laughed. "*Why* you're late?"

"Okay, not *why*…"

He reached for her and dragged her on top of himself, chest to chest. "You're not going anywhere." One of his hands smoothed along the undulating curve from Delilah's neck to her thigh.

She laid her head sideways, resting drowsily on Griffin's shoulder. "It's easier to talk with you when my pants are off."

"Aha! Apparently you're wearing pants all wrong—they're not supposed to go over your face."

She stifled a snort of laughter and gave him a gentle bite on the shoulder. "You're going to be amazing at dad-jokes someday."

An unexpected thrill went through him at the reference. "I kind of hope so." He kissed her hair. "I *definitely* hope so." His fingertips

Wylde Strangers

dragged along her spine. "Are you going to tell me about the thing that upset you today, before you came over?"

She scooted down to rest her chin on his chest, studying Griffin's face. "The big secret. I talked to Missy about it. She's, uh... my biological mother. You were right."

His eyebrows jerked up. "And your dad?"

"...is my dad. They had some kind of a fling. I didn't get details. But I was born in Arkansas, it turns out."

"Whoa." He combed her hair gently away from her forehead, and Delilah closed her eyes. "How do you feel?"

Her cool green eyes opened. "I'm not sure." She chewed pensively at her lip. "I don't think I'm ready to talk about it much yet. Is that okay?"

"Of course, beautiful." He lifted one hand with a teasing air of self-mockery. "You know where to find me when you need a shoulder."

Delilah's brow furrowed as if she was ashamed. "Don't say it like that..."

"It's fine. Couldn't resist being a little bit of a prick about it."

She smirked. "Nothing *little* about you there. And, uh... as for you offering a shoulder, they really *are* amazing shoulders."

Griffin rolled them both sideways and kissed her. "And as for *secrets*, I have two of my own."

She pulled her head back. "You do?"

"Mm hm." He delivered another kiss. "But I'll tell you both of them." He raised on one elbow. "I'm selling my half of Gold Lizard to Cleo, and I'm going to use the money to buy this building. I have a plan. You know how I was saying the saloon shouldn't change? I mean it. Not only because the locals love it, and it has history, but because all that new blood—the people moving here, the tourists and stuff—they'll *want* that local feel. The real cowboy-bar experience. But..."

Delilah's body had gone tense. Her brow had the telltale wrinkle Griffin had come to know, but he pushed on. Recalling Byron's advice, he was certain now was the time to lay his cards on the table.

Josie Juniper

"...but anyway, the place with the 'bullshit arugula,' as you so adorably call it, the indie music and craft cocktails... that's going to be *here*. I'll turn this building into something amazing. I believe Wylde can support *both* kinds of bar."

Delilah pushed herself upright, her body taut with alarm. "That's crazy! You can't do that—you can't give up your stake in the Portland business. That's your security. It's already successful, and you're drawing an income from it. Giving that up is insane." She shook her head hard. "*No*. I can't let you do that for a dream that may not even work. You'd lose everything."

His head tipped to examine her. "Not *everything*. I'd still have half of the saloon." He reached for her. "And hopefully I'd still have... *you*." Pulling her close, he continued. "That's why I'm going to tell you the second secret." He dropped a quick kiss on her forehead, steeling himself to get the words out. "Earlier, when you said 'Nine guys out of ten would be delighted for this arrangement,' or whatever it was? Well, the tenth guy..." He cleared his throat and met her eye. "The tenth guy is in love with you."

Delilah's silence was unnervingly long.

She got up and started putting her clothes on. One of Griffin's hands crept over his mouth in grim contemplation as he watched her get dressed. "That's not the reaction I was hoping for," he managed.

She picked up the wool coat thrown on the butterfly chair and poked her arms into it. "Don't sell the Portland bar," she said, her voice a rasp. "I don't want you to do that."

Griffin reached for a pair of plaid pajama bottoms and pulled them on, following Delilah as she went into the living room and headed straight for her boots.

"Dee, *stop*." His voice was stern enough that he surprised even himself, and she froze, holding the boots. "I probably spoke out of turn and freaked you out, and... I mean, sorry for the delivery. But I stand by the content. I love you, and I'm *in* love with you. I want to build something with you, here in Wylde. Not just a bar, or two bars, or whatever. But a *life*." He held out a hand. "You feel like home. I'm trusting my gut on this one. Not overthinking it, like you accused me of always doing. I'm taking a chance. I want you to trust me enough to take a chance too."

She went to the door, boots still in one hand, and grabbed the doorknob.

"Dee!" he said, his voice strained. "*Delilah.*"

She looked at him over her shoulder. Her face was so tense with something Griffin couldn't read—*anger, pain, embarrassment?*—that her teeth were gritted. "I hope you didn't sign anything yet." She opened the door and, without putting her boots on, hurried down the stairs.

chapter twenty-nine

He didn't text Byron until he'd stopped for gas in Eugene and was too far north to turn back. With the white roar of I-5 yawning in the background, Griffin leaned against the van, chewing on the last bite of a protein bar as he typed.

Griffin: *Up to PDX to wrap up a business thing, back tomorrow. Sadie's going to drive you to/from the bar. Want anything, as long as I'm there?*

Byron: *WHAT IS WRONG WITH YOU. Asshole!*
Byron: *Yah I want something. Maybe to come along?*

Griffin: *Dee needs you at the saloon*

Byron: *It's two days until christmas you dickhead*
Byron: *Seeing Dad would have been nice*
Byron: *Not that you care*

Griffin: *This isn't a Xmas trip. Dont get all aggro on me. Do you want me to bring anything back or not*

Byron: *Sure. Couple of dime bags*

Griffin got back into the van, but before pulling out, checked the text thread with Cleo again.

Cleo: *You know I'm not into drama, but this is too important for text. We should meet in person, since you'll be here to see the lawyer anyway.*

Griffin: *First of all, why do women say that??? NOT INTO DRAMA*
Griffin: *Because yes you are. You may not like it when it happens but you still make it happen*

He told himself, when he'd climbed behind the wheel back in Wylde, that he wouldn't listen to Elliott Smith on the stereo for six straight hours like a Sad Bastard. But it was the only thing that fit the hollow ache which had been lodged in his chest since Delilah had walked out, barefoot and haunted looking. He'd tried listening to something that might make him feel angry, or at least clever and capable. Nothing had worked. He rode out the last few hours steeped in waves of gloom.

The Willamette River was a wind-snagged stretch of brown as he crossed the bridge and headed for his apartment, where Cleo wanted to meet. Her immaculately restored green Triumph TR6 was parked across from his building, empty. He parked around the corner and pulled on his black hoodie before jogging through the downpour to the building's lobby.

Cleo looked up from her phone when he opened the big glass front door. She stood, long shapely legs planted on the tile floor, wearing an orange silk pencil-skirt, high heels, and a fuzzy sweater that created an effect almost like blurred vision. Griffin stopped and stared, then thrust his hands into the hoodie's pockets and slowly crossed the lobby.

"You're, uh… dressy. Plans after this?" he asked.

Her hair was up in two small buns out of which the blue tips of her hair protruded like fireworks. She tucked her phone into the designer bag hanging from the crook of her elbow, then turned and headed for the elevator. "Just felt like looking nice. Is that a problem?"

"Be my guest." He followed, pushing his hood back and ruffling one hand through his hair.

In the elevator, between the second and third floors, Cleo reached to pull the STOP knob. Griffin chewed at the inside of his cheek and surveyed her as she backed into a corner of the cramped cube. She reclined against her hands, braced on the mid-rail, and fixed Griffin with a speculative look.

"I broke up with Anton," she said simply.

"Congratulations."

They watched each other for a long minute.

"Is there something you want me to *do* with that information?" Griffin asked. Her nostrils flared and she punched STOP again to deactivate it. The elevator began to climb. As the car shuddered to a halt at the fourth floor and the doors slid open, Griffin added, "Okay, I'll bite—what happened? You obviously want me to ask."

Cleo paused long enough that the doors began to close. Griffin reached for them. He opened a hand to wave her through, and she ran a fingertip beneath the lower line of her lipstick, looking annoyed, before preceding him. They walked down the hall to the last door on the left, Griffin extracting his keys from the pocket of his jeans.

Cleo sighed. "Anton wasn't honest."

"Shocker." He rattled the key into the lock and pushed the door open, gesturing for her to go first.

"You were right. I was wrong," she admitted. "And… I'm sorry."

"All right. Uh, thanks." He threw her a cautious glance in passing. The apartment had a stuffy closeness after weeks unoccupied, and Griffin crossed to the window and tilted it open a few inches. He lifted a desiccated vine of the pothos on the table and inspected it. "Would this come back if I watered it?"

Cleo lifted a manicured hand, shaking her head. "No clue, Griff. You know Anya waters all my plants."

He took it to the sink in the open kitchen and set it under the faucet. Cleo pulled out one of the padded stools at the breakfast bar and sat. "Are you still dating that young girl?"

"Hazel? Nope."

She nodded as if she'd already known. The silence stretched between them. "Why do you really want to sell your half of GL?" she finally asked.

Plucking dead leaves from the plant, Griffin tipped them into the trash. "I told you—I have a business opportunity and I need liquid capital. Or at least *might* need." He attempted to fluff the listless vines. "It's complicated." He slanted a suspicious eye at Cleo. "You don't appear to have brought the paperwork with you."

Resting her little pointed chin on a hand, she drew up one corner of her mouth. "I didn't." She opened the side pocket of her bag and took out her pastel cocktail cigarettes, twirling the box by its diagonal corners.

Griffin leaned against the counter, folding his arms. "We're eight days from the end of the fiscal year. Wanna tell me why you're jerking me around?"

She trailed a fingertip across the rainbow of cigarettes and took out a blue one, rolled it between her fingers, and stood a silver lighter upright on the counter. "Do you think this relationship is as dead as that houseplant?"

He laughed. "Enough so that I wouldn't even use the word 'relationship.' Also, don't smoke in here." He took the cigarette from her and put it back in the box, upside down.

She righted it with a frown. "I want to pump the brakes a little on the sale."

A sardonic half-smile froze on his face. "Wow. I must be an idiot to have left this in your hands. Well played." Taking a purple cigarette from the box, he picked up the lighter and went to the window, sitting on the edge. He lit up, then exhaled through the gap.

Cleo followed, perching on the windowsill beside him. She gently drew the cigarette from between his fingers and took a drag, eyeing him sidelong with a look he knew well, before handing it back.

"Mrs. Robinson, you're trying to seduce me," he quoted, raising his eyebrows.

She smiled. "I'm only two months older than you."

He gestured with the tip of the cigarette. "But I think I'm reading your angle right." He pulled in another slow lungful of smoke, holding it like a secret before exhaling through his nose. "You only apologize when you want something."

Cleo tipped her head. "Oh? And why do you think it's *you* I want?"

He nodded at her outfit. "That's the skirt you were wearing when I met you. The only reason you'd wear clothes from... what, eight years ago? You're trying to provoke some sort of nostalgia."

She put her hand over his where it rested on the window ledge. He pointedly glanced at their two hands, then Cleo's face.

"I heard something through the grapevine," she confessed.

"The plot thickens."

"Sadie told me Byron mentioned something that implied you might've taken a relationship gamble, and... the 'business opportunity' was contingent on that."

"Huh. Sounds like you knew I'm not dating Hazel, in that case."

Cleo shrugged. "Guilty—I wasn't looking for the information."

"Sure. You wanted my reaction."

"Guilty again," she said, spreading her arms.

Griffin smoked in silence for a minute, studying Cleo with narrowed eyes, content not to offer the cigarette. "Interesting that you're putting so much stock in third-hand gossip routed through Byron, a guy you don't trust."

She offered a brittle smile. "Even a broken clock is right twice a day—isn't that how the saying goes?"

Griffin leaned toward her and stage-whispered, "He's not broken. And if you really are trying for seduction, you're doing a shit job of it."

Her fine nostrils flared again and her jaw cocked slightly, as if positioning something between her teeth. She took a slow breath and relaxed her face. Her gaze slid away, then back. "Let's start over," she suggested.

Griffin swept a hand out in concession. "Have at it. You go first."

"No, that's not—" She cut herself off, taking the cigarette from Griffin and smoking the last of it as she walked to the sink, her heels knocking like an insistent guest. She ran the glowing tip under the faucet and dropped it in the sink. With a hop she shimmied up onto the counter and crossed her legs slowly enough to provide a flash of black underwear. "I meant let's start *over*-over. You come back after Christmas, and when your lease is up here in March, we... um, you move back into the condo."

A thick numbness crept through Griffin. He sank his fists into the pockets of the hoodie and leaned his head back against the cold window. "You're gonna think I'm being vindictive, Mops," he sighed, the nickname escaping before he had time to rein it in, "but I honestly don't want us to do that. I'd say, 'it's nothing personal,' but of course it *is*. We suck together."

She folded her hands hard in her lap like an angry child struggling to display obedience. "Okay."

"Also I have... I have feelings for someone else."

Her precisely sculpted eyebrows lifted. "You've got to be kidding me." She let out a small laugh. "Don't make a fool of yourself with that little girl—take it from me. I know how everyone must have laughed at me over Anton."

"That's very telling," Griffin said. "You seem to think we're bonding here over some early-midlife-crisis. I *am* sorry Anton turned out to be a lying douchebag. But I'm not talking about Hazel. It's Delilah Kelley."

Josie Juniper

Cleo drew her head back. "The... wait, the redneck bartender?"

"I wouldn't characterize her that way, no."

"What are you saying?" Cleo waited. "Is this an actual thing?" She snorted. "You're dissolving our business partnership because you fell dick-first into one of the local yokels and caught feelings?"

Griffin put both hands over his face and shot Cleo a vicious glare through his fingers. "Jesus Christ, Cleo. You can be *so shitty*. It's almost funny, except for being absolutely *not*."

She hopped off the counter and walked over. Stopping a foot away, she poked him in the chest with one blue-lacquered fingernail. "Guess what, pal? We're two peas in a pod. You're a snobby sarcastic asshole whose taste in music serves the same purpose as my Botox—you use it so no one notices you're dead inside."

Griffin pushed her hand away in one slow arc. "Bullshit."

She sneered. "No? You got a three-month dose of folksy rusticity, and you're a new man? Gonna trade in your band t-shirts for a nice cowboy hat, go square dancing at the legion hall? Mosey down to the hitchin' post with someone with childbearing hips and a secret family recipe for cornbread? You're being a poser."

The gulf Griffin had always felt between them—even when he'd been desperately trying to bridge it with a cynical veneer—felt now insurmountably wide. Still, the mockery hit its target, and he turned away. He thought of everything he'd come to love about the quirky little Southern Oregon town. With a sodden defeat like a newspaper boat drowning in a bathtub, he recognized that he didn't deserve any of it—Wylde was Delilah's town, not his. Cleo's accusation of class-tourism choked him with a poisonous shame.

He stared out the window and across the street, at the pre-Christmas foot traffic on the trash-edged sidewalk. He didn't recognize anyone. All strangers.

It seemed fitting.

"Maybe you're right that I don't belong in Wylde," he told Cleo, his voice flat. "But I don't belong with you either." He went and opened the apartment door, holding it wide in unsubtle invitation for her to leave. "You've got three business days to get those papers to me to sign."

chapter thirty

Katie's mother had gone all out with the Christmas food, and Delilah and Katie sprawled in overstuffed bliss on the loveseat in the den, picking at slices of allahabadi cake and watching *Love Actually*. Plates that had formerly held palak paneer and malai kofta were stacked on the coffee table between their slippered reclining feet.

"Which love story in this do you think is the best one?" Katie asked, brushing crumbs off her sweater, which displayed a cartoon reindeer with its antlers tangled in Christmas lights.

"None of them. This is *your* favorite movie. I wanted a Jackie Chan."

"Quit being grumpy," Katie laughed. "And this isn't my favorite. *It's a Wonderful Life* is my favorite—George Bailey is 1940s-dreamy."

They stared at the TV for another minute. "I don't know… I guess the little kid," Delilah finally said.

"Stop it. That's absurd."

Wylde Strangers

"How's it absurd?" Delilah focused on the screen, scratching the sole of one foot with the heel of the other.

"Jamie and Aurélia are definitely the best. Why the kid?"

Delilah shrugged. "He's still young enough not to realize that love is bullshit. Also his mom is dead, so that makes it extra tragic."

Katie gave Delilah a critical side-eye. "You *would* say that."

"You asked." Delilah reached for another chunk of cake, took a bite, then handed it to her best friend. "Save me from myself. I'm going to explode."

Katie cheerfully polished off the last few bites. Her phone buzzed and she picked it up from the pillowy arm of the loveseat and grinned, texting back.

"Who's that?" Delilah asked.

"Nevermind." Katie set the phone aside.

Delilah sank deeper into the cushions. "You know, the first day… *he*… came to town, he said something about assuming I was the kind of girl to pick this as my favorite movie. He was surprised when I told him it's *Bullitt*."

"I thought it was *The Quiet Man*?"

"It is. But that's a romance, and I didn't want to seem like… *that* girl—picking a love story."

Katie rolled her eyes. "It's okay to like love stories. Also you're talking about him again. I thought you were such a total badass? No big deal—just have the best sex of your life with someone you're crazy about, then walk away. Piece of cake."

"Aaauuuggghhh, don't say cake…" Delilah joked, holding her stomach. She and Katie exchanged a smile before Delilah's face settled back into a bleak expression. "It was probably the best sex *anyone* has ever had—not just me. But I'm not crazy about him."

"Gotcha."

"And even if I was, I'll get over it. I can't destroy his future by making him chase some idiot pipe dream and go bankrupt and stay in Wylde resenting me. He's meant for a different life. If I let him go, in another year he'll probably move to New York or something, and live with some intense artist-chick who makes ink out of human tears and wears black berets and smokes clove cigarettes and throws things when she gets mad and speaks five languages."

"That is... *very specific*. You've really thought about this."

"Shut up." Delilah stood up and stretched.

"If you think Griffin's panting over a girl with a hot temper, that's you."

"Katie-bear!" Delilah protested, wounded. "I never throw things. I freak out for thirty seconds and then move on."

"There was the time you kicked that old man's car in the grocery store parking lot and told him to open the door so you could punch him..."

"He almost ran over a child!"

Katie's younger brother Lawson appeared in the doorway of the den. "I'm with Kate—you're definitely a psycho," he told Delilah.

"Says the guy who used to have a huge jar full of slugs under his bed," she retorted.

He tipped back his bottle of beer. "That was for a science experiment, and I was nine. Sometimes I hate living in a small town—no one ever lets you live anything down."

Katie's phone chimed again, and she snatched it up like the baton in the winning sprint of a relay race.

Delilah leaned close and tried to eye the screen. "Who got the pinball machine sound?" she demanded. "You hardly give anyone their own text tone."

The doorbell rang and Lawson separated himself from the doorjamb and took another swig of beer before heading down the hall. "Got it!" he called out.

Scrambling to her feet, Katie headed for the bathroom across the hall. "Be right back," she threw over her shoulder.

Staring after her, Delilah shrugged and reached for the remote, searching the bewildering expanse of buttons for PAUSE. As she found it, she heard male voices talking and laughing with Lawson in the front room. She jerked upright on the loveseat and froze, eyes wide, as Katie walked back in. She was smoothing her glossy black hair with her fingers, and had put on a touch of tinted lip gloss.

Wylde Strangers

Freshly applied mascara adorned her already Disney-animal-dramatic brown eyes, and a hint of blush dusted her golden coffee-with-cream skin.

"What the hell is going on?" Delilah asked, eyes narrowed.

"Byron wanted to stop by and say hi," Katie replied with affected casualness. "He and Griffin are having Christmas with that couple Byron's staying with, and we just… y'know, have been texting a little lately, and he said he wants to give me something."

"Ha! I'll bet he does."

"And he's become friends with Lawson, so…"

Moments later, Griffin rounded the corner and poked his head into the den. He pointed at the paused TV screen, where the character Mark held up a cue card that read: *And at Christmas you tell the truth*. He smiled. "Aha. Busted," he said to Delilah.

"I voted for *Drunken Master II,*" she retorted.

Katie looked from one of them to the other, stifling a smile between pressed lips. "I'm gonna go say hello to Byron," she whispered before edging away.

Delilah drew her sloppy ponytail out of the back of her sweater and wrenched it tighter. Griffin inserted his hands into the pockets of his jeans.

"You're really dressed for Christmas," Delilah observed blandly, waving at his t-shirt—blue with a picture of a washing machine that read "Sonic Youth," over an elbow-frayed white thermal.

"Not a big holiday guy," he said. Glancing at the window behind Delilah, he perked up slightly. "Hey, it's snowing again."

She spun around. "Huh."

"Wanna go for a walk? We should probably, um, talk anyway."

"Sure."

They went to the front room, where Katie and Byron—who wore a sweater that said "Ho Ho Homie"—took a quick step back from each other, standing near the flocked Christmas tree. Nat King Cole crooned on the stereo, and Lawson walked out of the kitchen, carrying steaming mugs to hand to his sister and friend.

"You guys want cocoa?" he asked Delilah and Griffin.

Josie Juniper

"No thanks," Griffin said, helping Delilah into her coat. "Maybe in a little bit. Back in a few." He shrugged on his own black and gray ski jacket and stepped into the boots he'd left by the door before they headed out into the slowly wheeling snowflakes.

When they'd reached the street, Delilah swung around and looked at the sprawling yellow ranch-style house, decked in white icicle lights, with lazily flashing colored bulbs around every window and door. Through the long front window, Delilah saw Byron lift the scarf Katie was wearing and coax her toward a doorway where mistletoe hung. Stopping, they both looked up and smiled before Katie melted into Byron's arms.

"I'm not sure if that's adorable or a terrible idea," Delilah said with a sigh, turning away and heading down the sidewalk. Griffin paused, then caught up.

"I thought you liked Byron," he said, zipping his jacket higher.

"I absolutely love him. And they're cute together. But she'll be a mess when he... when he leaves. You guys'll be heading back to Portland pretty soon."

Griffin gave a small hum of something not quite laughter. "That's what I wanted to talk to you about. Part of it, at least. Byron's, uh... he's staying here. It's just me going back. This week. I'm not sticking around until February after all."

She came to a stuttering halt as if she'd hit a crack in the cement. "What?"

"Ironic, right?" He looked up at the sky, then down at Delilah. "I wanted to stay here for you. But apparently that can't happen. Those two have known each other for about five seconds—" Griffin said, nodding backwards toward the house, "—and he's all in, going for it. Rolling the dice."

Delilah watched Griffin's troubled gray eyes. "I guess he doesn't have as much to lose," she finally managed. "So... that's probably fine."

With a bitter huff of laughter, Griffin started walking again.

"Hold on." She grabbed his sleeve, and he stopped. "We're still partners—*business* partners—so I don't want you to be mad at me.

You have to trust me about... about the other thing. You'll thank me in a few years for stopping you from doing something crazy. You'll still have security—"

"I won't have *you*," he cut in.

"That's... that's fine," she returned with a dismissive wave, closing her eyes. "You'll have someone better. The *right* person. A woman who fits. You'd never forgive me if I tank your life." She backed up a few steps and started walking again, turning the corner so they could proceed around the block. She heard the scuff of Griffin's boots as he caught up. Clearing her throat, she assured him, "I'll take care of Byron. He's always got a place in the kitchen if he wants it. And I heard that new young pastor over at Hope Church is going to do some kind of meetings... you know, for recovery. I'll nag Byron into going. Or Katie will."

They reached the end of the next block and turned again before Griffin spoke up. "When I first got here, you jumped all over my shit any time I was being arrogant and condescending. But it's the most arrogant thing I've ever heard, you thinking you know better than I do about what I want. You've got this pitying tone, like I'm too stupid to know what I'm blundering into, thinking with my dick or whatever, and you're going to save me from myself."

He shook his head and continued. "I'm not going to try to talk you out of it anymore. It is what it is." He glanced at her as they rounded the final corner to return to Katie's house. "But *that's* what I won't forgive, Dee—the fact that you refuse to let me try. If I'd botched this, lost my money, married and divorced you, gotten 'stuck' in Wylde..." He dropped his hands after making air-quotes, "that'd be my mistake. *Mine*. Nothing to forgive. But I *am* going to resent you for shutting me down out of cowardice, when for all we know it might've worked out great."

As they approached the front of the house again, he stopped and pinned her with a sober glare. "I think that's what you're actually afraid of—that it *will* work. All this other shit is just smoke and mirrors." He headed up the driveway. Delilah's eyes stung with tears, and after a second, she followed, catching up to him as he reached the back of the purple van.

Griffin pivoted, and before she had a chance to react, he grabbed her around the waist, lifting her and pushing her against the doors of the van, his mouth covering hers in a hot kiss. His cheeks were cold, and when his tongue gently parted her warm lips, she pulled in a gasp through her nose. She barely had the sense to think to herself that it was a good thing he was holding her up—her knees were so weak. Her arms went around his neck and she clung to him with a tiny moan, leaning back in to prolong the kiss as he started to pull away. Her response fired his, and his arms crushed her as he caressed her mouth with his, exploring every angle as they greedily enveloped each other.

Finally he set her down, her body sliding incrementally along his until her boots touched the gathering snow with a squeak.

"Merry Christmas, beautiful," he said. "Sorry I didn't wrap it. It's all I could give you."

He walked toward the front door.

She tried to stop herself, but the words escaped anyway. "What can I give *you*?"

He looked over his shoulder with a somber smile. "The only thing I want is a reason to stay."

chapter thirty-one

Missy wasn't much for fancy greetings or time-wasting small-talk when she had a bone to pick, Griffin had noticed.

"I expected better from you," she called through the Valiant's window as she pulled up to the tool-and-die works. She shoved the gear shift into PARK and shut off the engine.

"Uh, wow. Take a number, I guess." He swung the door of his van closed and leaned against it, moving the green plastic stopper-stick to the other side of his mouth. "Good morning to you too. What'd I do now?"

She climbed out of the car and squashed a purple knit cap over her gold-and-silver waves. "That girl's in love with you."

"Delilah?" He snorted. "I don't mean to be crass, but there's exactly one thing she loves about me, and she'd be content to schedule it like a goddamned oil change." He looked away, embarrassed. A gust of wind blew his hair into his eyes, and he tightened against the cold. The ground was a dirty lacework of thin melting snow, pocked with rain. "Come on inside and yell at me where it's warm. I have a pot of coffee already made."

Upstairs, Missy unbuttoned her rubber overshoes and wriggled out of them, exposing fleece-lined moccasins beneath, then took off her coat. Griffin poured coffee and met her at the sofa, handing her a mug.

"Hope you won't think it's rude if I keep packing," he said, walking to the bookshelf and bending to his task. "I'm leaving by three o'clock."

"Threw in the towel, huh?" she asked.

Griffin shot a scowl over his shoulder. "Hardly. I'm the fabulous hero who steered the ship off the rocks." He tossed a few paperbacks into a box. "Yay, me. I'd like my parade now." More books thumped onto the stack.

Missy slurped at the hot coffee. "You done cryin' yet?"

"Sure." He sat down beside the shelf.

"Because I'd like to get to the bottom of this thing."

Bracing one arm on his bent knee, Griffin eyed Missy. "Look, I don't want to sound like a dick, but even if you were Wylde's *actual* mayor and not just a resourceful local eccentric, you wouldn't be in charge of anyone's love life."

He was immediately afraid he'd gone too far, but Missy cracked up. "Man, you don't pull any punches, kid. I knew there was a reason I like you." The statement settled between them. Missy's tone was gentler as she asked, "So. Do you love her?"

His chest cramped, just hearing the words. He fanned the pages of the book in his hands. "I do. And she knows it. If Dee told you something else, that's pretty self-serving. She shot me down—not the other way around." He took a bookmark out of the book and fidgeted with it, then replaced it upside down. "What did she say?"

"Not enough. Which is how I might've got the wrong idea. Apologies."

Griffin shrugged with a dismissive wave.

"Tell me why you're leaving then," Missy requested.

He took a slow breath, his gaze traveling along the metal beams overhead as he tried to assemble his feelings into words. Everything he loved about Wylde crept into the barren places inside him, growing and filling in the cracks and shadows: Tammy's bad jokes and braying laugh when he went to get a latte, and the fact that she ordered oat milk just for him. The handmade signs in shop windows. Hearing the entire school bus full of kids singing along with the driver at a stop sign. The little finger-flick wave people did when cars passed each other—and which Griffin had started doing too after the first month. Old men gossiping in the barber shop, like some 50s TV show. Realizing he'd learned enough country songs that he hummed along when he heard them in the grocery store. The gorgeous desert sunsets.

And most of all, Delilah Jane Kelley.

"I can't keep pretending to be what I'm not," he muttered. "Acting like a phony, playing at a life I didn't earn. Or... so someone recently pointed out."

He remembered how Cleo had ignored him in passing when she'd exited his apartment, and how he'd stood at the sink later, staring at the sodden cigarette butt she'd left, and wondering if something about him made him deserve people like that.

"It's time for me to go home," he concluded. The words sounded wrong, as if they'd been uttered by someone else.

"Home is where you hang your hat," Missy averred.

"I thought it's 'where the heart is.'"

"That too. But it sounds like you already know your heart's in Wylde—I don't have to rub it in." She put her feet on the coffee table. "As for you supposedly being a phony, that says a lot more about the person who told you that crap than it does about *you*."

"How do you know it wasn't Delilah?"

"Because she wouldn't say that."

Griffin gave a skeptical look. "She's never missed an opportunity to tell me I'm a pretentious idiot."

"But an honest one," Missy said with a smile, "and that little gal's always given you credit for it. A week after you came to town, I asked how the two of you were getting on, and she said, 'His music's terrible and I doubt he owns a shirt with buttons, but he's as true as a compass.'" She chuckled and raised her mug. "Then her blush gave her away. I knew she was dead gone on you."

Griffin silently packed another box. Hearing that Delilah might have had feelings for him in October simultaneously pleased and saddened him. He flipped the box shut and tucked the flaps under, then went to sit in the easy chair, staring into his now-lukewarm coffee.

"For someone who allegedly thinks I'm so honest, she doesn't trust me worth a damn about my own feelings." He ran a weary hand over his face. "I'm not even gone yet, and I already miss her. Sometimes I think I miss her the most when we're in the same room—because she won't let me in."

"It's not you she doesn't trust, it's *herself*. Has she told you about Caleb?"

"No. Katie relayed the basics—Wylde's very own James Dean. Seems like a sore subject."

Missy nodded reflectively. "Well, it's not my story to tell. I just hope someday Delilah quits wearing that boy's corpse like an albatross and starts talking." She went quiet for a minute, then startled as if someone had tapped her on the shoulder, jumping to her feet.

"Are you okay?" Griffin asked.

Her green eyes held a faraway look. "I'm not given to superstition, but I do believe the old man might've just told me to start talking first."

***

Delilah's drive home after closing down the bar was silent. After years of avoiding A5 on the jukebox—her song with Caleb—Delilah found that Griffin's absence created an even *worse* music crisis... because every song reminded her of him. With some, it was because he'd made fun of them, such as the one about the barbecue-stained t-shirt. Others because he'd grudgingly admitted to liking them. And the rest simply because country songs told stories—it was what Delilah loved about them—and Griffin seemed to be woven into every story ever written, happy or sad.

There'd been four texts from him that night.

Griffin: *Home now (such as it is). Hope the bar has a good night. I'll check in once a week. You can text me any time if there's a problem, but I know it's best if I give you space so we can get past all the crazy shit that happened.*

Griffin: *I don't regret any of it though and hope you don't either. Enough said.*

Then, two hours later:

Griffin: *The silence in Wylde is so loud, like a symphony. I miss that. All the noise noise noise here is weirdly saying absolutely nothing.*

Griffin: *No need to text back, if you were planning to. I'm quite drunk.*

She hadn't replied, though the phone had trembled in her hands numerous times before being stuffed back in a pocket.

Watching Katie and Byron dance to Deana Carter's "Strawberry Wine" at the bar had made Delilah's heart ache, though she was happy for her best friend. *At least something good came out of this*, she thought to herself. She almost laughed when she realized that having avoided bankruptcy didn't enter her mind until far later.

When she turned the corner onto her street just after three in the morning, there was a car in her driveway. Her headlights swept across it, and she saw that it was Missy's. Further examination revealed her newly-discovered mother to be asleep in the front seat, covered in an afghan, with her hat over her face. Delilah tapped on the window gently, but Missy still jumped, swiping the hat away and rolling the fogged window down a crack.

213

"Why are you freezing out here?" Delilah asked. "The front door isn't locked."

"Wasn't ready to go inside yet. Not without you," Missy said with a sheepish smile, opening the door and stretching before she stood up.

It wasn't until Missy said it that something occurred to Delilah: the older woman, in all the years she'd known her, had never been inside Delilah's family home.

"Well, get the hell inside now and warm up. You're staying over tonight. I won't take no for an answer."

Inside the house, Missy looked around cautiously, like a child entering the hallway of a new school. Delilah cranked up the thermostat and turned on the living room lights—including the Christmas tree, though it was now the 27th—and gestured for Missy to sit.

"Something to heat your blood? Cocoa?"

"If you put a shot of whiskey in it," Missy said with a grin.

Ten minutes later they were on the old maroon sofa, sipping "medicinal" hot chocolate, sharing a quilt. Missy's gaze swept the room. Her eyebrows raised as she studied an early-1970s portrait of Colonel Kelley in his military uniform. His eyes were dark and intense with long lashes, his cheekbones high, his mouth stern yet shapely.

"That was probably a few years before I met him," Missy said, nodding at the photo. "I'd seen him around town, and admired him. Everyone did. He wasn't a tall man, but oh so much swagger... women stared, I tell you." She took a sip of her cocoa, wincing at the heavy pour of whiskey. "Then in 1976, when I was just a girl of twenty, he sold me the Valiant."

Delilah's eyes went wide. "Your car used to be *his?*"

"Yes indeed. Of course we didn't... uh, take up with each other until years later, when I was thirty-two. He'd say he was going on 'a fishing trip with the boys,' and we'd go camping. For three years. Man, I hated the winters, because we couldn't see each other for months. Then when I was thirty-five... you came along."

Delilah turned the mug in her hands, afraid to meet Missy's eyes. "What did he say about it?"

"I didn't tell him. Not for months. Then when I started to show a little, I went to Little Rock so no one would know. I didn't expect to come back to Wylde." Missy frowned and powered down her cocoa in one go, setting the mug aside with a resolved clunk. "There's something I have to tell you, but I'm worried that you'll hate me, and I'm afraid to lose you. But after a conversation I had with Griffin Isaacs this morning, I realized the only decent thing to do is to tell you about the mistake I made, so maybe you can avoid doing the same."

Delilah took a fortifying drink and tucked the quilt more firmly around her legs. "Okay..."

"When you and I took the bus back from Little Rock and your father drove to Medford to pick us up... he had suitcases in the back. He wanted for us to run away together. He asked me to take a chance on being a family. To take a chance on... our love."

The news tightened Delilah's throat like a fist. Her heart hammered and her lips parted, but the words in her head were a jumble that refused to be untangled.

"I was too scared," Missy continued. "My mother had gotten deep into my head with all her shame, and I thought: 'The selfless thing is to give that childless woman a baby. To pay the price for how you wronged her.' I knew Mose would be an amazing father, and he had a stable life—quiet homemaker wife, paid-off house, good income, respect in the community. Taking him away from all that, traveling to God-knows-where to start over, everyone back in Wylde forever talking about that tall skinny harlot who stole Colonel Kelley away from a good woman..." She shook her head soberly. "I couldn't do it. I broke his heart, and my own too. *I was wrong.* And I robbed you—because all I could see was having it blow up in my face, making a man I loved end up resenting me."

She put a slim hand on Delilah's knee. "It's the same nonsense I've heard you say about Griffin. I know you're scared, girl. If the statistics are to be believed, hell, you've got a fifty percent chance of failure. But if you never try, you've got a *one hundred percent chance.*"

Delilah's eyes burned, and the Christmas tree lights were glowing haloes through the blurred sheen of tears. Missy stood up. "You'll have to decide if you can forgive me. What'd make this terrible confession worth it—even if you never speak to me again—would be if in the morning your suitcase is by the door, packed to drive up to Portland and tell that man you love him as much as he loves you, and that you're ready to take a risk."

chapter thirty-two

When Delilah was an hour north of Eugene, she laughed to herself, realizing that it was much like Sam Gamgee leaving The Shire. Though Delilah had once been to San Francisco—and apparently Little Rock as an infant—she'd never been this far north of Wylde. In college she'd been invited on a trip to Seattle with friends, but had declined. A wave of insecurity shot through her now, wondering if Griffin could really be happy with someone whose life had played out mostly within a six-mile radius, with occasional forays into Klamath Falls, thirty miles west of home.

Three different scenarios had played out in her mind as she drove. The first had all the stirring drama of a foreign film, with tears and declarations and passionate lovemaking. The second was cautious and apologetic, with no one confident they were doing the right thing, but halfheartedly agreeing to give it a go. The third was the most realistic, Delilah acknowledged with considerable anxiety: she would drive around the city, lost and staring at the GPS on her phone as people honked at her, then panic and get right back on I-5 southbound. She'd slink home to Wylde alone, the highlight of her adventure having been that of trying a burger place she'd never been to before.

She was still in the parking lot of said burger place in Salem when she dropped an especially hot French fry into her lap, got distracted, and ran over the scattering of broken glass that punctured her tire. As she crouched in the windy rain putting on the spare—passersby gazing pityingly out their windows, but none offering to help—she told herself this wasn't a bad omen. First of all, she didn't believe in portents or signs. And if the event *was* to be looked at symbolically, it demonstrated her pluck and resilience.

Although not necessarily gracefulness, she allowed with a few colorful curses, after the lug wrench jerked free of its hold and she accidentally punched herself just below the left eye. By the time she got back into the car, her hair was a limp wet tangle, her carefully applied eye makeup had smeared into something resembling a demented lemur, and there was a nice pre-bruise pinking up on her cheekbone.

She later told herself it also wasn't a bad omen when traffic just south of

Portland was at a standstill due to a jackknifed semi, and her car overheated while idling. Or when she picked the wrong bridge and somehow ended up a quarter of the way to Astoria before realizing her error.

When she finally made it back into town and found the correct river crossing, a large boat decided to pass, and Delilah turned off the car while she waited for the bridge to slowly rise and drop. Standing in the downpour in the Y of the bridge entrance was an elderly man with a cardboard sign: *vietnam vet. anything helps. god bless.* Delilah cranked her window down and waved him over.

"My dad was a Vietnam vet," she told the man. "It'd kill him to see you standing here in the rain. Why don't you get in?"

The man blinked at her, water dripping off the end of his white beard, pale blue eyes squinted in surprise. "You must not be from around here," he said. "I'm a decent fella and everything, but I don't think it's too safe for you to be inviting strangers into your car. Thank you though—you're an angel."

Delilah reached over the back seat and grabbed her umbrella. "At least take this, and something to get dinner." She dug in her purse and took out one of the twenties she'd gotten from the ATM. The man opened the umbrella and wiped his face off with the inside of his coat cuff. She handed him the money and glanced at the lowering bridge, estimating how many minutes she had.

"What was your dad's name?" the man asked.

"Colonel Moses A. Kelley," she said. "Five tours."

The man's eyes widened. "Holy hell—Tiger Kelley was your dad?" He grinned and stuck his wet hand inside his jacket to dry it before offering it to shake. "I was practically a kid, but I met him once. What a small world. Jimmy Greene. I don't think your old man would've even remembered me, but I sure as hell remember him. Old Tiger Kelley—I'll be damned."

The bridge was nearly down, and people were starting their cars back up. Delilah grabbed her purse again and took out a matchbook with the saloon's address and phone number, then two more twenties, handing him the bundle. "You'll think I'm even crazier than when I invited you into the car, but… why don't you use that to get a bus ticket and come on down to Wylde? The guys at the American Legion would get you set up, and if you don't mind sweeping floors and such, I'll give you a job at my bar until you find something better."

He stared at her, his dry lips slightly parted, then glanced at the rumpled bills in his hand. "This is sixty bucks. How do you know I'll use it for a bus ticket?"

She started her car as the taillights of the SUV in front of her flashed to life. "I don't. But I'm glad I met you either way. I feel like something's telling me that today is a day for taking chances."

***

Josie Juniper

In the five days since Griffin had last been in Portland and tried to revive it, the neglected pothos had shed itself bald like a nervous dog. The curled leaves that lay scattered on the table caught his eye every time he walked through the room. But despite the fact that he'd been back in the apartment for over twenty hours now, he hadn't cleaned them up. The tableau of failure fit his bleak mood.

He sat at the breakfast bar with his laptop, trying to write a cheery reply email to his grandmother in Chicago, typing out sentences and then deleting them. He realized that once he cut out topics that might worry her, there was nothing left. After fifteen minutes of frustration, he had only: *Hi, Nana Shirley! Sorry this took so long. It's raining here today.*

His phone buzzed, and glancing at the screen, his pulse jumped.

Delilah: *What side of the building is your apartment?*

Griffin: *South side, fourth floor. Why?*

Delilah: *Look out your window.*

Far below, an unmistakable rain-drenched Delilah stood in her blue coat and what appeared to be Missy's khaki boonie hat. He tipped the window open and leaned out.

Delilah waved, then put her hands to her mouth and called up. "I don't think I can throw acorns that far!"

Griffin's hands tightened on the windowsill. His heart felt flattened against his sternum, clinging there like the wall-sticky toys he'd played with as a child. "I'll be right down," he called back.

He was as far as the apartment door, barefoot, when he changed his mind. He picked up his phone and texted her.

Push #419 on the panel beside the door and I'll let you in. Need to clean up a little. Elevator to the 4th floor, then turn right.

There was a long enough pause before the paint-flaked old intercom next to his door buzzed that he wondered if she hadn't looked at her phone. Once he'd let her into the lobby, he paced his apartment in a fretful circle. There was nothing to clean, aside from the pothos leaves. He glanced at his face in the mirror as he passed the bathroom door, then raked his fingers through his hair. There wasn't time to shave, and nothing could be done about the tired shadows smudged under his eyes. He heard the *ding!* of the elevator, and a tap on the door moments later.

He opened it, and Delilah smiled and pulled the hat off, crushing it in one fist. "Actual hat-in-hand," she joked. Her smile slowly faded as Griffin examined her without stepping back in invitation. "Can I... come in?" she finally asked.

"Of course." He drew aside and waved.

She stopped near him as he closed the door, unbuttoned her coat and hung it on a peg, then stepped out of her boots. Griffin leaned against the wall.

"I thought maybe you weren't hugging me because my coat is soaked, but I'm getting the feeling that's not it," Delilah ventured.

"Sorry," he said, pulling her into an embrace. Her hair had the warm astringency he loved, and her hands grazed up the back of his shirt and flattened on his bare skin. Her fingertips were cold, and Griffin's shoulders tensed.

She pulled away. "Um, you're... are you happy to see me?" She glanced deeper into the apartment. "Wait, is someone here? Is it *her*? Oh God—she's here, right?"

"Cleo? No." He walked into the living room. "Though she did ask."

Delilah followed, her steps slow. "Asked to get back together?"

Griffin dropped onto the sofa with a sigh. "Yep. When I was up here last. I turned her down. Because I was in love with you."

Delilah had been halfway seated when she rose back to her feet, pinning Griffin with a distressed stare. "*Was* in love with me?"

He refused to take the bait, and kept his face impassive. "Why are you here?"

She chewed at her lower lip, then backed away. She went to the window and looked out at the rain before starting a meandering stroll around the room.

"If you're holding out for *me* to tell you why you're here, you've got a long wait," Griffin told her. "I'm not playing this game with you again, where you hide in your silence, hoping I'll read your mind and then seduce you. I won't do it."

She wrapped her arms around herself, inspecting him cautiously as she leaned a hip against the dining table, where the dead plant sprawled. "You don't want me anymore?"

Griffin stood up and went to her, stopping unnervingly close. Delilah straightened, as if expecting to be kissed. He saw her gaze shift to his lips.

"I want you so much that in my head I've already had you on this table, that counter, the sofa, the bed—you name it," he said quietly.

She visibly took a deep breath and moistened her lips.

He narrowed his eyes, his heart hammering at her reaction, and went on. "I'd spend my entire life in your thighs if I didn't mind abandoning my self-respect. But I won't make a fool of myself over a woman who'll apparently drive three hundred miles for a hook-up, but can't manage one goddamned honest sentence about how she feels, aside from in bed. You know what that tells me? That you *don't* feel anything for me… except *here*." He put a hand between her legs for one heated moment, then removed it.

Her eyes went glassy with tears. "That's not true," she whispered.

"Yeah? Which part? When you came over after Missy told you the truth, I tried to call you out on this bullshit. *I tried.* Then you were all, 'Why are you making this difficult?' Well, guess what? I *didn't* make it difficult. The second you touched me, I folded faster than Superman on laundry day. I'm pissed off, Dee. And I have every right to be."

She looked down at her feet, in mismatched socks, and swiped the heel of one hand against her face. "I know."

"So start talking, or go home and let me get over you. The sex is great, but it's not enough. Believe it or not, getting laid isn't a huge struggle for me. You have to offer more than that." He went to the windowsill and reclined against it, worried that if he stayed near her, she'd touch him and he'd crack.

She pulled out one of the chairs and sat. The late afternoon sun through the blinds painted her in shadowy stripes. "Missy told me… about what happened with my dad. He asked her to take a chance with him and she was too afraid. She's always regretted it. So I want… I want to try with you. Come back to Wylde. And to… *me*."

Griffin shook his head. "If we're doing this, it won't be because of some dusty old sad tale. It's not our responsibility—to reanimate the corpse of someone else's failed love affair. Now quit stonewalling and tell me how *you* feel."

"I'm trying!"

"No. You're giving me excuses: 'it's because of such-and-such.' That's a load of bullshit. You want someone else to make the choice for you. It's never Delilah Kelley—hell no. Just like with the bar. *Every goddamned thing*, you have to fight me over it, even about shit where I know you secretly agree. It's your safety net in case it fails: 'Not my fault, I didn't choose it. I tried to talk you out of it.' How do you expect me to trust you, when you don't trust yourself?"

"You're making me really uncomfortable," she accused, getting up to tear off a paper towel in the kitchen and blow her nose.

He gave a wry sniff of laughter. "Good, I hope so. That's the first thing you've said that implies you actually care." He folded his arms. "I'm waiting."

Delilah glared at him and popped the roll of paper towels off its bar, bringing it with her to the table. "Fine." She blew her nose again. "Caleb wanted to leave Wylde and move to Los Angeles, my junior year—I was sixteen and he was nineteen then. He asked me to drop out and come with him. I couldn't do that to my dad. Pop already didn't approve of Caleb—my dating him had become a wound in our relationship. We'd always been so close, but after Caleb… we couldn't see eye to eye. I know it hurt him so much."

She got up and went to the kitchen and threw away a handful of paper towels, pausing at the refrigerator. She idly fidgeted with a button-shaped magnet holding down a grocery receipt, then came back and leaned on the table.

"Caleb was going to go to Los Angeles alone. But I... talked him out of it." She paused, her voice cracking. "I begged him to wait for me. I knew he'd fall in love with some exciting girl in L.A. and forget the hayseed kid back home. It wasn't his choice to stay."

"Of course it was," Griffin said. "Jesus, Dee... you were sixteen. You can't blame yourself for something you said as a lovestruck teenager."

She looked up with a skeptical frown. "Can't I? Really? I knew he was miserable there, working the line at Claymore Homes, bored and restless, drinking too much, shoveling pills and speed into himself right and left. Part of me knew I should tell him 'Okay, move to L.A.,' but I was selfish. I thought if I just kept him, you know... *satisfied*, that'd be enough. I think maybe that was when I settled on the idea that sex was a good substitute for... all the things that are hard to say."

Her face dropped into both hands. Griffin got up and went to her, coaxing her over to the sofa. He reclined sideways and tucked her back against his chest, pulling a blanket over them both.

"I can't do that to you," she managed, her voice high and tight. "I'm not afraid of failing for my sake, but for *yours*. I'm used to disappointment—I've spent most of my life settling. But then you came along, and it's the first time I've ever felt like things could be perfect with someone. You tick every stupid box." She turned sideways to lock eyes with him. "You're gorgeous and smart and honest, you can cook and fix things and talk about a bunch of dumb movies with subtitles... you climb literal mountains! Like some kind of fairy tale prince."

He dropped a kiss on her hair. "To be fair, not entire mountains. Just little pieces of them."

"Close enough." She put a hand on his cheek and kissed him, a tiny exploratory brush of her lips. "I really was trying to be unselfish by... not tying you to me, or to Wylde. But I love you too much to give up on this. Maybe we'll screw it up. So fine—let's screw it up together. I'd rather have a handful of perfect days with you than a lifetime with anyone else. I'm okay with not having a guarantee." She turned away and curled sideways into his chest as if too nervous to see his reaction.

He stroked her hair away from her temple with a thumb, then ran it over her cheekbone. "Is this a bruise? What happened?"

She gave a small laugh. "I had adventures on the way here. Trials on my quest."

"To find the prince?"

"To find the prince. I fought dragons and got lost in the wilderness and was heroically wounded and met a magical wise old soldier."

"No shit? This is quite the tale. I'd like details, Warrior-Princess Delilah."

"Okay, I burned my lip on a French fry and got a flat tire, hit myself in the face with a lug wrench, took the wrong bridge, and gave some money to a homeless guy."

He turned her around and drew her gently up to his mouth. "Where's this alleged French fry burn? I think I can help."

chapter thirty-three

Cemeteries, like country songs, told stories. For this reason, many times over the years Delilah had wandered the Wylde Pioneer Cemetery, browsing the age-eroded headstones—the earliest of which was from 1861—like the worn pages of a familiar book. All of her grandparents—none of whom she'd met, as they'd died long before her birth—were buried there. There was something comforting about knowing the ground in Wylde was filled with her people, like guardian ancestors. World War II hero Edward Kelley, beside Myra Thurston Kelley ("treasured wife and mother, a lady through and through"), their first child Elizabeth ("our little songbird, flown too soon"), and Wanda's parents Franklin Yeats (with the rather cryptic epitaph "distant thunder") and Corinne Bartok Yeats (her headstone bearing the backhanded compliment "she never shamed us").

Delilah tended to walk the cemetery in a spiral, starting with the perimeter along the rusty fence and concluding at the camperdown elm in the center. On this New Year's Eve, the bare trees stood motionless in the late afternoon sunset. Light touched the saucer magnolia near Caleb's grave in the southeast corner, with a subtle glow that was somehow even more dramatic than the pink and white flowers it bore in the spring.

It wasn't until her eyes did their usual scan of the headstone that she realized Caleb would have been the same age as Griffin now, and that their birthdays were three days apart. She reached into both coat pockets at once, taking out a single-shot bottle of Jack Daniels and a box of Good & Plentys.

"Hey, Cale. What's news?" she said, offering what had been his habitual greeting. Every time she said it aloud, it was with the soft elasticity his own voice had held, never having lost the Kentucky drawl of his childhood. Her gaze swept to the graves to his right and left—those of strangers, but ones Delilah now thought of as his adopted afterlife-family: Eugene Hatch, 1904-1962 ("friend to many, stranger to none"), and Mary Warren, 1912-1980 ("a life of service").

Caleb's own family had left him here, and the sense of injustice stung Delilah still. A few years after his death, his parents and younger sister had moved back to Kentucky, and Delilah knew they would eventually be buried there. Caleb was forever marooned in a town to which he'd moved as a mischievous black-haired hellion of a twelve-year-old boy. Her sense of perpetual duty to his memory had always sought to rectify that.

She cracked the screw-top on the Jack Daniels and tore the end of the candy box open. After raising the tiny bottle in toast, she took a swig, squinting against the burn, and then put one of each color of Good & Plenty in her mouth. Caleb had always eaten them that way—one purple and one white, until there remained only a few of a single color, which he wouldn't finish. She chewed meditatively, remembering the combination of flavors in Caleb's mouth—whiskey and black licorice. The taste still gave her a small thrill, recalling those years from fifteen to eighteen when she'd been recklessly in love.

Josie Juniper

She'd never forget the first time Caleb had offered her a ride on his motorcycle. With an appraising grin he'd scanned her curves and asked, "How old are you?" and Delilah had lifted her chin and asserted, "Almost sixteen"—despite having turned fifteen only two weeks before. Caleb had dropped out early enough that he and Delilah had never gone to the same school, but his reputation was well known around town, and Delilah was giddy with the sense of power that went with having caught his eye. In the girls' bathroom, written in red nail polish was: *Caleb Walsh has a big one,* and when Delilah had first seen it, she'd innocently assumed it referred to the motorcycle he rode.

She took a second drink of the whiskey, then held the bottle up to the light to check its level. Exactly halfway. She set the cap loosely on top and placed it on the grave with the box of candy, eyeing the pink-and-orange streaks of sunset feathering up the horizon.

"I'm in love," she said out loud. The confession felt too quiet for what she was really feeling, an intense storm of lust and tenderness, pride and curiosity for the future. She cleared her throat and continued. "He's the one. I feel it in my teeth." The phrase had been Caleb's unique take on *I feel it in my bones,* and she'd never known whether it was a regional variation from where he'd grown up, or just a personal quirk. Like so many things about him, it had been something she admired without comment, as if knowing too much would pull back the curtain on his magic and make him just a regular person.

"I think you'd like him. You'd probably call him an 'egghead,' but still enjoy a few beers together." She took two steps back. "I'll bring him to see you some time. This is his home now, so he has to meet everyone." She blew a kiss to the grave before turning away, the same way she'd always done before Caleb would ride off. It was still a comfort, to this day, that she hadn't forgotten to send one final kiss flying after him the last time she'd seen him alive.

***

Wylde Strangers

"Holy shit, they made these things heavy," Griffin managed with a grunt as he lifted the antique baby buggy from the back of the van and set it down in Sadie and Weston's driveway. "No surprise it's from the 1940s—they must have assembled these in the same factory as battle tanks."

Delilah tucked two baby quilts—which she'd begun sewing weeks before, when Griffin had told her Sadie was expecting—inside the buggy. Both were fashioned of fabric from vintage 60s and 70s pillowcases, and Griffin smiled as he ran a hand over them, impressed at how Delilah had so intuitively made something exactly Sadie and Weston's style. He grabbed the handle on the buggy and tried to push it, but the pitted terrain of the driveway impeded the wheels. With a sigh he hoisted the white-wheeled black buggy and lugged it to the door.

"You know they're not actually going to use that for walking around," Delilah said with an indulgent sidelong smile.

"I know. It's just a cool thing. They can use it for decoration in the nursery—keep stuffed animals in it or whatever." He set it on the porch. When he'd seen it two days before, while showing Delilah around Portland and wandering through an antique mall she'd wanted to check out, he hadn't been able to resist the giant leathery contraption, black as a bat and with an appealing springy metallic creak.

As he was about to knock on the door, Katie's silver Honda turned into the long driveway, sending up a new rooster-tail of dust to replace the one that had just settled from Griffin's van.

"Katie-bear!" Delilah exclaimed, going back down the steps to meet her friend. She hugged Katie as she climbed out, and they linked arms and started back for the porch. Delilah threw a look over her shoulder at the car. "Why do you have a suitcase?" she asked.

Katie delivered a casual shrug. "Just an extra one I don't need—I'm dropping it off at the thrift shop. It's got some old clothes and stuff inside." Thrusting her hands inside the buggy, Katie plucked up a quilt and gasped over it. "Oh my God, these are adorable!"

Delilah was immediately distracted, launching into a discussion of quilts and antiques, but Griffin watched Katie warily, sensing something a bit too effusive. The front door flew open, and the second Griffin turned and saw Byron's face, his eyes narrowed in suspicion. Byron picked Katie up by the waist and swung her around, kissing her. Griffin exchanged a look with Delilah, who smiled and rolled her eyes.

As he set Katie back on the porch, Byron glanced from Griffin to Delilah. "What?" he asked with a shrug and a grin. "I can't keep my hands off her. Look at this girl." As Griffin pushed the stroller through the door, Byron delivered a flick to his ear. "Like you're any better, bro—*please*. 'Pot, meet kettle'…"

***

The vintage buggy and quilts were a huge hit, and the food—pizza made in the brick wood-fired oven Weston and Byron had built—was amazing. Missy had showed up just before dinner, with a big pink box of pumpkin bars and pecan tarts from Tammy at Sweet Dreams. Despite the evening's chill, they all sat on the back deck, bundled up in hats and scarves and blankets—Sadie holding the new baby quilts tucked over her round six-month belly—and watched the stars.

Sadie and Weston were side-by-side in Adirondack chairs, their hands linked. Missy sat on the railing, quietly strumming "Knockin' on Heaven's Door" on a worn old acoustic guitar. Katie and Byron were wrapped together on one long lounge chair at the far side of the deck, the blanket's shifting attesting to their inability to stop petting each other and exchanging little nuzzles and pecks, seemingly oblivious to everyone around them, only six days after their first kiss under the mistletoe.

Delilah sat sideways on Griffin's lap, his arms around her, a fleece blanket swaddling them like a cloak. She leaned to his ear.

"I think those two are up to something," she murmured.

"Yeah, trying for third base under everyone's radar."

She laughed and gave him a pinch. "You know what I mean."

He nodded. "I think they are too."

Delilah narrowed her eyes and threw another discreet glance at the couple. "I know Katie though—if I'd kept after her about that suitcase, she'd be so on guard that I wouldn't have been able to catch another clue."

Griffin brushed his face back and forth against Delilah's neck, savoring her scent. The crisp cold pines, faint residual wood smoke, her warm weight on his lap, the gentle vibration of her voice against him... everything felt perfect. It was minutes before midnight and a new year, and the fullness of it all swelled in his chest like warm bread rising—nourishing and luscious.

As he heard Katie giggle, one tiny bead of anxiety, like a drop of ink falling into clear water, marred Griffin's peace.

He took a slow breath. "Byron means well," he began cautiously, his voice low, "but there's no denying the fact that he has a spotty track record. I know he won't actively *try* to be an asshole—if anything, he's always been a people-pleaser to a crazy degree. But..." His thumbs grazed her palms fretfully in their tangled hands. "...if he screws this up and disappoints her, will you want to murder me?"

Delilah raised her eyebrows with amusement. "How do you know *she* won't be the one to screw it up?"

"Fair point, but let's get real."

Dropping her head to Griffin's shoulder, Delilah sighed. Her fingertips absently combed the hair at the back of his neck, sending shivers through him—for the past three mornings when they'd awakened together, Delilah had reached immediately to touch his hair like that. The thought of the drowsy dawn-shadowed lovemaking that followed made his arms tighten with longing around her.

"I've done a lot of thinking about that," she began introspectively. "Not Katie and Byron specifically—I just mean the issue of being responsible for what other people do. I've wasted years on this weird push-pull, going back and forth between thinking

Josie Juniper

I have to be in control of everything, and hunting for an emergency exit so I *won't* have to."

Griffin drew a tendril of hair away from her face as a passing breeze tugged it across her eyes.

"I couldn't fix my dad after the strokes changed him," she continued, "and I never let myself stop kicking against the unfairness of how it altered what was left of our relationship. I couldn't make my mother love me the way I wanted to be loved, and I probably missed out on the relationship we *could've* had, with her just loving me to the best of her abilities. And I couldn't let go of the past enough to see that the bar needed changes. Hell, I wouldn't even swap out jukebox songs that were almost as old as *me*."

Her smile faded and she shivered, pulling the blanket closer. "And... I couldn't save Caleb. Because it wasn't my job, and Caleb needed to save *himself*. Just like you can't fix Byron—*he* has to do it. Whether he and Katie make each other happy or miserable, that's their responsibility. I won't blame you or myself for their choices." She rested her forehead against his. "It's not going to be the work of a moment, but... I'm trying." She smiled. "And it's not just me—you're a royal pain in the ass too, so don't think you're off the hook on change."

His hands swept up her body under the covers and came to rest on either side of her face. He smiled and kissed her, long and slow. "I kinda love that you don't let me get away with anything. My fiery wildcat."

She gave a small laugh. "You won't necessarily love it every day."

"Maybe not. But what I *do* love is hearing you say the words 'every day.'"

The clock must have reached midnight, as suddenly there was a distant riot of fireworks bursting and echoing. Missy placed a hand over the guitar strings and stood up with a weary sigh. "Oh, holy hell. Everyone in town knows those damned things are prohibited this year." She stretched. "Well, the mayor's got work to do. Sounds like it's coming from the direction of the Carlton boys' place—no surprise. I'll head over there and crack some skulls before they burn the town to ashes."

Delilah stood up and gave Missy a hug before the older woman went inside to get her guitar case. Griffin watched from the corner of his eye, trying not to intrude on their moment.

"Happy New Year, Mama," Delilah said.

"You too, little gal." Missy squeezed Griffin's shoulder in passing. "Looking forward to maybe having this one as a son-in-law before the *next* New Year's."

Griffin opened his arms and wrapped Delilah in the blanket again, and together they listened to the Valiant fire up with a rattly purr and drive off. The headlights winked out, leaving the desert dark, like a chalkboard on which anything might be written.

About the Author:

Josie Juniper is a former journalist, part-time algebra tutor, and full-time hopeless romantic who likes her romance heroes like she likes an assortment of number types—complex, real, natural, and occasionally irrational. A Pacific Northwest native, she's worked in a variety of fields from the downright wholesome to the unmentionably scandalous. She loves writing, reading, origami, rain, tattoos, running, animals, swearing, and lost causes. If you met, she'd probably love you too, and write her next book with your exact fantasy romance in mind. (Hey, come to think of it, why don't you tell her about it? Website, Twitter, Facebook, Instagram... let's talk! It's "Josie Juniper Author" on all) She lives in Portland with her dashing artist husband, weird cats, adorable dog, and a bunch of rescue chickens and turkeys who are surprisingly unreceptive to how much Josie would like to hug them.

Books In This Series:

Wylde Hearts Series

Wylde, Oregon is a small town with big personality. Peopled with a dynamic cast of characters—irresistible sexy rakes, smart fiery women, charming eccentrics, heart-of-gold locals, and nefarious love-to-hate villains—it's a place you'll want to visit again and again. Each book in the six-volume series explores a new heart-stirring love affair, always with a dash of delicious mystery and intrigue. Join our mailing list and never miss a trip to Wylde!

Wylde Secrets – coming in December, 2021

An impulsive Reno wedding. A marriage that breaks all the rules. A dangerous secret from the past, and a desperate gamble on the future. Can these star-crossed lovers prove that they belong together, in a world that's trying to tear them apart?

Made in the USA
Columbia, SC
28 November 2021